A TASTY TREAT

"Of course you're safe . . . in my arms."

Dimly, she knew that was the most dangerous place of all. Their hips brushed as he slid to a stop.

The cold, hard stone on one side of her hip accentuated the warm hardness on the other side that proclaimed him very much a normal man. And blood surged through every inch of her in response, bringing her nipples to tingling life again. Life so bright and sweet she hurt with its poignancy. She'd never felt so alive as in the arms of this man who looked like a fallen angel but could be . . . something much worse.

But the rumors and warnings were impossible to heed at this moment, beneath these stars. Strange, even in starlight he shone golden, his hair and eyelashes glittering as if with moon dust.

Then the stars above her head tilted crazily as he swept her high into his arms as if she weighed nothing. "Safety is such a boring word, don't you think?" The husky purr of his laughter brushed warm air above her bosom. His head bent lower, lower. "No, my dear Angel, I don't need the banality of utensils to eat you. I only need my tongue. . . ."

The Trelayne Inheritance

COLLEEN SHANNON

LOVE SPELL NEW YORK CITY

To my biggest fans: Jason and Devon Jeske.
Thanks for believing in me and the power of dreams.

LOVE SPELL®

November 2002

Published by

Dorchester Publishing Co., Inc.
276 Fifth Avenue
New York, NY 10001

ISBN 0-505-52493-7

The name "Love Spell" and its logo are trademarks of Dorchester Publishing Co., Inc.

Printed in the United States of America.

Visit us on the web at www.dorchesterpub.com.

The
Trelayne
Inheritance

Chapter One

Maximillian Britton, Earl of Trelayne, poised the stake exactly over the center of the heart. He pounded down with the mallet, calmly watching as the creature's eyes opened. It hissed, reaching toward his throat with long, sharp nails, but on the next downthrust, it went limp. From bitter experience, Max knew to pound several more times. He watched blood spurt from the hole, but only when he felt the stake strike the stone sarcophagus under the spine did he stop.

Max wiped off the gold-handled mallet passed down to him by his older brother, and set it carefully in its rosewood case next to several yew stakes topped with engraved gold handles. Locking the case, Max looked down at the blood on his hands. He was almost overcome by the urge to taste of the headiest blood of all—vampire blood. But he hastily washed his hands in the freshwater bucket he'd brought for just this purpose. He dried his hands and checked his superfine coat. No stain, not even on his blindingly white and pressed cuffs.

Of course, he should be meticulous at the art by now.

Then he pulled out his unusually large gold pocket watch. The outside bore a bossed motif of a bat with its wings wrapped around a dove. Max checked the time and made a detailed note in the tiny journal that never left his side.

"Sydney Blythe. Dispatched two o'clock of the afternoon, May fourteenth, 1880, Blythe Mausoleum, on the outskirts of Oxford." He put the notebook and watch back in his pocket.

Then he shut the sarcophagus lid and shoved the heavy casket back into its crypt.

The danger of his lonely quest for justice added urgency to his daytime wanderings. But he didn't repine. Such was his fate as the Trelayne heir, and the fate of his brother before him. Kill or be killed, and succeed where so many others died trying. Surely the loss of this latest playtoy would draw out the oldest, deadliest vampire ever known on English shores.

Unafraid, Max made his way into the sunshine, his hand around the smooth comfort of his pocket watch.

The comforting crackle of the letter in her pocket was Angelina Blythe Corbett's only reassurance as the elegant barouche bore her to her destiny—a destiny she both feared and coveted. She stared out at the lovely, rolling hillsides picturesque with spring grass, fat sheep, and blooming wildflowers.

How many times had she pictured this lush, green land in her mind's eye?

Oxford, England. The land of her mother's birth. A land she knew only in pictures.

Fitting enough, as her only remnant of the face she barely remembered was a picture, too. It had faded over the years. Angelina pulled the worn daguerreotype from her reticule.

The night's haunting questions seemed all the more urgent now that they had a hope of being answered in the bright spring day.

Why had her mother fled the elegant comfort of her father's Oxford estate for the peril and poverty of life alone in America?

Why had she taken her own life when her daughter was eight? Surely her shame and grief over the fact that her lover had refused to wed her and give the product of their illicit affair a name had long since faded. Angel had spent the rest of her formative years in an orphanage, grieving and wondering what children always wondered: had something she'd done driven her mother to suicide?

Most curious of all, why had she left instructions that her daughter was to have no contact with her English relatives? The questions that had been her most beguiling and disturbing childhood companion were finally, praise God, about to be answered.

"I promise not to leave until I understand," she whispered to the picture in her hand. Her mother had been poor, but she'd been strong, and if she'd known how her daughter would grieve and ponder the mystery of her own birth, she never would have left such stringent instructions.

Angelina traced a finger over the fading contours of that lovely countenance: the high-cheekboned face framed with thick mahogany brown hair; the slanted eyebrows that complemented slanted dark eyes; the exquisite porcelain skin that never freckled and never tanned. A face, everyone told Angelina, that was the exact image of her own.

Nonsense, Angelina thought. Her mother had been beautiful.

Carefully, Angelina put the picture back in her reticule. She smoothed the ugly gray serge fabric of her dress over her knees and quelled, with her usual ruthless self-control, the old longing for taffeta.

Orphans could afford no such luxuries. Especially orphans who supported themselves as lowly assistants in university laboratories. Angelina had to fend off quite enough advances from professors and students without bedecking herself in feminine frills.

She hadn't traveled across the ocean to become the sort of miss she detested: silly, simpering, pining for a man. She'd traveled across the ocean to solve a mystery and to convince her mother's brother, a former Oxford don, that she was worthy to assist in his science lab.

They were tasks for which gray serge was far better suited than taffeta.

Angelina stared resolutely forward.

And almost missed the gates, they went by so quickly outside the window. The sight was accompanied by a muffled scream, an expression of mortal agony Angel felt more than heard.

She pressed her nose to the glass, staring back. The carved marble gates were rapidly receding and the scream had faded into the quiet afternoon. She banged frantically on the roof with her fist, yelling "Stop! Stop, please!" to the coachman. "Someone's been hurt."

The coach jolted to a stop.

Angel bolted out and ran toward the marble gates of the cemetery.

"But miss, we be almost there," protested the coachman.

Angel paused briefly. "Didn't you hear it?"

"Hear what?" He scratched his head under his cap. When the pretty girl only stared toward that ghastly place, her face flushed with an excitement he didn't understand and didn't like one bit, he crossed his arms over his chest. Be damned if he'd offer to go with her into the hellish nest all the locals avoided. "Suit yourself. Give us a good yell if you need anything."

She ran toward the cemetery.

"Yanks," he muttered, spitting in the grass for good effect. But he waited, knowing Lady Blythe would have his hide if he didn't. He cradled his blunderbuss in his arms. Just in case. The tales he'd heard about the goings-on here and at the two landed estates in the area fairly curled his hair.

And he'd been bald these many years.

Heedless of the coachman's nervousness, Angel sprinted through the gates marked simply BLYTHE. Her mother's maiden name. The place of her final rest, for that had been her mother's last request—that her remains be sent back to the land of her birth.

Angel stopped inside the gates again, listening intently. Had she imagined the scream? The place was quiet.

Deathly quiet.

No birds trilled. There was no sound of running water from the river Thames, which flowed so close by. Odd, that. It almost seemed as if this strange place, twined with ivy, shadowed by enormous oaks, filled with ornate headstones and mossy mausoleums, encompassed a universe outside the normal bounds of reality.

Telling herself true scientists never let imagination run amok, Angel walked slowly among the headstones. Her heart pounded as she read, searching for her mother's name. The Blythe family seemed to have an unusually tragic history, if one could judge by the ages of the people here interred. The younger they were, the more massive and ornate the headstones.

Somehow, Angel knew to look for a simple marker for Eileen Blythe Corbett.

The need to feel some connection to the woman she barely recalled seemed stronger than ever, forcing Angel deeper into the cemetery. That it was a macabre need that went beyond filial honor never occurred to Angel.

Maybe only bones lay here, but they were still tangible. They were Angel's only earthly connection to the mother who'd given her birth.

The same mother who'd willingly deserted her by taking her life with her own hand.

Angel finally saw it. Small, almost overgrown by weeds. A very simple granite headstone. EILEEN BLYTHE CORBETT. And then the dates of her birth and death. No "Dear daughter," no "Dear sister." No touching epitaph.

Falling to her knees, Angel stared at the name. She felt no urge to weed the headstone and bare it to the harsh light falling over her shoulder. Her mother had been shrouded in mystery for all of Angel's life. Finding her so, trapped in shadows for eternity, seemed only fitting. Angel wasn't fond of sunlight, either.

Nevertheless, some dark instinct made Angel bury her fingers in the damp soil beneath the weeds. The smell of fecund earth was heady to Angel's unusually acute senses. The scent fired her imagination, drawing her down into the soil. She ached with the need to see her mother, just once, to hold her in her arms. "Mother," she whispered.

The frenzied urge to dig with her bare hands, to pull this woman up and confront her, almost overcame her.

Why did you leave me?

Warm moisture on her cheek recalled Angel to herself. She angrily dashed her tears away with a dirty hand. A shadow fell across her from above. She looked up.

A tall male figure blocked the sunlight from atop a mausoleum under construction. He stood on its roof, one arm casually around an avenging male angel. She looked between the angel and the man. There was an eerie resemblance between them in the shape of their perfect heads, their large hands, the strength of their legs.

The angel's wings were half-furled, and it looked weary as it stared down at something in one hand, while holding a sword high in the other. However, there was nothing weary about the man. He stood above the cemetery, yet curiously, he seemed ruler of it as well.

Even with his back to the sunlight, he looked strong, invincible, a being born of day and brightness. His hair was a hue so golden it seemed to absorb the light of times present and times yet to come and cast it back again, a lure and a promise to any woman bold enough to catch it in her hands.

While she gaped at him, he lightly jumped the twenty feet to the ground, so resilient to the shock of gravity that he was walking toward her the second his feet touched down. As if he ruled the forces of nature, too. She heard no crackle of broken twig or bent grass.

Then she could see his expression. . . . Angel leaped to her feet and backed away, both repelled and mesmerized by the look on the perfect face that matched the perfect form.

He stared at her with utter fascination. Not with curiosity—with recognition.

He looked down at her mother's headstone and back at her face. Then he gave her a courtly bow. "Welcome, Eileen's daughter."

Shelly Holmes walked rapidly along the Thames. Big Ben tolled the hour in the distance, its normally robust bong muffled by the choking fog. *Three P.M.,* Shelly thought. *I'm late.* Her footsteps were soundless on the wharf even when she broke into a run. Heavy droplets mixed with the noxious coal fumes so pervasive in this disreputable part of London, forming an insidious fog, faceless, nameless, creeping through rotted doors and rag-covered windows. More than one poor consumptive soul had suffocated during these foul spring months.

However, Shelly was fleet of foot and breathed easily in the thick pea soup. Her eyes, glowing green, saw images of heat and movement beyond mortal senses. She passed not a single soul as she wound deeper into the rabbit warren of warehouses lining the East India Docks.

These past two years had confirmed the belief of a lifetime: females who gave up their independence to a man lived to regret it—or worse. Her mission was proof enough of that verity.

The victims had been young.

They'd been female.

They'd been beautiful.

They'd been poor.

They'd been virginal.

Most telling, all had gone alone to meet an anonymous admirer. The strange courtships always began the same: with flowers, and lovely poetry, and finally gifts, some lavish. What destitute young girl in these dire times of 1880 could resist such lures? But when they finally agreed to meet their suitor, late, alone . . . they suffered an end grisly even to Shelly, who'd investigated strange phenomena the world over.

But these latest murders were unique in her lexicon of serial killers. What possible creature, the *Daily Globe* had demanded only this morning beneath a lurid drawing of a vampire, could suck every drop of blood out of a body? Could the myths be true?

Two years ago, perhaps, Shelly would have scoffed at the very idea of the undead stalking undetected through the most populous city in the world.

Until the moors of Cornwall.

Until she met, face-to-face, not one werewolf, but two. She knew for a fact now that creatures of the night sometimes hunted mortals.

Shelly quashed the regret that was as much her companion now as loneliness. She couldn't change the past. But she could help protect the future. Today, with or without Scotland Yard's consent, she'd do all she could to catch the killer.

The Beefsteak Killer. A name coined by one of London's more lurid rag sheets. This killer liked rare meat—bloody, as it were. The name stuck, to Shelly's regret, for in this age, the poor were already jealous enough of the wealthy. If this predator did indeed prove to be a titled lord, the sordid truth would be inflammatory enough.

A breeze drifted down the brackish Thames. Shelly's prominent, sensitive nose wrinkled at the stench of hundreds of thousands of tons of raw waste that had been dumped into the river only today. What did one say of a government that allowed such filth, then bemoaned the diseases that ran rampant through the poor?

One word: idiocy.

The fine lords of Parliament should be forced to bathe in this stuff, drink of it, wash their clothes in it. Laws would change quickly enough then.

If there was indeed a dead body to be discovered today, as the anonymous tipster claimed, linking one of England's wealthiest earls to the carnage, these murders would move from the back pages to the screaming headlines where they belonged. But the truth needed a judicious hand. If the yellow journalists got hold of the scandal first, not even Parliament would be safe.

The killer had to be stopped before another poor young girl died.

As her destination finally came into view, Shelly paused. Quite aside from her determination to better the lot of both her city and her gender, she admitted, at least to herself, that she had two overriding motives for her presence here.

One, just as civilization was built one brick at a time, so was society saved one soul at a time. Her wide mouth lifted in a wry smile.

Two, Shelly had always wanted to know if vampires truly existed.

Under the hulking warehouse, the foul stench of sewage faded to a bearable level. Shelly's glowing eyes beamed through the blanketing fog to read the almost indistinguishable peeling black letters on the side of the sturdy wood and stone warehouse: JASPER BRITTON AND SONS, IMPORTERS AND EXPORTERS, EAST INDIA COMPANY.

Shocked to see the owner of the address chosen for this meeting place, Shelly stopped. She glanced warily around. A trap, perhaps?

Nothing. Shelly stepped closer. The warehouse door was ajar. She reeled back as she scented something more disgusting than raw sewage.

It came from inside the warehouse.

The stench of death . . . overlaid by a menace so ancient even her formidable mind couldn't grasp its ageless hunger. Lifting her scarf over her nose and mouth and pulling the horse pistol out of her capacious coat pocket, Shelly plunged into the darkness.

She had only to follow the depressingly familiar odor of death and decay. Her heart sank at what she found. A lovely young girl, eyes open, staring with horror straight ahead. Her body was arrayed on top of a crate, her clothes ripped, her throat almost torn open. But she was ashen from head to toe, her blood obviously drained. She was also in the advanced stages of rigor mortis and had begun to decay.

She'd been dead, Shelly judged, at least two days.

Killed here, or arrayed here as a ruse by the anonymous tipster who'd left the note under Shelly's lodging door? From the looks of it, this warehouse was seldom used anymore, so it could be either.

Shelly bent and examined the fang marks.

Sure enough, one mark was slightly twisted, as if the fang that made it was crooked.

The Beefsteak Killer had done this.

Shelly looked at the stamp on the crate: Britton and sons.

Since her suspicion that the killer was of the nobility had been increasingly borne out by the facts, Shelly had made it her business to discreetly inquire about the more suspicious members of the ton. Few were as scandalous as Maximillian Britton. He was the sole surviving heir of this import-export company.

He was, by all accounts, a merry fellow, quick with a laugh, yet though he had many acquaintances, Shelly got the impression he had few friends. He slept with numerous women, but loved none. He traveled frequently and seemed to have a curious fixation with cemeteries, where he was often found.

He was obscenely wealthy, obscenely handsome, and obscenely tempting to women. The perfect lure to the lovely but penurious.

His estate was just outside Oxford.

Leaving the body exactly as she'd found it, Shelly left the warehouse and walked rapidly toward Scotland Yard. As usual, they wouldn't be glad to see her. But as usual, they'd listen, for she'd long since proved her investigative skills to them.

Then it was time to check the train schedules for Oxford. She'd been hankering to visit Oxford's renowned Bodleian Library anyway.

As she stared, transfixed, at the gorgeous male striding toward her, Angel was torn between the need to flee and the need to run her hands over those perfect features to assure herself they were real. She had never, in her entire life, seen such a good-looking man.

He glimmered with gold, from his hair to his golden skin to the gold studs in his ruffled shirt and cuffs and the huge, old-fashioned pocket watch and fob chained securely in his pocket, right down to the gold buckles on his shoes. In fact, his dress was a blatant defiance of propriety, for he wore a crimson damask vest and form-fitting pantaloons that had been in style some years back, not the severe black tie and fitted suit of a Victorian gentleman.

His chin was strong, dented with God's loving fingertip, his cheekbones high, almost Slavic. His nose was bold, a bit too long, his mouth so perfectly shaped and lush with sensuality that, masked, he could have been a girl. But he was far too tall and powerfully built to be female.

Angel was tall herself. Still, he towered over her. Most telling of all, no one looking into those clear green eyes could call this man anything but a male on the prowl.

His gaze was fixed on her, unblinking, consuming, hungry. Even as her temperature climbed and her loose clothes felt too tight, she knew she'd have felt less threatened if he'd suddenly flashed a tail and claws.

Then, when he smiled with the alert, hooded gaze of a predator, his gaze falling to the rapid pulse in her throat, for an instant she thought she saw fangs. . . . Gasping, she backed up until her hip knocked into her mother's headstone.

The tangible reminder of why she'd traveled so far gave her strength enough to snap, "Do all English gentlemen unclothe women with their eyes on first acquaintance?" She went red at her own boldness, but something about this man made her skin crawl. Her very nerve endings were alive with affront.

Or was it affront?

A slight smile curved that lush, sensual mouth. He removed a clean kerchief from his pocket and dampened it with his tongue. Heat curled through her at the sight, but then . . .

The kerchief was still warm with his wetness when he used it to wipe the dirt from her face. "No, I usually wait until second acquaintance, but you, my dear girl, are a Blythe. The only rule with Blythe women is that there are none."

She backed away a step, further embarrassed as she saw the kerchief come away stained brown. "How do you know I'm a Blythe?" She scrubbed at her cheek with the heel of her hand. Why did her flesh burn there where his essence had touched her?

"You look exactly like your mother. You stand over her grave. And I heard you were coming." He gave her a charming bow. "Maximillian Britton, at your service."

His name meant nothing to her, but the air with which he said it spoke volumes. He was a lord.

And lord, was he trouble. Exactly the sort Angel had become adept at avoiding.

She turned to leave, but paused despite herself. She'd probably never see him again. Curiosity. It was both her best trait and her worst failing. "Why were you standing on that mausoleum?"

"Ascertaining its construction. I'm considering using the same freemason for my own crypt. One never knows when one's end draws near."

Claptrap. Angel didn't say it aloud, but she didn't have to. His smile only widened. His gaze raked her again, telling her what other charming lies they could say to one another. She turned to stalk off.

He stopped her, his hand gentle on her arm, no teasing about him now. His impossibly handsome fallen-angel face was serious, almost severe. "Tell the coachman to take you to London. Book the first passage you can find back to America. For your own safety."

"From you?" Again, the words were out before she could stop herself.

This time he didn't take the bait. But his green eyes darkened as he looked at the full breasts even her severe garments couldn't totally disguise.

Angel drew away and ran the remaining distance to the impatient coachman. He looked behind her, alarmed when he saw the lord. He pointed the blunderbuss at that haughty, naughty face.

Max stared him in the eye. The coachman cowered back, the gun sagging.

Flinging open the carriage door, Max ordered, "Take her back to London."

"Take me to the Blythe estate!" Angel contradicted, slamming her own door.

Through the carriage window, their gazes met and held.

Green and brown. Life and earth. Bound together, the one giving life to the other.

Angel blinked, breaking the power of that immobilizing gaze. "Why do you wish to get rid of me?"

"Oxford isn't safe for the likes of you."

Likes of you? What the devil did he mean? Then the carriage jolted into motion. Max stepped back, one unusually large hand uplifted in a wave.

We'll meet again, stubborn girl. He didn't say it, but Angel heard it nonetheless.

And even as she told herself she didn't care, a chill feathered down her spine.

Of fear? Or anticipation?

Both. She was already in trouble. And she hadn't even met her uncle yet.

Lady Sarina Blythe paced her salon. "Why is it taking so long?"

Sir Alexander, as usual, pored over the results of his latest experiment. He pushed his spectacles to the top of his thick head of black hair. He looked somewhat like a studious Lord Byron, but Sarina hadn't married him for his looks.

He said for the third time that afternoon, "The train schedules have been sporadic of late because of new construction. I declare, one would think she were your relative instead of mine."

Sarina bristled. "Who found her, might I ask, and suggested her visit?"

"I did write the letter inviting her."

"Under my instruction."

He slapped his spectacles down on his papers. "I put my own trousers on quite well before you came into my life!"

Sarina immediately went to him to knead his broad shoulders. At the first touch of her fingers, the tension in his muscles eased away. Really, men were such babies.

All the affront had left his tone when he said drowsily, "Don't worry, my dear. She'll be along soon enough, I make no doubt."

The clatter of carriage wheels punctuated his statement. Sarina flew to the window. "She's here!" She ran out the salon door and down the stairs, her footsteps so light with joy they scarcely clattered on the wooden steps.

Sir Alexander followed more sedately.

Waving the butler aside, Sarina flung the door open herself. She extended both hands to the shy, lovely young woman who stood there. "Welcome to Blythe Hall, Angelina."

The girl's fingertips just brushed hers. Sarina ignored her hesitance and swept her into a soft, perfumed hug. "I've been on pins and needles awaiting you!" She drew her inside the door. "I'm Sarina, dear child. Alexander's hussy of a wife."

When the girl blinked in shock at this plain talk, Sarina added with a gurgle of a laugh, "But hussies are so much more interesting than prim and proper ladies, do you not agree?"

"All the men around Oxford certainly think so," Alexander said, walking forward, one hand properly extended. As Angel took his hand, he bowed over hers even more properly, a thick lock of hair flopping over one eye. That same eye dropped a sly wink as he rose again. "Making me, the bookish Oxford don they used to scorn, the envy of them all. A situation quite to my liking, for it's me she comes home to after breaking all those arrogant hearts."

Looking between the couple, who now stood, arms affectionately linked, Angel laughed. "The English must be more romantic than reported if all married couples are so open and honest with one another."

"No, it's something far more prosaic," Sir Alexander said without missing a beat. "The weather's so often disagreeable that it behooves one to find someone amiable to cuddle with." Sarina whacked his arm.

Angel laughed again, the last of her shy look easing.

"You look exactly like your mother, my dear. I used to adore watching her laugh," Alexander remarked.

Abruptly, Angel's smile faded. A ripple of something passed over the girl's perfect porcelain face. But the girl disguised it quickly. *Good.* She didn't carry her feelings on her feathered cap, like so many young girls. Sarina's estimation of her character went up a notch.

Alexander noted the response too, for he quickly added, "But based on the document you sent me on the experiments you helped conduct at the American university, you are much more than a pretty face."

The girl's unease faded into an expression of pure pleasure. Ah, here lay her weakness. She wanted to be admired for her mind, not her looks. *How quaint,* Sarina thought. But it was also somewhat endearing and bespoke an independent spirit Sarina couldn't help admiring.

Sending her husband a look of gratitude, Sarina drew a soft breath of relief. It was important that their dear guest feel at ease. Sarina was renowned throughout England for her abilities as a hostess, and Angel, the sweet, lovely young thing, could only add to the acclaim. Sarina was already plotting where to seat her at the party the following weekend.

"You must be exhausted, my dear Angelina," Sarina said.

"Angel, please," she corrected.

"Angel, please forgive us for keeping you standing in the hall. Let me show you to your room."

Alexander looked at the small bag at Angel's feet. "Are you having the rest of your luggage sent on?"

Angel went beet red. An uncomfortable silence ensued, but Sarina filled it skillfully.

"When one travels abroad, one does so lightly, Alexander. This will only give us an excuse to go shopping."

Alexander covered a snort with his hand. "As though you need an excuse for that."

"Go back to your experiments, Alexander," Sarina suggested sweetly. "We'll be down directly."

But this time it was Angel who balked at being led up the stairs. "When will I be able to see your laboratory, sir?"

Alexander glanced at his wife before he said blandly, "In due time. There's no rush. You're with us for the summer, are you not?"

"I wouldn't want to wear out my welcome, but if the position of lab assistant should be offered, I'd consider staying indefinitely. There's nothing for me back in New York." Then, as if she'd said more than she intended, she turned and hurried up the steps.

Sarina followed.

Angel stood in the door of the room, trying not to let her mouth sag open. To a girl who'd grown up in an orphanage, her privacy consisting of one bed in a long row, this was a suite of dreams, not a room. A plush fainting couch covered in a fur rug stood before the fireplace. A small fire crackled a welcome, taking the early May chill out of the air. The carpet was green, the walls covered in burgundy silk, giving the suite a pleasing array of jewel tones that brightened the spirits.

The four-poster bed was covered in plush dark blue velvet hangings embroidered with golden thistles. The heavy burgundy drapes were tied back with gold tassels that matched the tassels decorating the tops of the bedposts. The lamps were stained glass, the rugs Aubusson, the figurines genuine Dresden.

It was a room Angel had once dreamed of.

But that dream had died, too, along with her hopes for a home and a family. Angel bolstered her faltering willpower.

Dreams were as futile as the need for love. They hurt rather than healed. But tasks . . . those were far more easily accomplished.

Smiling brightly into Sarina's questioning eyes, Angel reminded herself that she had two tasks here, and two tasks only. One, to find out why her mother had killed herself. Two, to bury herself and what remained of her dreams in the only work that had meaning to her.

Scientific work. Where emotion held no purpose.

"It's not to your liking?" Sarina asked, watching her closely with those enormous blue eyes so long lashed and huge they reminded Angel of a doll's eyes.

Feeling guilty, for this woman had certainly done all she could to make her feel welcome, Angel smiled even more brightly. "It's the loveliest suite of rooms I've ever seen." That, certainly, was true.

Sarina relaxed slightly. "Excellent. I'll send my maid along directly to assist you in your unpacking. If you wish to bathe, I'll see that water is brought up."

"Oh, yes, please. And forgive me if I seem . . . distracted, but—"

A slim white hand cut her off. "You've traveled far to a strange land to stay with people you've never met. You can spend as much time or as little with us as you like, until you are comfortable. I'll see that you're assigned a horse and groom if you'd rather ride about outside tomorrow than be sociable."

For such a beautiful woman, she certainly was understanding of human nature, Angel decided as Sarina walked toward the door. She was dressed all in white and looked very young, not much older than Angel, in fact. She'd been so kind that Angel felt comfortable broaching what could have been, with someone less warm, a touchy subject. But she had to know. Angel cleared her throat. "Might I ask you one question?"

Sarina turned back immediately. "Certainly."

"Why is there no epitaph on my mother's grave?"

Shock appeared in those huge blue eyes, but it was quickly veiled by the long lashes. "You've already been to the cemetery?"

"Yes, we passed it on the way here and I

asked the coachman to stop. I hope I didn't intrude."

"Of course not. I cannot answer your question, however. Your mother was buried there some years before I came. But I shall ask Alexander."

"And who is Maximillian Britton?"

This time Sarina's shock was so great she couldn't hide it. "You met him? In the cemetery?"

"Yes."

Sarina swallowed, her swanlike neck looking as if it needed to regurgitate a ball of feathers. "He's the local rake, I'm afraid. I'd take anything he said to you with a grain of salt."

"Not garlic?"

Sarina smiled. "Ah, I see my coachman talked to you. He's a primitive creature full of superstition. But myself, I don't put much stock in tales of creatures who drink of blood and can't be seen in mirrors." Sarina brushed back her hair in the mirrored image above a bureau. "Surely if there were such an indomitable, ageless creature, it would be smart enough to find a way to make itself appear corporeal in mirrors, too." She turned back to Angel. "And find a way not to fry in sunshine. How inconvenient and depressing to only be seen at night."

Angel nodded, but she felt a bit uncomfortable with the subject. Sarina seemed quite knowledgeable about the mythical vampire.

Sarina finished briskly, "No, my dear, I'm afraid the danger Max poses to one of your tender years is of a rather more worldly kind. You may see him from time to time but I'd recommend that you give him a wide berth. Now, enough unpleasantness . . . We shall see you at dinner. We eat promptly at eight." With a last luminous smile that seemed brighter than the jewel-toned room, she added, "I am so glad you are here." She left.

Angel unpacked her own clothes, thinking about what she'd learned. Or rather what she hadn't learned. Sarina had certainly been vague about this Max person, and genuinely shocked to hear he'd been in the Blythe cemetery.

Angel couldn't shake the feeling that he'd been there with an air of purpose. He'd so resembled that avenging angel on the mausoleum. And the way the coachman had reacted . . .

The lurid accounts of the deaths that had struck the Oxford countryside and London were whispered about even on the packet ship long before she arrived. Angel had been more intrigued than frightened.

Once, Angel had even been foolish enough,

on first hearing of the fantastical creatures of the night, to research them in one of the many libraries she haunted. She'd closed the tome in disgust. Clear, cold science, where things were empirically proven, could not account for such nonsense. And science had become Angel's touchstone.

The only family she had lay in cold repose in that strangely compelling cemetery, remembered by not so much as a "Dear sister." Angel hung the last of her meager garments in the armoire. When she was finished, she went to the roaring fire, chilled despite all her logical arguments with herself.

She'd come here to face the truth, no matter how unpleasant, and lay the ghost of her mother to final rest.

But in these gruesome deaths was a peril even logic couldn't explain. What else but a vampire could drain all the blood from a human being?

"Bats. It must be bats."

Her voice was a still, small echo in the drafty room. But the memory of Maximillian, avenging angel, vampire, or human rake, as he stood there, part of the sunlight rather than subject to it, warmed her more than the fire. No matter which being he was, he was the most enticing, fascinating man she'd ever met.

30

She had to stay away from him, as Sarina suggested.

But she didn't want to.

No logic in the world was powerful enough to reason away that truth.

At two in the morning, Sir Alexander soundlessly entered the crypt where Sydney slept, his acute senses on full alert. As if the stone sarcophagus weighed nothing, he pulled it out and opened it. What he found made him reel back with both shock and hatred.

Damn that Britton degenerate. Sydney was just a lad . . . the latest convert. Harmless.

They say I'm ruthless, Alexander thought, staring down at the stake buried in the crumbled, powdery form. When a vampire suffered impalement like this, even his bones deteriorated to dust. Alexander felt sick to his stomach and knew he must feed soon.

But he was sick with more than hunger.

What manner of ruthless creature could so coldly, efficiently, kill its own kind? Maximillian Britton. A vampire young in years but old in cunning. He wanted to rule England supreme, and he didn't care whom he had to dispatch to do it.

Gagging, Alexander shut the lid and shoved the casket back. His throat was dry, and his fangs ached as he read the warning as intended.

He needed to feed. He needed strength for the battle to come. He hurried out, soundless as he blended with the night.

Some miles away, in his own estate, Maximillian Britton, Earl of Trelayne, needed to feed, too. He pulled up the sealed bottle of blood from the well in his suite, but the familiar sight of the stoppered bottle, its contents more black than red, sickened him. He just managed to set it down before he dropped it in disgust.

He reeled back, his stomach roiling, and knew he'd vomit soon if he didn't feed. But he didn't want to drink . . . he wanted to suck. He wanted the warm spurt of blood, not the chill, almost coagulated soup that was increasingly distasteful to him.

The memory came to him of that lovely neck, tilted away in such pride and aloofness. Angel. Eileen's daughter.

His fangs ached beyond the roots, down into his jawbone, gnawing hunger into his gut.

Grinding his back teeth together, Max stared at the silver-plated family shield his father had never let out of his suite. Each of his brothers had once treasured it too, until finally it passed down to Max himself, the youngest and last surviving Britton.

The family motto was embossed and gilded in blazing gold, as if to forever imprint itself on the eyes that read it: *Tomorrow is a gift, but today a blessing.*

In other words, make every day count as if it could be your last. Max had lived his adult life according to that credo, finding joy where there was sorrow, and pleasure where there was pain. Most of all, hewing always to the straight and narrow path set first by his father and his siblings, and then by the other Watch Bearers. He'd come too far along that lonely road to be tempted aside now by a chit who hadn't a clue of her sexual power.

Staring at the motto until his eyes watered, Max forced himself to drink of the disgusting pap. Forced himself not to think of that lovely white throat and its delicate, throbbing vein.

Chapter Two

Feeling, for some unaccountable reason, uneasy in the hall, Angel took advantage of Sarina's offer and rode about the countryside on several occasions, sending her groom back to the mansion over his protests. "Gustav will whip me, belike."

"Gustav? Who is that?"

"He be the head groom, miss, and a right tight stable he runs."

"Tell him it was my decision." Angel wheeled her mount away and rode off.

Out here, she felt safe enough. The spring nights were chilly, but the days were magnificent. It almost seemed to Angel as if Mother

England herself wanted to indulge its newest daughter.

Winding country roads led from charming villages to delightful hamlets. Cottages were interspersed with grand mansions. Lush sheep meadows were bounded by ancient trees. Spring lambs cavorted with their ewes while rams grazed, oblivious to their offspring.

On this, the third day after her arrival, Angel wrapped up the remnants of the lunch Cook had prepared for her. She shut the book she was reading and bookmarked it with her finger, intending to finish the chapter before making her way back to the hall. Surely soon Sir Alexander would invite her into his laboratory.

But she paused to watch a tiny lamb, still shaky on its legs, stumble over to what it apparently took for its sire. The lamb lifted its adorable curly head, sniffing the much taller ram. The ram bleated its displeasure and lowered its horns, preparing to butt the baby. A ewe ran between them, taking the butt instead. Apparently unharmed, she gently herded the lamb away.

"And that," Angel said under her breath, "is as good a polemic as any I've ever heard espoused at a suffragette gathering on the division of labor in the typical marriage."

"Ten seconds of pleasure for the man, a lifetime of toil for the woman?" The voice came from above Angel's head.

Astounded as her thoughts were so neatly completed by the disembodied female voice, Angel at first wondered if her own opinion had somehow taken corporeal form. But as she turned her head, she saw someone drop lightly down from a tree, an apple core in one hand. Only then did Angel note the horse tied to a tree some distance off. This . . . entity had obviously eaten an impromptu lunch in the tree, watching the same bucolic scene as Angel.

And come to the same tart conclusion.

Fascinated, Angel stared. *Woman* didn't seem quite the right word for this . . . person. True, this person was female, even though she wore breeches. True, she was imposing, even though she was plain. And certainly true, she was intimidating, even though Angel was not easily intimidated. The person obviously read Angel's unease, for her wide mouth curled in a self-deprecating smile.

"Don't mind me and my cynicism, young woman. Marriage is not always so," the person said, her green eyes cool and analytical. "I have observed that it can be mutually pleasurable and beneficial, though I cannot empirically prove it with my own experience."

Angel's lips twitched. "You speak as if marriage belongs beneath a magnifying glass, where it can be studied as the strange anomaly it is."

"Indeed, if I had my way, every woman would dissect her prospective husband, in-laws, home, and prospects before subjecting herself to potential eternal misery." The woman tossed away the apple core as if disgusted at the mere thought of such misery. Then she offered a rather large, very strong hand. "Shelly Holmes."

Switching her book to the other hand, Angel shook it. "Angelina Blythe Corbett."

"Blythe? Ah, then you must be able to direct me to Blythe Hall. I fear I took a wrong turn somewhere."

"You surprise me."

The gray eyes stared at her enigmatically.

"I'd expect you to have your way mapped to the smallest detail."

"Ah, there you do me an injustice. Even those of us of a scientific bent"—she nodded, acknowledging Angel to be of the same bent—"can enjoy the journey as much as the destination. Why else should one make the trip?"

Angel laughed, liking this redoubtable woman immediately. "Would it be rude of me to inquire as to your mission at Blythe Hall?"

That full mouth widened further into an even broader smile. "I like the way you think. How did you know I'm on a mission?"

Angel looked at the mare loaded down with bags, at the dust covering Miss Holmes's clothes, and at the spark of excitement behind her smile. "You've come far, to stay long, and are in such a hurry that you've not tarried to clean the dust of the road away. You packed your own meals. When you got lost, you decided rather than wandering about hoping to find a marker, you'd sensibly wait for a local resident and ask directions to one of the more famous estates in the county. All bespeak more of a mission than a visit."

Miss Holmes clapped. "Excellent! I do declare, for such a young person, you've an admirable head on those pretty American shoulders. New York, I opine."

Angel blinked. American was not difficult, because of her accent, but how did she know . . . ? Miss Holmes tapped her fingers against her chin, appraising Angel. "It's not just your accent. The research tome you hold, *Blood—Its Strange Properties and Exigencies*, was written at New York University, I believe. It's a subject of some interest to me as well, you see, and I'm familiar with its content. Given your own analytical abilities, I further opine that you are a researcher too, and have your own mission at Blythe Hall."

Not sure whether to be offended or amused, Angel reluctantly nodded. "Correct on all counts. I was actually a lab assistant at the university. My superior wrote this book, though I am, I confess, an uncredited editor."

"No man is a superior to any woman merely because he has the requisite genitalia." Shelly smiled wickedly. "Though even I admit to a certain appreciation of gender differences at, shall we say, propitious moments."

The blush started at Angel's toes and worked its way up her knees to her shoulders to her face. Now, finally, she was speechless. Never in her life had she heard a woman speak so frankly, especially on such short acquaintance.

Hearty laughter echoed so loud it startled the ram. He veered sideways into another ram, who took affront. He got butted for his impudence.

"Serves him right, too," Shelly said, swallowing back another laugh. "Forgive me, my dear Miss Blythe Corbett, but you were so smug in your intellectualism, I had to overset you a bit. It's something I know a deal about, you see." The smile faded. "Rational thought, as critical as it is to our kind, even more, I believe, than to males, is still no substitute for softer feelings.

We were constructed to need those. Denying them only leads to unhappiness."

Without another word, Angel turned back to her mare, away from those green eyes that seemed, at this moment, to reflect Angel's own troubled countenance.

Even Sarina had not been so insightful.

Obviously unperturbed at Angel's abrupt coldness, Miss Holmes ambled toward her own horse and mounted. "Do you mind if I ride with you back to Blythe Hall? Just so I don't get lost, you see."

"I guess not." Angel kicked her mare into a lope, hoping the quick pace would forestall further conversation. Angel had come here to learn, not to be a curiosity to others.

When, some time later, they rounded the long, curving drive that led to the house, Miss Holmes drew her mount to a stop and admired the gray edifice. Blythe Hall was new as such mansions went, being a mere fifty years old. Consequently, it was more modern than other mansions in the county. It boasted gaslights, an actual watering closet in the master suite, so Angel had heard, and a steam-activated lift to the tower.

The hall had three triangular pediments in front, topped with a square tower in the middle. Each lower floor had diamond-paned bay windows, and tall chimneys abutted the ends like authoritative exclamation points.

Look at me, the hall seemed to say. *An upstart I may be, but I'm someone to be reckoned with.* The grounds were equally imposing, artfully arranged in circular fashion around the house itself until it seemed the very center of the universe, not lost in it.

"Impressive," Shelly said.

As they rode around back to the stables, Angel noted that Shelly sat straight in her saddle, sharply appraising every mounting block, groom, and horse in the paddock.

A man dressed in finely made but serviceable breeches came to the stable to watch them ride past. He had dark hair, a dark face, and a dark air about him that made Angel uneasy. He also carried a crop in one hand with an air of authority, and he snapped an order at a stableboy, who hustled off.

Gustav, Angel presumed. She watched Shelly give the man the same appraising look and decided there would be fireworks between the two before many days had passed.

When she dismounted, Shelly gave Angel a smile very different from her earlier ones: bland, impersonal—she all but bobbed her head. "Thank you most kindly, Miss Blythe Corbett. I must run along now. I see I'm sorely needed here." Strangely, she was looking toward the Blythe cemetery, barely visible on a rise, as she spoke. Then she stalked off and stopped before the head groom.

Angel couldn't hear the exchange, but it was obviously lively.

At nuncheon, Sarina verified Angel's conclusion. "Yes, Miss Holmes is our new stable manager. She comes highly recommended."

"I see." But Angel didn't. Why would a stable manager be of such a scientific, analytical bent? And what was her self-appointed mission?

The answers came, appropriately enough in this comfortable but most unsettling world, when Angel wasn't looking for them.

Enlightenment, in her prior experience, came through laboratories and dusty books, not through crystal chandeliers and heady wines. But as there was nothing typical about Blythe Hall or its master and mistress, there was even less typical of the legendary balls they gave almost every sennight.

"Why," Sarina's maid nervously declared that Saturday evening as she helped Angel dress for her first such ball, "I saw two ladies fight over an invitation once. They ripped it clear in two, they did, and most put out with them were their mamas. The richest blokes in three counties come to these fancy dos. Who needs the ton and the upper ten thousand when we have our own marriage mart right here in Oxford?"

"What happened to the two young ladies who ripped the invitation? Which was allowed to come?"

"Why, both, miss. The lady Sarina is such a tenderhearted creature, she had her secretary write out a fresh invitation for each of them."

"And did they find suitable husbands?"

The maid suddenly got busy brushing off the hem of Angel's pristine gown.

Angel got the distinct impression she heard the question but didn't want to answer it. Before she could figure out why, a gentle knock came at the door. Sarina entered.

Angel met her huge blue eyes in the cheval mirror. Sarina's gaze dropped as she appraised her husband's niece. Angel saw a strange spark that made her eyes glow like blue-hot embers for a bare instant, but when Sarina looked at her again, her eyes were limpid. Mischievous as usual. "I do declare it's fortunate I am not the jealous type, or I wouldn't allow you to come. You will quite overshadow me. I'm glad the new gown so suits you."

Staring back at her own image, Angel tugged

for the tenth time at the red silk bodice, trying to pull it up. Sarina and Alexander had insisted on purchasing her a welcoming gift in the form of the first—and probably only—ball gown Angel would ever own. The low-cut, heart-shaped bodice was trimmed in gold brocade and buttoned with gold frogs that were intended to give it a slightly military look that instead accented the femininity of Angel's lush curves. The same brocade rimmed the vee inset of a deeper shade of silk that bedecked her full skirts. The hussar-style sleeves were also fastened with gold frogs.

Angel eyed herself doubtfully. The red silk had seemed daring when she stood before the dressmaker feeling like a stuffed pheasant about to be displayed over a mantel. She felt even more so now that she stared at the finished effect. *Poor flamboyant creature, strip the feathers away and she's just another piece of meat at the market.*

Sarina laughed at the look on her face. "I had a Pekingese once who used to ogle the edge of my bed exactly so. As if she aspired to reach it but wasn't sure she was quite up to the task. I made the mistake of lifting her up that first time and did it ever after until the poor thing expired, too young and too fat . . . and too dependent." Sarina gently caught Angel's shoulders and whispered, her fresh breath stirring the upswept dark hair at Angel's ear, "You are your mother's daughter, my dear. Up to any task you set yourself."

Her smile was so glowing, Angel was infected with some of her enthusiasm. She stared at herself again, moving from side to side. The swish of silk seductively cooed over the crisp rustle of taffeta, soothing Angel's nerves. She'd longed for taffeta and silk just a few days ago.

Abruptly, she felt feminine, eager to dance. And, for the first time in her life, beautiful.

Angel's return smile glowed more than she realized. "Are there handsome men at this ball?"

"The best-looking in the entire county. And they shall all be fighting over the last space on your dance card. Come along." Sweeping her own full white skirts aside, Sarina led the way out.

Not for the first time, Angel noted how Sarina's taste in clothes was oddly virginal. Still, white was flattering to her and did what Sarina obviously wanted—kept her looking young.

Angel felt positively seductive by contrast. She wasn't so sheltered that she didn't realize Sarina probably planned for her to feel that way. To put her at ease, perhaps, or try to help her land a rich husband.

They joined Alexander, resplendent in black velvet that brought out his saturnine good looks, on the landing leading to the second-floor ballroom.

He bowed. "Charmed, my dear. Shall we enjoy a bracing aperitif before we greet our guests?" He led the way into the second-floor salon and walked straight to the liquor tray. He fussed for a moment, and then handed Angel a glass of tawny port. She sipped, making a moue of distaste, but he laughed and insisted she finish it. She swallowed it down, coughing slightly.

Taking the glass, he patted her hand and put it back at her side, his eyes moist as he obviously recalled his sister when he stared at her. "If I'd come across you on the street, I'd have recognized you immediately as Eileen's daughter. You make us both proud, child."

Angel's throat closed up, and she could only nod. Remote relatives or not, this couple had been so kind to her that she felt ashamed of her occasional unease with them. This ball would make that right. Since they seemed to want her to be a femme fatale, again for some mysterious reason she couldn't fathom, Angel resolved to repay their hospitality by being charming to every man she met. For once, she'd not brood or fear for the future. She would only enjoy the moment.

The words crept unbidden into her heart. Words she'd tried all her life to believe, with limited success.

Tomorrow is a gift, but today a blessing.

That little homily had been embroidered on Angel's christening cushion, sewn by her mother's own hands. Tonight, Angel vowed, she'd live its true meaning.

Alexander proudly escorted his wife on one arm, Angel on the other, as they made their way to the ballroom. Glittering gaslights reflected in myriad mirrors and crystal chandeliers revealed elegant bejeweled ladies and gentlemen in shining evening shoes and severe black tie and tails.

As Sarina had predicted, when the receiving line ended, Angel was besieged with admirers wanting to sign her dance card. Angel felt flushed and flattered by all the attention, the avid desire in the eyes of the men who stared at her. Usually she shunned such attention, but as if even her body sensed that tonight would be different, she acutely felt the touch of silk against her own skin. Her nipples tingled, and there was an unfamiliar warmth between her thighs.

A dark young man eagerly fetched her a

glass of punch. Angel swirled it from side to side, admiring its deep ruby-red color in the bright gaslights. She brought it to her lips to taste. It was snatched from her hand. A glass of champagne was substituted.

A hush fell over the ballroom. She looked up into brilliant green eyes.

He stood right in front of her. As if he belonged there.

Max set the punch glass down on a waiter's passing tray. Taking her dance card from her limp hand, he boldly wrote his name over it on a diagonal, imprinting himself over all the others.

A few of the surrounding men muttered a protest, but then he looked at them. They seemed to shrink in stature under his gaze. He was so tall that he overshadowed them.

Angel was embarrassed for them. Collecting her scattered wits, she opened her mouth to put him in his place, but it was too late. The other men, who had seemed so gallant, melted away like mist before a fiery sun.

The analogy was apt, Angel had to admit as she looked back at what appeared to be her only remaining dance partner. Max was a blazing contrast to the local gentry. In total contempt of their fashionable black tails, he wore old-fashioned cream-colored silk pantaloons and a heavy cream tapestry jacket shot through with gold threads. The garments were a perfect setting for that strange pocket watch he wore, and an even better setting for a face and form that seemed to have more in common with Apollo than a mere English lord.

As she looked at him, Angel's breasts felt so full and heavy she almost cupped them to stop the aching before she caught herself. That green gaze settled on her, and the sound of the orchestra, the whispering of staring guests, even her sensitivity to Alexander's obvious outrage at Max's boldness, all faded away. There was only this moment, and this man, and the singing joy fulfilled: she'd known she'd see him again.

He held out an imperious, perfectly shaped hand. "Dance with me."

Tomorrow is a gift, but today a blessing. Her mother's favorite saying allayed the last of Angel's wavering inhibitions.

Mesmerized, she was reaching out when Alexander protested, "Now see here, Britton, you can't barge in without so much as an invitation—"

Carelessly, Max put a gold-edged invitation in Alexander's jacket pocket with one hand while he took Angel's hand with the other. Alexander jerked the invitation out, glaring down suspiciously, as if he believed it could be forged.

Max's deep voice purred, "Your secretary will vouch for its authenticity. She wrote it out for me over a very nice picnic on your grounds." Max's smile widened at Alexander's outraged expression. Max gave a strangely quiet Sarina a short bow, took Angel's hand, and led her onto the dance floor.

The guests parted like sheep before a wolf, which made her, Angel reflected wryly, his prey. Odd that she didn't feel like prey, unless prey longed to be eaten.

And then his hand was around her waist. Her legs brushed against him in the intimate sway of the waltz. She looked into those admiring green eyes, so full of life, and joy, and admiration, and she felt like what she suddenly, surely knew she was: a desirable woman, wanted by a desirable man. That was all he was, after all. A man. Surely no creature of the night could be light incarnate, or make her laugh even as he made her wary.

"What are you thinking?" Max asked softly, his gaze locked with hers.

"I'm wondering how a rabbit feels before it's a last meal."

"You mean before it eats a last meal?"

"No, I mean before it *is* a last meal. For a wolf."

Laughing, Max whirled her in a complicated maneuver that averted disaster with another couple on the crowded dance floor, his mirth whirling above her head, its tempo and meaning equally complicated. When he brought her back to his chest, he said, his solemnity spoiled by sparkling eyes, "You're safe for the nonce. I supped before I came."

Angel looked around at the packed room, half of its occupants staring at them.

He read her mind with his usual ease. "No, I care not what others think. And someday, I hope, you shan't either. Besides, how can I eat you? I forgot my knife and fork."

Without missing a beat, Angel rejoined, "From what I hear, you don't need them."

His eyes went flat. Ominous. "Even naive American girls should know better than to listen to nasty English country rumors."

"American I may be, naive I may be, both through circumstance, but listening is a skill I choose. And perhaps it's one you could hone as well."

The slight stiffness in his movements eased. That thread of golden laughter glittered under his severe tone when he whispered, "Oh, I hear you. You try to put me in my place by hinting of the rumors you've heard of me. And you're quite correct. Rumors often have a vestige of truth." He bent his head to whisper, his warm breath stirring the hair at her temple, "They also say I'm a great lover. Do you wish to be curious about that as well?"

Challenge. She'd longed for a change from her boring routine. Well, here it was with a vengeance. Was she bold enough to take it? Her gaze locked with sparkling green, Angel automatically matched her movements to his. She felt the cool brush of night air and realized he'd danced her toward the open French doors leading to the second-floor balcony.

"This time, my coolheaded little scientist, I don't need knife, fork, or even spoon to eat you." Still dancing, he ably closed the doors behind them with his foot as they passed. Without missing a beat, he led her toward the stone railing that lined the second-floor balcony.

Her heart pounding at the subtle intent in his slow, deliberate movements, Angel managed, "Then I'm safe."

He glanced at the double stairways leading below, and her heart skipped a beat.

Was he going to whisk her into the night? And if he did, would she scream?

To her mingled relief and regret, he ignored the stairs, continuing their slow glide toward the railing. "Of course you're safe ... in my arms."

Dimly, she knew that was the most dangerous place of all. Their hips brushed as he slid to a stop.

The cold, hard stone on one side of her hip accentuated the warm hardness on the other side that proclaimed him very much a normal man. And blood surged through every inch of her in response, bringing her nipples to tingling life again. Life so bright and sweet she hurt with its poignancy. She'd never felt so alive as in the arms of this man who looked like a fallen angel but could be ... something much worse.

But the rumors and warnings were impossible to heed at this moment, beneath these stars. Strange, even in starlight he shone golden, his hair and eyelashes glittering as if with moondust.

Then the stars above her head tilted crazily as he swept her high into his arms as if she weighed nothing. "Safety is such a boring word, don't you think?" The husky purr of his laughter brushed warm air above her bosom. His head bent lower, lower. "No, my dear Angel, I don't need the banality of utensils to eat you. I need only my tongue...." Lifting her higher, he sucked the nipple thrusting high and taut, beading the silk, into his mouth. Delicately, wetting the silk with his heat, he licked and tongued as if she were the most delectable candy.

She melted in his warmth, sugar-spun . . . and oh, so glad to be eaten. She slumped against him, so dazed by the strange sexual sensations she almost missed the last taunt whispered against her nipple, "Better yet, I need only teeth." Gently, delicately, his teeth enclosed her nipple and tugged.

Through a haze that made everything but the intimate circle of his arms seem far away, she heard angry voices approaching. The French doors rattled. Her uncle's voice came faintly.

"Now see here, Britton, unhand my niece!" The doors rattled even more loudly.

Angel heard them as the veriest tinkle, all her sensations concentrated on the tiny circle of flesh leaping up to meet tongue and teeth. Then came the breaking of glass. Raising his proud blond head, Max leaped over the second story railing in a single bound.

Night air whistled past her heated cheeks. Was she flying?

Vaguely Angel sensed a great rush of movement rising toward them, but the thud she expected came lightly, as if their combined weight was welcomed, not punished, by the earth. Only later would she realize he should have been embedded ankle-deep in mud.

As he carried her off into the night under a bright, full moon, Angel looked back. Sir Alexander stood there, his figure outlined by the blaze of light behind him, as Maximillian bore her off into the night.

Odd that he didn't run after them. Odder still that she saw no imprints marking their passage in the lawn. She blinked, wondering if she was drunk on one glass of port. Clouds skirted across the moon, and by the time they cleared, Max was on the pebble-covered drive and Alexander had disappeared back inside.

Angel struggled with the eerie sense of unreality that had been growing since she'd arrived in Oxford. Was this night all a dream? Or was this man—or this being—carrying her into the night, the preface to a nightmare? Angel knew she should struggle free. Since her uncle made no hue and cry after them, she should demand that Max put her down and not ruin her reputation.

But then Max lowered his head again to tease her other nipple. And the dream became her only reality. She slumped back into his arms.

The sunlight of his presence filled her as the night swallowed them up.

* * *

From the second-story salon window she'd opened earlier, Shelly Holmes watched Maximillian Britton, Earl of Trelayne, carry poor Miss Blythe Corbett into the night. Her eyes glowed as they caught the light cast by the full moon. She felt the change coming over her and ducked back, whipping the thick curtains shut. The hairs sprouting on the backs of her hands disappeared, and the claws growing on the ends of her fingers were sheathed back into her skin.

Over the past couple of years she'd managed to exert formidable control over when and how she changed, but in full moonlight, when she was stressed or upset, she couldn't always control herself.

Tonight she was both.

She liked Miss Blythe Corbett. Which was why it bothered Shelly exceedingly to know that the poor girl was the prize in a game she didn't even know she was playing.

A game the masters of which were, quite possibly, two powerful male vampires. Earlier, from the front drive, hidden beneath a tree, already suspicious of the master of this house and his strange nightly perambulations, Shelly had watched Sir Alexander pour three glasses of wine.

Then, his back to Angel, he'd sprinkled a

white powder into one glass and swirled it around. He gallantly offered it to Angel, who looked like what she was in her seductive red silk: a siren who didn't know it yet. Strange way of showing familial devotion, for an uncle to drug his own niece who'd come thousands of miles to meet her only remaining family.

She'd heard the commotion he made on the ballroom balcony as Max jumped down with his prize. But if Alexander had really wanted to stop Max, he'd have summoned servants or led a rescue group down the balcony steps.

He did neither.

Now Shelly went to the liquor tray and appraised the three glasses there. Closing her eyes, using her powerful olfactory senses, Shelly smelled the residue in the bottom of each glass. The first held nothing but the scent of expensive port. Nothing in the second glass, either.

But in the third . . . Shelly sniffed and almost gagged, jerking the glass away from her nose. Over the many years of her investigations, Shelly had learned the stench of various aphrodisiacs by smell alone. This one was very old, very powerful.

She forced herself to sniff again. Persian, if she recalled correctly.

The question was, Why would Sir Alexander

give his own niece an aphrodisiac and then let his greatest enemy carry her off? And were these two powerful males truly vampires, or men who liked to pretend they were vampires?

Most critical of all, if they were vampires . . . which one of them was the Beefsteak Killer?

Shelly felt the urge to go after the girl and warn her if possible, save her if need be, but she squelched it. She really didn't think Angel's life was endangered. At least, not yet.

Angel felt herself float down to a cloud. No, not a cloud, cushions. She forced herself to open her heavy eyelids. A carriage ceiling met her gaze, its plush black velvet lining surrounding a coat-of-arms medallion. The medallion had writing at the bottom, but it was dark and she couldn't quite read it. Then the carriage jerked into motion, and a strong, hard male body lowered over hers, jolting her back to reality.

And the danger of what she'd thus far allowed without a protest.

When Max's hands covered her breasts, tugging at the fabric, and his tongue and teeth teased her earlobe, from somewhere she found strength enough to quiet her raging body.

She caught his hands. "No."

He froze. "No? Then why did you allow me to carry you off like this?"

"How could I stop you?"

He sat back, his knees straddling her hips on the wide seat. "A simple no would suffice. No matter what you've heard about me, I'm not a demon. I'm but a man, with a man's needs." He caught her hand and kissed her fingertips, bringing them dangerously close to the proof of male desire imprinting his pantaloons. But then he dropped her hand and finished coldly, "Needs I control. Can you say the same?"

Shamed, she covered her aching breasts with her hands, but he gently tugged her hands away. She tensed, but instead of devouring her again as he had promised he could—with tongue and teeth—he moved aside, sat up, and pulled her up next to him.

"Tell me to turn the carriage around, and I shall." Leisurely, giving her time to pull away, he kissed his way to her wrist, undoing with his teeth the frog that stopped his progress.

"T-tur . . ." The words would not come.

To her horror, she watched a disembodied arm, for it certainly couldn't belong to her, half-bared as the sleeve gaped open, lift to twine about his neck. And it was joined, most improperly, by another arm in a properly closed sleeve.

Then she was kissing him.

Passionately. Not because he seduced her.

Because she wanted to.

And that made her truly lost.

Lost to propriety, lost to independence.

Lost to hope of escaping this sensual web so powerful surely only an unnatural creature could weave it.

Did vampires really exist? She had a feeling she was about to find out.

Chapter Three

Angel had been kissed before, but she'd never been the aggressor, and she found the new experience heady. Perversely, now that she'd quit fighting his masterful seduction, he'd lost interest. He sat unmoved as she shyly pressed her lips to his. When she leaned back, frustrated, he rimmed his teeth with the tip of his tongue.

"Port. He gave you port. With an added little taste for my benefit." He reached to open the carriage window and she realized he was going to tell his coachman to turn the carriage around.

She couldn't bear that. The need throbbing in her lower parts had become unbearable since he'd suckled her breasts. Her reputation was ruined anyway. Half the local gentry had watched from the ballroom windows as he carried her off. She caught his hand in hers and used her instincts—the strange, overtly sensual instincts she usually repressed. Her mother, she'd been told, was an equally sensual creature, and because Angel didn't want to end as tragically, she'd deliberately smothered the needs that sometimes awoke her, lonely and empty in the night.

But now . . . now she sat alone with temptation incarnate. There was no one to see or care if she followed the path of her mother in the land of her birth.

Angel didn't kiss his fingertips, or bring his hand to her breast. Instead, she licked the artery throbbing at his strong wrist. He inhaled sharply, making a fist, moving away from the window to give her more of his skin. He did taste delicious. "No fork, no spoon," she teased huskily against his smooth skin. "Only tongue and teeth." She glanced up through slitted lids.

He stared down at her, thunderstruck. She realized none of his previous night toys had been so bold as to use his own tactics against him. She was different. Maybe he was bigger, stronger, faster, and much more experienced, but she matched him in willpower, intellect, and sensuality. As he'd soon discover.

Delicately nipping the bluish vein, she pried open his fist. Then she nibbled her way down his fingers, pausing to suckle them daintily, one by one. At last, she was giving the instincts she'd stifled all her life free rein.

Groaning a muffled protest, he pushed his free hand through her thick hair, caught the nape of her neck, and lifted her face to his. He kissed her full on, making no allowances for her innocence and no excuses for his needs. His lips were hard, and sensual, and demanding.

She sank back against the squabs, half frightened at the passion she'd incited, but then he softened slightly. The tip of his tongue delicately rimmed her mouth. Her lips tingled as much as her nipples. Automatically she opened to the pleasure like a trumpet vine thirsty for morning dew.

He filled her with a far headier moisture in the intimate thrust of his tongue. It was the first time she'd been kissed so. For an instant, the analytical part of her brain took over.

The French had reputedly started this type of kiss. She'd wondered how it could be pleasurable to have a slippery tongue inside one's mouth. She'd avoided the intimacy with her few previous suitors, but they hadn't been masters of the art, either.

How appropriate that this silver-tongued devil should taste so sweet. Maximillian Britton was as good at kissing as he was at everything else. He wasn't slippery; he was soft, strength sheathed with velvet that knew exactly how to fill her yearning warmth, caress her, and make her open wider to accommodate him.

And the images filling her head, she knew, were the ones he intended her to picture. This wildly sensual, intimate act was but a foretaste of the greater pleasure to come. Would he feel so good there, too? Fill her so utterly, pleasuring them both?

But then her appraisal of these strange new sensations ended. She couldn't think. She could only feel. Tingles danced from her lips, her tongue, down her neck, through her torso, centering in the softness that yearned to be likewise filled.

He dipped and swayed, and coaxed her to even greater boldness. Then she was doing battle with his tongue, learning the most thrilling victory of all.

In this intimate war of foreplay, there was no loser—only two winners. For, strangely, the more she gave, the less he took. And the more he tried to please her.

Boneless, without will or identity, Angel sank back against the squabs and reveled in sinful pleasure as the carriage bore her away under the stars.

From a crouched position, Shelly Holmes vaulted to the top of the stone wall surrounding the Britton estate. There had been a time when she'd wished to cure herself of her lupine ailment, but of late, especially at times like this, she found her curse quite useful. Lycanthropy endowed her with abilities far beyond those of a normal human, giving her a unique chance of catching the Beefsteak Killer. Who had better odds of defeating an old, deadly vampire: a woman skilled in the detective arts, or a werewolf skilled in the detective arts?

Her husky chuckle came out like a whine. On all fours, easy now in her bristly canine skin, she jumped the twenty feet to the ground. Soundless, she crept through the heavy brush, her gray eyes glowing phosphorescent green in the night. She saw tiny living things scurrying away under grass and leaves. For an instant, as a rabbit made a terrified dash for its hole, the primitive instinct to swoop down on it and consume it whole, bones and hide included, almost overcame her.

She quelled it. Her quarry here this night was larger and far more dangerous.

No matter how much she'd lectured herself that Miss Blythe Corbett deserved the disaster she courted, Shelly hadn't been able to return to her room above the stables, close the curtains against the lure of the moon, and go to sleep. The girl, with her unusual blend of intelligence, determination, and scientific skill, merited a better destiny than becoming vampire fodder, which was what would ultimately happen if she allowed herself to fall under Britton's sway.

Shelly couldn't allow that. No, even knowing she was imperiling the more important investigation, Shelly still had to follow the credo that had led her on this unusual path—where there was mystery to be solved and innocence to be saved, Shelly Holmes would act.

Undressed for the change, Shelly had opened her windows wide and exulted in the siren call of the moonlight. When the transformation came over her, she embraced it. Leaping down, she ignored the frantic stamp of terrified horses, narrowly evading one of her own drunken grooms rounding a corner of the barn. He blinked after her, crossing himself. She paused long enough to bare her fangs at him. He stepped back, knocking his foolish head into a tree, and passed out cold.

Just as well. He'd think he'd hallucinated when he came to.

But on the second corner, she came face-to-face with Gustav. He froze, staring at her with more astonishment than fear. She sniffed him, aware he had a stench that reminded her of a vampire, yet was a bit . . . different. He was an odd one, but now was not the time to debate his character. Brushing past him, knocking him to the ground, she ran out to the open road.

Her easy lope had soon caught up with and surpassed the black Britton coach. She planned to beat them inside the estate and find a way to avert the tryst Britton obviously intended. The vial of powder she'd taken out of her medicinals bounced comfortably on the leather thong encircling her neck. She'd mixed the palliative herself and hoped it would reverse the effects of the aphrodisiac, as promised in her ancient text.

However, she had no illusions about her task. Shelly knew this enemy was the most dangerous she'd ever faced. Far worse than the murderers she'd helped put behind bars when she was a mere woman, worse even than the werewolf she'd helped defeat on the Cornish moors two years ago, when she'd become a werewolf herself by being bitten in the process.

Colleen Shannon

If all went well, Miss Blythe Corbett wouldn't even realize she'd been rescued by the bold, irritating woman who spoke too frankly and saw too much. And the killer, if Max Britton was the one with the slanted tooth, wouldn't even know who'd subverted his dastardly plans.

The hulk of the ancient estate blocked the moonlight. Shelly looked up. No modern architectural marvel, this. Britton Castle looked like exactly what it was: the estate of landed gentry who'd shed generations of blood to keep the pile of stones.

Shelly used her nose to ease open a casement window. She slipped inside.

The carriage had stopped before either of them realized it. There came the rattle of the stairs being put down. Angel and Max, who'd been lying entwined on the seat, sat up, lethargic with a seductive heat that was slow to wane even as cold night air coasted over them.

The coachman stood respectfully aside, face turned away, awaiting their descent.

Angel raised her heavy lids. She looked at the man holding her in his arms as if he couldn't bear to let her go. His mouth was lax and wet with their passionate kisses. The lamplight beaming outside the door seemed caught

68

in his golden hair, bestowing a halolike glow around his head. Again, she was struck at how much he resembled a fallen angel. But then she realized those eyes, dilated and dark, were fixed on her neck.

Angel looked down. Somehow her bodice had slipped, revealing her chemise and the deep swell of her bosom. Any other man would be staring at her cleavage.

Maximillian Britton looked at her neck, his eyes dark with a savage hunger that should have terrified her.

It didn't. She was a bit worried by that, especially when Max licked his lips. For an instant, she thought she saw fangs.

That didn't terrify her, either. Before she could face that appalling truth and wonder at it, the chill night air seemed to recall him to the proprieties.

Shoving his hand through his hair, he turned that brilliant smile her way. No evidence of fangs now. He stepped down and offered his hand, saying formally, "Welcome to Britton Castle, Miss Blythe Corbett. Would you care to join me in a glass of wine?"

Without hesitation, Angel accepted his hand and descended. She wasn't sure what they'd started this night, but she knew it was too late to turn back.

*   *   *

In human form, attired in the long duster she'd also rolled about her neck, Shelly hovered over the liquor tray in the salon. Which would he choose to offer the lady? Surely not the brandy. Not the Irish whiskey. By all accounts, Maximillian Britton was probably a vampire, but he'd been raised as a gentleman. No, it would be the ratafia or the sherry.

Shelly held the vial of powder up to the light. She had enough for one bottle, not two. She could hardly hide behind the couch and sprinkle the powder into the chit's glass at the propitious moment. The more urgent his desire for the girl, the more likely he'd be to hew to the proprieties when he could. Ratafia was the generally accepted nightcap for a proper lady.

Shelly took a chance on the ratafia.

Dumping the contents of the vial into the crystal decanter, she swirled it around, watching it dissolve. A smile curled her wide mouth as she wondered if the palliative would affect Max too.

Her laugh echoed in the lovely room as she pictured the look on his face if he couldn't perform. She clapped her hand over her mouth as she heard someone enter the black-and-white marble foyer. Time to go upstairs and search his chambers.

She might as well kill two birds with one stone. If Max was a vampire, he'd need the requisite soil to sleep on. That would be all the proof she needed. She'd already verified that Sir Alexander was a vampire by following him one night and watching him suck blood from a doe.

She'd intended to hide and examine the creature after he was finished to see if he left a crooked fang mark. But when he was finished, Alexander had tossed the poor dead thing into the river, which was running hard with the spring rains.

To hide the evidence, no doubt.

After the way Max had whisked the girl to his lair this night, Shelly feared she already knew which of the two men had a taste for lovely young virgins. But to justify arresting a peer of the realm, she needed physical evidence, not circumstance.

She also wanted to remain within screaming distance, in case the girl needed additional help. Shelly went out a side door as the main salon door opened. She waited until the hall was empty of servants and then stole upstairs.

As she went, she appraised her surroundings. She'd have expected the inside of the house to match the grim exterior, but the walls were painted white, and Britton's predilection for paintings ran to sunny seascapes and portraits of happy families. The decor was bright and cheerful, and gaslights glowed everywhere.

As she walked upstairs, Shelly looked closer at the enormous painting that held pride of place between the second- and first-floor landings.

It depicted a dark man who looked most unlike Max next to a lovely blond woman with Max's perfect features and bright green eyes. The five rough-and-tumble boys ranged beside them looked to be anywhere between fifteen and eight, and they were all dark like their father. One lovely young blond girl stood with her hand on her mother's chair arm. The youngest child, a blond baby, chubby and gleeful, on his mother's lap, was obviously Max. She didn't need the brass plate, saying simply, *The Tenth Earl of Trelayne and Family* to know whom she stared at.

She didn't remember hearing about any siblings. And the way the family was dressed ... it was the garb of over a hundred years ago. Unless they were costumed, she was looking at incontrovertible proof, hung bold as you please for all to see, of Max's advanced age.

He *was* a vampire.

* * *

Inside his cheerful salon, Max was finally able to master the dark hunger that had almost consumed him there in the carriage. Thank God his coachman had interrupted. Max looked at the girl, so sensual yet innocent as she stood blinking in the light. Didn't she know what she did to him?

He was struck by the unwelcome thought that perhaps she knew precisely what she did to him. Her gown hung precariously low on her shoulders, and only the peep of white lace at her bosom protected her modesty. Max clenched his hands to prevent himself from finishing gravity's job. He swung aside to the liquor tray and grabbed the safest spirit there.

He hated the stuff, but he was too polite to swig brandy, as he longed to. He poured two glasses of ratafia. He handed one to the girl. She set it aside, raising her arms to him, her mouth lifted for his kiss.

His head lowered until he felt the heat of her skin, scented the womanly essence their embrace had aroused. His nostrils flared, but he stumbled back and drank his wine in one gulp.

She pouted, her lips already red from his kisses. "Why did you bring me here then?"

In a word—madness. It was madness to want to save her from Alexander's clutches, madness to want to make love to Eileen's daughter, whom he—Max violently shoved the dark memories away. He lifted the glass to Angel's lips. What a ridiculous name for her when she was more like Lilith incarnate. "Drink."

She took one sip, made a face, and pushed the glass away. She wandered the salon, appraising the bright yellow–striped divan facing two cherry-red padded Sheraton chairs. The carpet underfoot had the same touches of red and yellow that gave the room its tasteful but bright atmosphere. She touched a delicate figurine on a white marble-topped table and then whirled on him.

Apparently she, like almost everyone who saw his recently redesigned house, expected something different.

"Where's the dungeon?"

His lips twitched. "Next to the seraglio where I have my harem imprisoned."

She didn't crack a smile, merely nodded emphatically. "I thought so. Do I get to see it?"

"I save the thumbscrews for special occasions."

"This is my first ball ever. Isn't that special enough?"

"Next time you come, I'll let you try out the iron maiden." He gave her a provoking look. "A device tailor made for one of your bent, I might add." There. He'd finally silenced that saucy tongue.

She shot back, "You assume I'll still deserve that appellation after tonight." She broke into lilting laughter at the look on his face.

Damn, did nothing disconcert this American miss? Most women were tongue-tied when he played these verbal games with them. Not Angel. She tossed his bon mots right back.

There was a better way to handle her. Surely the aphrodisiac would be losing some of its effect by now. He strolled across the carpet to set his hands lightly on her shoulders. He nuzzled her ear, safely avoiding her neck, then trailed the tip of his tongue over the outline of that lush mouth, whispering into it, "Bold words require bold deeds, my little iron maiden. You play a dangerous game, but I'll join you gladly if you like." He gently cupped her breast. He expected her to pull away now that he'd called her bluff. She was still an innocent, after all.

Instead, she leaned into his touch. "My mother always said 'Tomorrow is a gift, but today a blessing.' I don't think I ever understood what she meant until tonight." She twined her arms about his neck, closing her eyes as she kissed his strong chin, so she didn't see the shock in his eyes.

Eileen . . . Max's semihardness, which had been strangely softening since he drank the wine, went flaccid. God, memories he had aplenty, regrets even more, over his long life, but none made him ache with sadness like his memories of Eileen. Even Angel's wandering lips couldn't distract him.

He remembered the last time he'd seen Eileen before she left for America. He'd tried to talk her into staying, but she'd insisted, hoping the new land and new air so far away would help her find a cure for her ailment.

She hadn't succeeded. He knew that better than anyone. For he'd been the last one in England to see her alive.

He looked down at her daughter, kissing the hollow of his throat with more enthusiasm than experience. He'd been immediately drawn to Angel because Eileen had passed her looks, her strength, her sensuality, to her daughter, along with her love of his family motto.

How would Angel react if she found out the saying of her childhood was emblazoned on the Britton crest? He set her away from him. "Stop it. You don't know what you're doing."

He dragged her before a mirror so she could see her own scandalous image, her dress half off her shoulders, her mouth red with his kisses. Her cheeks flushed and eyes sparkling, she looked nothing like the cool, contained scientist she claimed to be. He wondered why his own passions didn't soar out of control, for she was so sensuous, so ripe for the taking . . . maybe he wasn't too old for gallantry yet. "Ask yourself why your uncle bought a maid a dress that should only be worn by a woman of the world."

"Because he wanted me to look my best."

He shook his head. "No, Angel. You're not dressed like that to please yourself. You're dressed like that to tempt me."

Shock finally dimmed the fevered glitter in her eyes. "Why?"

That was much harder to explain. When he turned aside to drink another glass of ratafia to collect his thoughts, she wandered the room, touching a statue here or a pillow there. Learning, he knew, by the touch of her hands, his things, his likes, his needs.

He turned back to her, glad the wine had dulled his raging desire enough for him to be able to think clearly. His hand clenched hard about the wineglass.

Angel had her head back now as she stared at the bucolic mural he'd recently had painted on his ceiling to further brighten the salon. Her long neck was arched, her jugular vein exposed. All he had to do was lunge forward and sink his fangs into that warmth and life. . . . No amount of wine could assuage that need.

Growling in physical pain, Max jerkily turned aside from the one thing forbidden to him. His hand went for comfort to the unusual watch in his pocket.

Angel turned in time to see it. "Why do you carry that huge thing?"

"Why do you ask so many questions? If you're finished with your wine, I'll have my coachman take you home." He turned to the door.

"No."

He stopped abruptly, giving her that haughty look that made princes nervous.

She stared right back. "If I've sacrificed my reputation to your whims, you have to accede to one of mine." She strolled toward him, her eyes dilating again as she neared. "I want you to kiss me again. With your tongue. I enjoyed it."

He felt the urge to duck behind the couch but quelled it. Dammit, what was wrong with him? Normally he'd have found temporary surcease, at least, in her lovely body. She was so determined to become a woman tonight, no matter the cost. And she was quite possibly right. Her reputation could already be ruined, so who would know the difference?

He would.

Alexander must have given her a very powerful dose. He wouldn't take advantage of her. In fact, when she pressed that lovely form against him and pulled his head back down for a kiss, he knew *wouldn't* wasn't a strong enough word.

Couldn't better suited his feelings at the moment.

Max stood nonplussed, his hands holding her waist, his mouth just out of her range as she stood on tiptoe trying to reach his lips. Now he knew how a pretty woman felt when she was wooed against her will.

It was a most unique experience. He didn't like it. The girl—no, woman; innocent or not, this female was all woman—had the arms of an octopus. When he removed one small, determined hand, the other was soon in its place, twining about his waist, or slipping behind his neck as she tried to tug his head down into her range.

Max caught both her hands in his.

She stopped, but only briefly. "This is a new experience for you, isn't it?" She cocked her head on one side, her eyes sparkling with mischief and desire.

She looked so like her mother. He waited for the usual surge of interest. It didn't come. Embarrassed for the first time in a long time, Max began to back toward the door. Maybe if he screamed . . .

She cut him off at the door. "Craven," she taunted. She approached him, sensuality in every measured movement.

He liked pursuing much better than being pursued. That was why he couldn't respond to her at this moment, he told himself.

He dodged her and ran for the side door.

"What kind of rake are you?" she complained, her arms crossed over her prominent nipples. She rubbed herself, obviously still aching.

"The sensible kind who knows when to run." The door snapped shut behind him.

Telling his coachman to take her home, he climbed the stairs a few minutes later, totally confused. Not once in the past hundred years, had he ever had a lack of . . . interest. And Angel fired his interest more than any woman since Eileen.

If this got out, he'd never live it down. . . . He glared at the offending portion of his anatomy, which remained fully *down* at the moment.

What the deuce had just happened in there?

Shelly's sensitive ears caught the sound of his footsteps before he'd climbed three steps. She stood over the well in his room, staring down at the bottles of blood she'd pulled up. She'd tasted one just to be sure. Calf's blood. The taste was familiar to her from her own forays into meadows when the wildness took her.

The bottles were almost icy with cold. There were six of them, filled to the brim. Enough, she was guessing, for a week. Even though he tried to keep it chilled, the blood had a thick, unpleasant taste. He must find it hideous compared to the silky warmth that came out of a living vein.

She could think of absolutely no reason for a virile vampire with a taste for young women to make do with calf's blood out of a bottle unless . . . he was resisting his vampirism. Which put rather large ravels in the tapestry of motive she'd been trying to weave around the Earl of Trelayne.

His steps neared. Shelly glanced at the window. If she hurried, she'd have time to leap outside to the ground. Instead she stood calmly, waiting. Even her strong heart pounded nervously as she realized what she faced alone. She wished she'd thought to tie a crucifix about her neck, too. But there could be no better time than now, during a full moon, to face him.

Maybe he'd be so stunned, she could surprise him into telling her the truth. As a precaution, she opened the curtains to the moonlight, ducking back away from its allure. If she had to embrace the change, she would.

Perhaps tonight would answer another question that had been bothering her of late—which was stronger: a werewolf or a vampire?

Despite his confusion, Max immediately felt the alien presence in his chambers. He instantly became well-nigh invisible. He was unable to totally become mist, but able to shift light about his form until he appeared as a haze to others.

He was so surprised to see who awaited him that he took human form again. He recognized her instantly: Shelly Holmes. She was famed as an investigator for Scotland Yard, so famed that he'd seen her picture in the *Times* on more than one occasion.

Famed for solving murders. Which should have alarmed him, since she'd sneaked into his chambers to search them. She obviously suspected him as the Beefsteak Killer.

Her eyes glowed strangely in the darkness. She stared straight at him, tall, apparently unafraid. But he felt the throb of her heartbeat even from where he stood. She hid her fear well.

Blast, he'd had enough of intrepid women for one night. Anger began to surge through him at her temerity. No one, not even his own servants, trespassed in his chambers. How had she gotten past the complicated opening device at his door? One had to know just which piece of molding to move to fit into another. . . .

"It's not difficult to find the opening. A tiny crack lies between two pieces of molding that are inverted. When you twist them, they fit neatly together."

The fact that she read his mind so easily angered him further. In one bound, he stood over her. His breath warmed her face. "If you know what I am, you're mad to come here alone."

She looked back at him steadily. "If you had a taste for fresh blood, you wouldn't have bottles of the stale stuff awaiting your consumption." She flung a hand out at the carriage rattling away down the long paved drive. "And you wouldn't put Angel in a carriage to send her home so soon. Intact in every way, I suspect." A strange smile played at the corners of her mouth.

Sheer fascination began to ameliorate Max's anger. How did this woman read him so clearly when most of the people in the county, common folk and gentry alike, were terrified of him? "But if I'm a killer some five hundred years old, do you not think I'd be smart enough to build up a stock . . . just in case I have to resist my darkest urges to escape capture?" He was delighted to see her steady gaze waver. No, she hadn't thought of that.

He pressed his advantage. "Or maybe I'll just feel the urge to make an exception in your case. Unless you tell me why you're here." He closed a strong hand about her throat, letting her feel the strength of his fingers. His nails began to grow, grazing her skin.

With a surprising strength of her own, she used both hands to pull him away. She sidled several steps until moonlight pooled at her feet. "If you tell me what the grudge is between you and Alexander, perhaps I won't go to the authorities." Then she struck at his weakest spot. "Or tell Angel what you are."

Silence descended between them, neither giving an inch. Max showed her his fangs, but she eyed them analytically, with more interest than alarm. He noted she inched into the moonlight until it covered her . . . bare feet. Why were her feet bare?

Unable to terrify her as he did others, he turned away in disgust. "Get out, while I'm inclined to let you go. I won't be so forbearing next time—Miss Holmes." He was delighted to see her hesitate on the way to the door.

She peered at him. "How do you know my name?"

"Anyone interested in the investigative arts in England knows your name."

"I am to conclude that you're interested in the investigative arts?"

"You're to conclude exactly what you always do, I expect—whatever your evidence supports." He glanced meaningfully at his well.

She ticked off the facts on her fingers, one by one. "One. Vampires are apparently thick on the ground in this part of England. Two. There's a war between two of the most powerful ones. A war over a woman? A war over a kingdom? No doubt I shall learn, eventually. Three. Angel is the prize in that war, though she doesn't know it yet. Four. Whoever wins is most likely the Beefsteak Killer." She dropped her hands. "Can you tell me why you and Sir Alexander hate each other so? Just so I don't draw the wrong conclusion—and have the wrong man arrested."

Max laughed. "Do you really think you can toddle a vampire off in chains and expect him to let himself be imprisoned?"

"There are ways. Sunlight—"

"We don't like it, but over the years, some of us have found ways to battle its effects."

"Garlic—"

"My favorite spice," he lied. He detested the stuff.

"Crosses."

"I attend church every Michaelmas." And he could get past the holy water only because of those disgusting bottles in his well and the magical, invisible glow of his watch. Any vampire who supped on human veins couldn't bear to look at a crucifix.

"Stakes."

Max was silent. He glanced at the hidden compartment beneath his bed. It looked secure. He suspected he'd interrupted her before she'd had time for a thorough search. Which was a good thing, because she'd really be intrigued if she found a vampire-killing kit in the room of a vampire.

She turned back toward the door. "We all have our weaknesses, my lord." With her hand on the knob, she paused, looking back over her shoulder with that odd smile. "I suspect you discovered one of your own tonight. Your . . . dalliance didn't last long."

He blinked, truly chilled now. How could she possibly know?

She did, as she proved with a bland, "Did you enjoy your ratafia?"

For an instant, he was too stunned to be angry. "You put something in the wine?"

"I knew Alexander gave Angel an aphrodisiac, and I wanted to give her a fighting chance
to resist you. I'm glad to see it worked."

Max knew he should be angry. If nothing
else, he had a reputation to live up to. But now
he finally understood why she'd invaded his
home, even suspecting she faced a vampire
without so much as a crucifix.

She'd come to Angel's rescue.

He'd always had a soft spot for the coura-
geous, especially when they fought for the innocent. Staring at her widening smile, Max
admitted ruefully, "She didn't drink the disgusting stuff. I, on the other hand, had three
glasses."

Her hearty laugh joined with his own as relief swept the last of his anger aside. At least
there was nothing wrong with him.

In that moment, Max realized he'd met two
very unusual women tonight. One he could
love. The other he could call friend.

His mirth faded quickly. And both were dangerous to him and his solemn oath.

He flung the door open. "Get out."

The sympathy in her eyes remained with him
long after the door shut in her face.

He tried to feed after she was gone, but one
taste of the chilly, vile stuff and he put it aside.

Max prowled his room, staring at his coat of arms and its motto. That was a saying he'd spent over a hundred years trying to live up to. He could bear what he'd become only by living each day as it dawned and not repining over the many dark days already past. Days when the natural optimism of his nature found it harder and harder to remain hopeful.

Maybe tomorrow, or the next, he'd find the missing clue, the link that would prove beyond all doubt that Alexander or another of his cozy circle of vampires was the Beefsteak Killer— the quarry Max's family had been hunting for over a century. The reason for the grudge was, appropriately enough in a war between vampires, the spilling of blood. Innocent blood.

His own lovely, virginal young sister had been, to Max's knowledge, the Beefsteak Killer's first English victim.

Max's father, a learned man who'd studied myths of every type, including vampirism, found his daughter dead, her blood drained, two black holes in her neck, one crooked. At first the earl went to the authorities and tried to convince them that the ancient rumors were true: yes, vampires had come to England. More vampires were created as the killer brought across some of his victims, he tried to explain. They had to stop this killer, not just for the Brit-

tons, but for all Englishmen and English-
women.

Max's father became the laughingstock of
England. Humiliated, he vowed to find the
killer himself. Binding all his sons in a blood
pact, he made them vow to carry on and stop
what couldn't be stopped if he failed.

Max was still a baby when his father left
home to pursue the killer. When he returned,
he came home in a coffin, his own blood
drained. One by one then, the other Britton
brothers took up the grisly Trelayne inheritance. One by one, they doggedly followed
slim clues, chasing the killer all over the world.
Cairo. Monte Carlo. Mexico. Rome. London.
Persia.

One by one, they were slain.

Now the mantle had passed to Max, the
youngest child, the favored child, the apple of
his family's eye. He was the mischievous boy,
the brightest and most beloved for his sunny
nature. The one who used to put ink in his
nanny's tea, the one who knotted his older
brother's slippers together.

But as his brothers disappeared in sunlight
and in darkness, blackness consumed his life.
As men, even the Earls of Trelayne were not
strong enough to fight such evil. When his
youngest brother came home in pieces, Max,

the last of his line, the last heir of the terrible Trelayne inheritance, knew there had to be a better way. And he'd found it, after much searching and much danger, in the science that had filled his life before he became earl.

Staring at Eileen's miniature next to his bed, Max choked back a bitter laugh. Was he about to become what he hated most? It might have happened this very night, if that witch Shelly Holmes hadn't drugged his wine. She'd done him a favor and didn't even know it.

For all his long life, he'd struggled against the bitter cost of this legacy he'd chosen. So far he'd been incorruptible, using humor and his enjoyment of women, sports, and art to keep the darkness at bay. He'd struggled as he'd been warned he'd have to do, the price he'd paid for becoming a Watch Bearer.

But this . . . He'd never faced a temptation as rich as Angel.

She was what he hungered for and what he feared most: a sensual, beautiful woman designed for his touch for a very simple reason, though she didn't know it yet herself—she was half vampire.

The one being, as Alexander knew, who could tempt Max away from his lonely path. That was why Alexander had dressed her like a slut and drugged her.

Max fumbled for his watch, but it didn't offer him the usual comfort.

It was cold and hard, a symbol of his loneliness. And he wanted something soft and warm and sweet.

Angel . . .

Bile rose up again. Grimly, Max forced himself to drink.

Chapter Four

The next morning, the minute she awoke, Angel blushed. Strange how she could recall last night with crystal clarity. Every touch, every kiss, every caress. For the first time in her life—and she hoped the only time—she'd understood the sheer power of carnality.

Was this why all those men followed her around, peeking at her in ways that made her uncomfortable, making her wish for a higher collar and a thicker layer of undergarments? She'd never understood what dark urges drove them.

Until last night.

The baring of her bosom hadn't been shocking because she'd wanted to expose herself, to revel in sin and forbidden delight. To know firsthand the power of the urges mothers warned their daughters to resist until the gold ring glittered and the marriage sheets beckoned.

But Angel had no mother to warn her. . . .

"Maximillian," she whispered.

Just the sound of his name seemed to bring moisture to that forbidden spot between her legs that good Victorian women were not allowed to think of, much less touch. At the sound of his name, for the briefest instant, she could have sworn she actually saw him, at least in her mind's eye.

His head flung back, he bathed himself standing in the nude, scrubbing briskly under one long, golden arm, then rinsing and rubbing the soapy sponge over the muscles of his impressive chest. He glittered gold from head to toe. The image was so real she reached out to touch him before she could stop herself. As she did so, he turned his head to smile at her.

That knowing smile, that glowing smile that caused a soft curling in her lower belly. It was almost as if . . . he knew she watched him. As if he were reaching into her mind across the miles between them. She bolted upright, her half-closed eyes flying open. The image dissipated.

But the heat it inspired remained.

Angry at herself, Angel tossed her covers aside and rose, only to have to throw her arm about the bedpost. She was still quite literally weak-kneed. But she forced herself upright and walked steadily to the ewer. She poured water into the big ceramic bowl and rinsed her face, lecturing herself all the while.

This weakness was nonsense. Not in her nature at all. It was the wine, or the sheer novelty of the experience of being the object of such a dynamic man's attentions.

She'd always been attracted to dangerous things. She'd experimented with opium, she loved to gallop full-tilt over stony terrain, and she'd even climbed a steep cliff once, just to see if she could. The jagged-toothed rocks and crashing surf far below had only contributed to her exhilaration once she made it to the top and saw the folly of the path she'd chosen.

Had it been folly to leave the only home she'd ever known to venture to the land of her mother's birth and remote relatives she barely knew?

She pinned her hair up severely and dressed in her plainest attire, telling herself that, so far at least, she had no regrets. And since Maximillian seemed to turn her spine into mush, she'd be wise to avoid him. Besides, she'd rusticated long enough. She'd come here to be a scientist.

It was time to beard Sir Alexander and press the issue of her employment.

She found him in his study poring over his notebooks. He slid several under cover of his newspapers, making her wonder what he was trying to hide.

"Good morning, my dear. How was your outing last night?" He folded his glasses to smile at her.

Outing, was it? She cringed as she wondered what half the people at the party were whispering about her this morning. The other half were probably gossiping openly. And this man who smiled so genially, her mother's brother, hadn't lifted a finger to stop it.

She was cooler than she intended when she rejoined, "Illuminating." And she left it at that, secretly satisfied at his nonplussed expression.

She proffered the book she carried. "Sir Alexander, if you recall from our correspondence, I also wanted to offer my services as your lab assistant. As I mentioned, I helped write this book and compile the research that led to its publication."

He took the book, glancing down at the title, *Blood—Its Strange Properties and Exigencies,* and set it carelessly aside. "Yes, yes, most interesting, but surely you see now that I could never allow my own lovely niece to waste away in a smelly laboratory. You, like your mother, my dear Angel, are meant to dance by candlelight, not toil by it." When she made to protest again, he rose and took her hands, kissing the backs of her knuckles. "No, no, my mind's made up on the matter. Now go along and let me work." He sat back down.

If he'd patted her on the head and called her a good little girl he couldn't have angered Angel any more. She'd been here only a bit over a week, but she'd already figured out that nothing was as it seemed.

Kindly, protective Alexander had his own hidden agenda and wasn't above using his niece's reputation to achieve it. And his wife, ever youthful, ever joyful, had a dark side that sometimes glistened in her eyes when she looked at Angel. The stable manager had her own self-confessed mysterious mission. And the surly head groom always seemed to be where he shouldn't, poking about even in the house, where she'd caught him on one occasion.

As for the local rake . . . well, of him Angel didn't want to think. Especially not now when she needed a clear head.

Angel hovered a moment longer, but when

Sir Alexander never even bothered looking up again, Angel took her worn tome and tattered dignity where they'd be appreciated.

That was how Shelly found her an hour later, playing with the puppies born only the week prior to Sir Alexander's prize Irish setter. Angel held one soft, squirming little red body to her cheek, whispering to it, "Tell me, little one, what's it like to have all these brothers and sisters and a mama who loves you?"

The words had scarcely escaped her before the pup's little brother latched onto his sister's toe. The pup howled. Angel gently pulled the little fellow away, holding it by the scruff of its neck. "On second thought, perhaps I should be glad I'm an orphan." He licked her nose. Angel giggled, glancing up at the soft laughter from the stable doorway.

"I should imagine if the dog could talk, he'd complain that you were giving his troublesome little sister so much more attention." Shelly sauntered inside the stall door. With capable hands, she checked the mother's teats for milk and shoved a fat little puppy away so the runt could have his share. "And so many siblings inevitably divide a mother's love, with the result that one or more offspring feel left out. Being alone is not always a bad thing. Mayhap one doesn't have a mother's love, but one doesn't have to compete for self-assurance if it springs from within."

Steady gray eyes met Angel's. How could this strange woman see so clearly into Angel's heart?

To avoid that stare, Angel set her pup down and watched it squirm through the bodies for its own teat. "You speak with the voice of experience, I imagine." Angel sliced her eyes up in time to catch Shelly's look of surprise.

Then offense settled down over that strong face. Shelly stood to her full, imposing height and stuck her hands on her hips. "Are you implying, my girl, that I'm a runt?"

Angel stood also to her equally imposing height. "No, I'm saying that we both like our solitude perhaps a bit more than is good for us."

A yelp made them both look down. The runt, pushed aside, had latched onto the aggressive little male pup's ear and taken over his teat. Angel and Shelly both smiled down at the dogs, then back at each other. Their look seemed to say that rejection did tend to make one strong, in both the canine and Homo sapiens communities.

Shelly turned to the door. "I'm famished. Would you care to join me for a bite to eat?"

They lunched that day on cold chicken and

warm conversation. The more she got to know Shelly Holmes, the more Angel liked her. And the more she let down her guard. However, when the subject of Maximillian arose, she knew not how, Angel looked away.

"I don't know him well. And I suspect I'd be most unwise to pursue further acquaintance with him."

"I suspect you are quite right." Shelly wrapped her bones in her napkin and stuck them back in the sack. "But I also suspect that, as long as you remain a guest at Blythe Hall, you'll have little choice in the matter. As happened last night, the veriest chance will throw him your way."

"Are you suggesting I should leave?"

"It might be wise."

"And where, oh Solomon, would you have me go? I sold every stick of furniture I owned for traveling money to get here. I quit my position and gave up the lease on my flat." Angel angrily wadded up her own half-eaten meal. "No, I came here of my own free will and so I will remain. Despite the dangers."

"Because you feel you have no choice?"

"There's always a choice. In this case, staying here is my most palatable option."

Shelly toyed with the edge of her shirt in a nervous gesture that seemed most unlike her.

"And if I proved to you that your behavior last night was the source of neither choice nor chance?"

Angel blushed. So it was true. Even the stable mistress knew of her wantonness.

Again, Shelly showed that uncanny ability to read her mind. "There's always gossip after Blythe Hall's parties. Last night was positively tame in comparison to some of the tales I've heard. While a few will no doubt condemn you for leaving without a chaperon, others have done far worse far more blatantly." At Angel's confused look, Shelly said baldly, "I was there, Angel. In fact, had I not been there, at this moment you'd likely be a resident at the Trelayne estate, mistress, in the pejorative sense of the word, of its last heir."

"But I don't understand."

"Your wine was spiked."

Angel frowned. Spiked?

"With an extremely strong aphrodisiac."

Angel's eyes widened. Blood left her face in a rush, and then flooded back in a sea of outraged color. "Maximillian drugged my wine?"

Shelly's hesitation was all the answer Angel needed. Angel surged to her feet. "That bastard!"

Shelly stood to face her. "No, Angel, it wasn't Max."

"Who, then?"

Shelly stared at her implacably.

Angel turned away. "No."

Shelly patted her shoulder. "Unfortunately, yes. Sir Alexander and Maximillian are locked in some kind of fierce power struggle, and you, my dear, are both the pawn and, if you're not very careful, the prize."

Covering her ears with her hands, Angel ran. She didn't believe that. She wouldn't believe that. Why, Sir Alexander was her mother's brother. He was her own last remaining kin.

What possible gain could he win from her ruin?

Tears blinding her, she stumbled away from the hall, but her feet seemed to have an unerring sense of direction. When she stopped to gain her bearings, wiping her eyes on her sleeve, she stood within the gates of the cemetery. Over her mother's grave.

Falling to her knees, Angel let grief and betrayal take her. And with them, they carried the knell of certainty.

Deny it though she tried, she'd just solved one of the mysteries of her childhood: this was why her mother had fled the land of her birth for an uncertain future in America. Because she knew her own kin were not to be trusted. . . .

*   *   *

The niggling awareness of her pain came slowly to Max. He stiffened with dread this time, the second time it had happened. The first time, when he'd been bathing, thinking of her, he'd felt the brush of her awareness. He knew she'd seen him because he'd wished it so. However, the strange mental bonding was not always a matter of his will. And it happened only with those who touched him in some way.

Mentally. Physically. Emotionally. Since Angel touched him in all three ways, he'd been expecting this.

But now? He had not expected it to come upon him unawares, as he pored over his own research. At a time when nothing typically troubled him. But the more he tried to deny the tingle, the clearer the image grew.

Angel. Crying. He closed his eyes and saw her on her knees, her arms cradled around her middle as she rocked back and forth. He let the eerie sight take him, the image broadening until he saw the headstone. She was alone. In the Blythe cemetery.

And darkness fast approached.

He dropped the books, flung open his windows, let the wind take him, and flapped away on soundless black wings.

*   *   *

The ageless hunger grew unbearable. Time to feed. But not just any blood would do. It had to be the right age, the right gender, the right shape.

The right girl.

Angelina Blythe . . . The taste of her was already a torment on the tongue. That last drop of blood they shared would turn the pasty-faced prude into the true creature of the night she was destined to be. A companion for the ages. Most important, a companion who would be the death of the hunter.

The hunger was so piercing now it became pain. The Beefsteak Killer doubled over briefly, but through a fierce effort of will that was second nature now, it denied itself. For five hundred years it had learned to wait when patience was unbearable, to hunger when satiety was near.

Since the time of the Crusades, it had thrived, growing strong on fear and hatred. Nothing stopped it, nothing frightened it.

Except the vampire who killed vampires.

They were both the last of their line. Both hated each other with a fierceness endowed by all the blood that had been shed in their ancient battle.

But as much as fury raged to hurry, to strike now, the Beefsteak Killer knew it was too soon.

It wouldn't do to get hasty after so much careful planning.

It wasn't yet time for the end of Maximillian, the last Earl of Trelayne.

But the girl . . . it wouldn't hurt to torment her a little. To ready her for the melding.

The Beefsteak Killer turned into vapor and melted into the night.

By the time grief faded enough for Angel to realize it was almost dark, she remembered too late the whispers of the servants when they thought she wasn't listening.

Don't be alone after dark.

Don't wander outside the hall.

Most particularly, Don't go near the cemetery.

Angel got slowly to her feet, eyes searching through the gloom. She heard what sounded like a brief rustling. She turned in that direction, half able to see despite the almost total darkness unrelieved by so much as a sliver of a moon.

She'd always been blessed with unusually acute night vision, perhaps to compensate for her odd sensitivity to the sun. She started backing toward the gate, still watching the shadowy outline of a catafalque. She'd seen a flash of movement behind it, she swore she had.

Angel . . .

"Who's there?" She froze midstep. She'd felt the voice more than heard it.

Chill bumps pimpled her skin. The voice was soft, a whisper so magnetic that she couldn't tell if it was male or female.

Angel, come to me . . .

Angel tried to run toward the gate, but her feet were stuck in molasses. Cold molasses as congealed as her blood. And then she was moving . . . but not toward the gate.

Toward the catafalque and the unseen presence. A strangely alluring presence, despite her fear of it. But one always feared the unknown, she told herself.

As she drew near, the lid slid open smoothly.

Welcome . . .

Angel climbed inside the cavity to find smooth stone steps leading down into total darkness. It was then the scent brushed her nostrils, a chill damp almost like mist. Mist that carried the whiff of rotting things.

Part of her, the cool, scientific part, gave her strength enough to recoil.

"No." The sound of her own voice was bracing. "I can't see."

You don't need to see. Only to feel.

Angel's rational half was swept away in a deluge of dark curiosity. Her destiny lay here in this place of her blood. She knew it. She couldn't walk away without finding the source of this voice. Some instinct that went deeper than bone and sinew told her that if she solved the mystery of this voice, she'd also solve the mystery of her own birth. Why she was different, why she'd always been alone.

Angel walked down the steps.

The second he flew over the headstones, Max felt the presence. But it shocked him so that the change wasn't as smooth as usual. Half man, half bat, he fell with a thud to the ground, his arms slowly forming out of the bat wings.

The Beefsteak Killer. He was sure of it. Once before, as his investigation led him to a victim a few minutes too late, he'd come upon this presence. It felt like nothing else he'd ever known, either human or vampire. But when he tried to chase it, it evaporated.

Like mist. As long as he'd been a vampire, that was one skill Max hadn't yet mastered. The handiest skill of all, to become part of the night itself. Even when cornered, such a being could still escape. You couldn't drive a stake through mist.

But the bitter taste of evil was here again, upon his tongue. It was ageless, deathless, utterly without remorse or mercy.

And Angel was here.

Max forced his mind to clear of his own burgeoning panic, not for himself, but for her. As his mind cleared, his body rapidly completed the change. He sprang the short distance to the catafalque, where he sensed Angel had disappeared.

Indeed, as he neared, he saw that the heavy lid was thrown back.

The presence grew stronger.

Max cursed his inability to bring his kit with him. Ripping down a half-dead tree branch, Max broke it into several pieces that would have to serve as stakes. If the creature would threaten Angel's humanity, it would have to take human form.

Max followed Angel's footsteps, glowing before him like a beacon, into the murk.

She was strong. Strong enough to resist the allure of her own nature?

Hurrying now, Max would have said an exceedingly rusty prayer if he hadn't known it would be sacrilegious.

The vengeful God of his childhood wouldn't want prayers from unnaturally immortal creatures who survived on blood. No matter how valiant, he was still a vampire.

Suddenly, the rough stakes in his hands seemed woefully inadequate.

*   *   *

As she walked deeper into the tunnel that led away from the steps, Angel realized she was beginning to see. Odd. There was no discernible light.

Angel rounded a corner and found herself in a lovely sitting room. The outlines of the furniture were dim, but when she touched a gilded arm, her fingers came away coated with dust.

A crystal decanter, covered with spiderwebs, sat on a sideboard. Angel felt a sudden urge to wet her dry throat. She walked toward the decanter, noticing a shadowy movement above in the mirror. She looked up. Her breath caught in her throat.

Twin spots glowed redly at her. Eyes. Watching.

Angel backed away, shaking her head. The eyes moved from side to side. Angel froze, her eyes widening. The reddish eyes widened, too.

She stared at herself. Those eerie, glowing eyes were *her own.*

Angel covered her mouth to stop a scream, but then that alluring voice came again, calming her slightly.

Accept your gifts. . . .

Angel resisted. She stared at her own glow-

108

ing eyes. Why had she never noticed them before?

You're growing stronger. . . .

"Who are you?" Angel begged. "What do you
want of me?"

Drink. . . .

Angel looked at the decanter. One minute
she was halfway across the room, the next she
was lifting the heavy crystal vessel.

No! Max's voice came clearly. She turned,
expecting him to be in the room, but she was
still alone. *It will make you sick. Put it down.*

Angel moved to put it down, but the other
voice came stronger, harder, more powerful.

DRINK. . . .

Angel took off the stopper.

It's not wine, Angel. Max's voice in her mind
was soft, pleading. She saw him standing as if
in a shaft of light, that golden glow beaming
from his hair, his skin, his soul. In that instant,
she understood what was happening.

There was a battle of wills going on, and just
as Shelly had warned her, she was the prize.

But who was good? And who was evil?

*It's a lie . . . he's a vampire . . . drink to pro-
tect yourself from him. . . .*

Angel poured a small drink in a glass. Her
hand felt numb, and when the two crystals
rang as they connected, the sound seemed to

vibrate through her, too. As if she were an empty vessel also. Waiting to be filled, and used.

Angel lifted the glass.

Then he was there, in body as he'd been in her mind. There were no footsteps, no rustle of clothes to presage him. He reached out to knock the glass away, but then he grasped his throat, choking.

Angel saw someone, something, tall but cloaked, grab him from behind.

Immediately the siren whispering in her mind went quiet. Angel set the glass down, shaking. Fear made her move for the door, but she stopped. Max had come here to protect her. She knew that as certainly as she knew she couldn't trust him.

Vampire or not, he needed her help.

But he didn't. . . . Even as she lifted a heavy figurine and tried to circle around behind the cloaked figure, Max's nails grew into long, disgusting claws and dug deeply into the hands choking him. The cloaked figure gave an unearthly screech and backed off. Max whirled and jabbed with the stake that had suddenly appeared in his hand.

But he touched air. The cloak floated harmlessly to the floor. A column of mist grew.

For an instant, the stench was so strong Angel had to cover her nose with both hands.

Then the mist trailed toward the door, growing thinner, finer . . . and it was gone.

Only then did she realize the smell of death remained.

And Max was the only one left in the room.

He tossed the stake away in frustration, turning toward her.

With the mist went some of Angel's strength. She was a scientist, but the events of this night had no rational explanation.

Two unnatural beings had invaded her mind, fighting their battle within her. As to why she, of unusually strong mind, had not been able to fight them off . . . well, she'd have to ponder that later. For now, she knew only the urge to flee. Max stood quietly, staring at her.

His eyes glowed redly, too.

If she'd needed further proof of who and what he was, here it was. She was drawn to this enticing, enigmatic man because he was a vampire.

She sidled toward the door. One minute he was in front of her; the next he was against her, pressing her back into the sideboard. So quickly, so artfully, did he move.

He held her just as artfully, no claws in evidence now as he lifted her chin with a warm, seemingly normal masculine hand. "I came here at considerable risk to myself. Why this sudden coldness toward me?"

"You'll excuse me if I don't know my proper crypt etiquette, but I don't number many vampires amongst my acquaintance." She tried to ease away, but he caressed her throat now. She shivered, hating herself for liking the silken stroke of his hands. His eyes glowed at her redly, but she was growing increasingly accustomed to the gloom, and here, even here, perhaps most of all in this place that still smelled faintly of death, he shone with starfire.

His golden vibrance and bright smile contrasted so with the reddish eyes and claws that more befitted the legends of his kind. Which were harbingers of his true nature? She still didn't know which of the two strange figures who'd battled for control of her was good, which was evil.

The other presence had only spoken to her. It had made no threatening moves. Whereas Maximillian had only to touch her to set her heart to racing. Like now.

"How do you know I'm a vampire? Do I look like one?" That bright smile deepened.

She felt his sensual tug at her very womb. "No, but you feel like one. And nothing else can explain the way you move without sound, leave no footprints, the glow of your eyes—"

"Your eyes glow, too." He swung her about, holding her framed against him to force her to look into the mirror.

Indeed they did. Almost as brightly as his. To block the sight, she closed her eyes, her mind reeling with more possibilities than her shocked sensibilities could take. There was some simple explanation for that odd reddish tint. A lack of pigmentation, perhaps, that gave her albino tendencies. Her skin was very fair.

"Very fair, indeed, in every sense of the word. But that can't account for your ability to see in the dark."

She jerked away from him. "Would you stay out of my head?"

"Why? It's getting crowded in there, since you seem to be of two minds yourself. How fortunate that I like crowds."

She wanted to hit him until she saw the wry curve of his luscious mouth. Her own mouth relaxed slightly.

A fingertip brushed her lips, barely grazing, side to side. "Ah, you look so much better when you smile." His mouth lowered to brush the same path until her lips tingled with his starfire. "And the taste of your smile is addictive."

She opened her mouth to him, unable to deny the dark allure of this bright, impossible-to-understand . . . But he wasn't a man. Not really. But ah, of all the nightly gifts he gave, kissing was the best. Then his light little nibbles trailed from her lips down her chin, where his tongue explored the small indentation, to the soft, scented hollow of her throat. His tongue dipped there, too, as if she were not only honey, but surcease, hope for happiness.

The crazy thoughts spun, windmill-like, in her brain. And then she felt the brush of his teeth against the side of her neck. He shuddered, a small breath warming the place where his lips and teeth nibbled. Then, with a groan that seemed to come from depths where he let no woman reach, he crushed her to him, kissing her wildly, passionately, with a need that seemed more desperately human than vampire seductive.

As he deepened the kiss, a faint sound came from the corridor.

He was instantly alert. "Stay here." He seemed to float more than walk to the door.

She'd never been a good one for orders. She waited, heard only a fainter rustling sound, what sounded like a low moan, then dead silence. She had to know what was happening. She crept to the door after him, surprised at how soundless her own feet were on the cold stone floor. Odd. Her slippers had hard soles.

When she reached the door, she stopped, gripping the jamb with both hands. She saw the body with her mind, smelled it with her nostrils, before she forced herself to look down at the tunnel floor. It was dotted with dark splotches of blood.

Fresh blood.

Max knelt over the figure. The poor thing still had oozing holes torn on each side of the long, previously flawless neck. Holes torn so violently, blood spurted from the jugular. It still oozed sluggishly. Max stared down, his expression peculiar, obviously so intent on the girl before him that he'd momentarily forgotten the one he'd left in the sitting room. Then he started to bend toward the feeble flow. In that instant, she saw fangs.

Gasping, Angel leaped over both of them with a strength and agility that startled her and ran as if her life depended upon it.

As it probably did. If not for that poor girl on the floor, she could have been the one lying in a pool of blood.

Max snapped to when he felt Angel jump over him. He sprang up to follow her, realizing she'd seen his brief battle with temptation. And misunderstood. Exactly as the killer had intended when planting its latest victim in the tunnel.

How did the Beefsteak Killer know how much the enemy hungered to taste of human blood? Warm human blood. Just once . . .

Shame burned through Max as he looked down at the poor, unfortunate girl. She looked as innocent and lovely as the rest. Alexander was quite choosy, as usual. Max covered the girl with a quilt from over the settee, closed her staring eyes, and then sought fresh air.

When he emerged, torchlight almost blinded him. But his eyes adjusted quickly. He was shocked to see quite a gathering: several burly farmworkers, the village smithy, and Gustav, the head groom from the Blythe estate, a surly fellow Max had never trusted. Even the local parish priest. The priest held a huge silver crucifix high, as if the feeble silver glow could protect all of them.

And in the distance, he just made out Alexander escorting Angel away into a carriage. The horses galloped off, leaving Max alone to face the mob.

But it wouldn't be the first time. It also wouldn't be the last time Alexander had used his own people in his war against the Trelaynes.

The crucifix trembled slightly. Max's lip curled. He bowed, one hand in his waistcoat. "A welcoming party? Just for me? How kind."

His sally only earned even grimmer looks.

The Blythe groom sneered. "We found her scarf against a tree, one shoe outside the steps where you did your foul deed. You're going to the lockup, your lordship. We'll have no more of these killings once you're behind bars."

Max looked at the red scarf, the small shoe. If he hadn't been so concerned about Angel upon his arrival, he would have noticed the convenient trail. He'd noticed nothing but Angel's footsteps. . . .

"And how, pray tell, do you know there's a victim, much less that I'm a killer?"

The words were scarcely out of his mouth before two men struggled up from the gaping hole in the catafalque, carrying the dead girl.

"We was warned," said the smithy, his beefy arms folded over his broad chest. Max had always admired the fellow. He had a "come through me, not around me" look to him that few wore before the Earl of Trelayne.

"And if I told you I merely stumbled upon her, quite literally?"

The smithy spat his response. "And bathed in her blood, belike?"

Max looked down at his clothes. The flow of blood had stopped more slowly than he'd realized. "Nevertheless, I killed no one." Not tonight. "But I shall be happy to live down to your

117

lurid expectations. Who's first?" Max leaped forward in a huge bound, whipping the stakes from his cloak.

The dare had the effect he hoped. The priest almost dropped the crucifix. The torches trembled. Even the smithy backed away a step. Only Gustav stayed firm, and for a brief instant, Max could have sworn the head groom bared fangs.

Max took full advantage. One more bound took him behind a huge tree. There he climbed soundlessly into the branches.

By the time the villagers clustered at the base of the tree, casting torchlight up to peer into the branches, Maximillian, Earl of Trelayne, flapped far above their heads on noiseless wings.

But he left frightened whispers and resentful mutterings behind him.

Chapter Five

Unable to sleep, Angel paced, her night robe
flowing behind her. She had to know what had
happened to Max. She'd been shocked to see
the gathering, had pointed automatically when
Gustav asked if she knew if anyone had been
killed.

"And the Earl of Trelayne? Was he there,
too?" Gustav had asked.

Angel froze, finally thinking clearly again.
That was an odd question for him to ask, unless
. . . unless someone had sent him.

Telling him first that Max would be there.

Thinking back, Angel remembered how
quickly Alexander had appeared, sweeping
her into his carriage without a question or,

119

come to think of it, a great deal of concern. He patted her shoulder on the brief journey to the hall, seeming to take no offense when she shrank away. She longed to confront him with what Shelly had told her, but if tonight had taught her anything, it was to bide her time and her tongue.

If Alexander were truly her enemy, it would be far better for him to think she still considered him a kindly uncle. But that didn't prevent her from trying to find out what was going on.

She cocked her head and listened. She'd never ventured out of her quarters in the wee hours before, even when she occasionally heard an odd noise. But she'd never been so restless before. Frightened, curious, oddly exhilarated all at once. The danger she'd experienced tonight had strangely enlivened her and stirred up her blood.

She'd come here for adventure, hadn't she?

If nothing else, she wanted to see inside the lab in the cellar that her uncle refused to let her enter. She threw off her night robe and rail and dressed.

As soon as he was out of sight of the others, Gustav threw off his heavy coat and overpants to reveal his fine serge wool jacket and matching pants. This distasteful role of servant thrust upon him was a necessary charade, but that didn't mean he had to relish it. And it certainly didn't mean he had to wear mean clothes and mean manners for the coming meeting with his peers.

He'd led the villagers to the earl and done his best to stir them up. The plan had been to use weak humans to put a bloody period to the last of the tenacious Earls of Trelayne. And it might have worked if Trelayne had turned to run as expected, falling into the net the villagers had spread for him. Instead, the youngest vampire in the area had outsmarted even him. He'd bounded *forward*, and then disappeared into a tree.

Gustav glanced at his watch. One of the morning.

And the piper to pay. They wouldn't be happy with him. If they even let him into their sacred conference of blooded brothers.

He'd have to grovel. But that was part of the charade, too. . . .

The downstairs was darker than Angel expected. Every rustle made her start. But the whisper of fabric was merely curtains flapping in the breeze. Why were the windows open?

A slight scraping sound made her gasp, but then she realized her own foot had brushed against a chair, bumping it gently over the parquet floor. She stopped, for once thankful for her excellent night vision, for it was apparent she was the only one stirring in the side hall that led to the stairs into the basement. She clutched the chair back, wondering where her bravado had gone.

Right out the window, along with her loyalty to kith and kin. For a moment, she seriously considered going back to her room, but then she stiffened.

She had nothing to feel guilty about. Sir Alexander was her uncle and he'd used her as a pawn since the day she arrived here. Perhaps he had reason. Perhaps the oh, so handsome, oh, so bold and bright Earl of Trelayne was the true Beefsteak Killer.

But whatever the battle between them, and whatever the outcome of her own role in it, one irrefutable fact made her put one foot in front of another again: she needed—no, she wanted—to get into that basement laboratory.

There lay hard physical evidence of what Alexander truly studied. It was the only truth about her mysterious relatives Angel trusted.

Taking a deep breath, she set foot on the first step leading into the basement.

Only then did she see the eerie glow.

Almost, she turned and ran back to her

room, but she heard not a whisper of sound and assumed that perhaps someone had left a lantern burning. Even if Alexander were working this late, she could make some excuse, say she'd been unable to sleep and had come in search of him to ask questions about her mother.

He was her uncle, wasn't he? He should comfort her.

She walked rapidly down the steps.

For the fourth time in as many minutes, Max gagged on the disgusting, cold blood he was trying to consume. No matter how he tried—he stared at his fireplace, where his own blood-spattered garments burned—he couldn't forget the silky texture and warm feel of that poor girl's blood.

For over a century he'd kept to his vows as a Watch Bearer. He'd not once partaken of living human blood, though he had on occasion been reduced to robbing from experimental laboratories where doctors experimented feverishly. They were trying to deduce why some humans could safely pass their blood on to others, and other individuals who seemed even healthier could not.

But he'd tried to avoid that necessity because the taste was different from sheep's blood, or cow's, or pig's or goat's. It was silky-smooth and sweet. Like clotted cream on the tongue.

Angel . . . What did she taste like?

The image of that long throat thrown back for his delectation jabbed at his temples like one of his own stakes. Shame at his rare weakness gave him strength enough to gag down his meal. Then he lay back, exhausted, on the bed that rested over the earth of his forebears.

That part of the vampire myth was true. Every vampire had to rest upon the earth of its birth or weaken. Which meant if he could find where the Beefsteak Killer rested, he could at least force the vampire into flight, or to the stash where it kept its second coffin. One thing Max was sure of: the Beefsteak Killer was the same legendary vampire the Watch Bearers had been pursuing for five hundred years.

It was the only one known with a slanted tooth. It had first appeared in the historical accounts—myths, really—when it preyed upon the fair young daughter of a Crusader who'd taken his family to Constantinople with him.

The creature was likely an unholy product of the East, with its exotic wiles and exotic ways. Where could it keep its coffins? Not in the mausoleum, for Max was reasonably certain he'd been over every inch of that.

He'd also searched the Blythe estate during those wild parties. He'd found nothing, not even in that pathetic excuse for a science lab in the basement.

Max sat up abruptly. Angel . . . walking toward the lab.

Now, at this very moment.

Damn the girl; this was twice in one night he'd have to rescue her! For all the good it did him in her esteem. He'd seen the way she let Alexander whisk her off, leaving him to face the mob alone. But he was used to that.

He wasn't used to having his willpower so tested. Having a feeling that he was going to regret this night, Max leaped out of bed and went to the window, his bat wings already forming.

Angel was relieved when she saw the brace of candles someone had left burning on a small table outside the laboratory. The feeble light felt brilliant after her eyes had so well adjusted to the dark. She was about to turn her attention to the strange locks on the laboratory door when she heard voices.

She cocked her head, trying to deduce the source. Definitely not the laboratory. She followed the sound more easily as the voices grew more heated. She found herself winding through a darkened corridor until she finally faced—a blank wall. Or what seemed to be a blank wall.

She felt for cracks and crevices as she listened with all her might to what she sensed was a clandestine meeting that would help illuminate the mysteries going on around the estate. At first only a faint hum was evident. . . .

Then she heard a voice she recognized. "Dammit, I did all I could to see the bastard captured!"

Gustav. The head groom.

Angel vaguely recollected glimpsing him at the head of the villagers who'd collected in the cemetery. Before she'd had an opportunity to learn their purpose, Alexander had whisked her off.

Unable to find an opening, Angel pressed her ear to the wall. Her heart skipped a beat as she clearly recognized Alexander's smooth voice. "Then I should be appalled to see a half effort from you, Gustav."

"You haven't had any better luck cornering him," Gustav retorted.

The voices abruptly went silent.

There was a choking, gargling sound that chilled Angel enough to make her run down the corridor back toward the glow of light.

She didn't hear the "What's that?" that came from inside the room.

Almost, she went back to her chamber to cower under the sheets. But that wall didn't seem to open on this corridor, and she doubted if she'd been heard. Besides, these damnable locks were suddenly symbolic of all the blank walls her life had consisted of to date. She was tired of being manipulated.

Her mouth twisting defiantly, Angel pulled from her pocket the long, wicked metal skewer she'd filched from the scullery for just this purpose. It wouldn't be the first time, no, nor the last, she'd pry open a locked door.

There were a few advantages to being an orphan, and a female determined to succeed in a man's world. The first lock was easy, the second far harder. She wiped sweat from her brow.

"Isn't it easier with this, my child?" The voice came over her shoulder, silky-smooth and so bland it almost concealed the menacing undertone.

Almost. Trying to disguise her terror with a cough, Angel turned to see her uncle dangling a key from the chain at his waist.

Her orphanage escapades had also taught her that bluffing was the best policy when caught red-handed. Angel straightened to her full height, calmly reached out, and removed the key from the chain. "Thank you." She immediately turned back to the last lock, but his stunned expression told her she'd finally surprised him.

"Were you wandering down the corridor just now?" he demanded.

The fact that he was worried enough to ask warned Angel to lie. She glanced over her shoulder at him, then quickly looked back at the lock. "I've been struggling with these for nigh onto thirty minutes. Why, did something happen I should know about?"

"No."

Pretending not to hear the doubt in his voice, she fumbled the lock open, picked up the candles, and entered the lab. But she looked back over her shoulder at him. Because of the bright glow blinding her, she couldn't see his face, but she trusted the strange instincts that had come to her more and more strongly of late.

He wouldn't hurt her. At least, not yet. "Please, would you show me around finally?" she asked lightly. "Normally I wouldn't dream of intruding, but you've been so kind to me that I . . . well, I just want to repay you. And I'm an excellent lab assistant, truly." As she spoke, she moved farther into the room.

He followed her, moving so soundlessly that he was right behind her when she turned to set the candles down. With a great effort of control, she managed not to shrink back, but to her relief he only held out his hand for his key. She handed it over without a quibble.

"What do you wish to see?" he asked with ill grace. "The dead bodies I have removed every Thursday?"

Angel tapped her chin with her finger. "Hmm, since this is Friday, I suspect I'll have to make do with boring notebooks instead of an interesting autopsy." Her retort surprised a fleeting smile from him. More of her fear eased and she smiled back.

"You truly are Eileen, the best and worst of her. She was as curious as a cat also." He moved up, making her heart skip a beat, but he only tapped her cheek. "Sassy as brass, too."

"And you'd have it no other way, darling, as you well know," said Sarina from the doorway. "Now let the poor child explore and learn the dastardly truth of Blythe Hall." Sarina held a finger to her lips, her blue eyes dancing in the candlelight. "Shhh . . . you will keep our secrets, won't you, dearest Angel?"

Her tone said, *We have none, but I understand your need to look.*

Angel relaxed further. Somehow she always

felt better when Sarina was near. Stronger, more capable, as if the older woman brought out the best in her. "Please forgive me," Angel said, finally shamed. "But, indeed, I did come here to work in science and—"

"No need to apologize. I've been telling Alexander for days that you are not the typical milk-and-water miss. That you don't mind getting your hands dirty and your mind cluttered." Sarina sauntered forward and pulled several heavy notebooks from a shelf. "But if you can read this drivel for more than an hour without falling asleep, I shall find myself surprised."

Angel accepted the dusty notebooks as if she were offered the Ten Commandments, ark included. "Thank you." She took them to a table, set the candles down, and opened the first one. She began to read, immediately engrossed in the dry recitation of the experiments Sir Alexander had conducted on his own calves, trying to determine the differences in composition between bovine hemoglobin and Homo sapiens hemoglobin.

He'd reasoned that if he could define vast differences first between species, the finer points of what differentiated various human types would slowly become evident.

Specious reasoning, as far as Angel was concerned. She kept her head down as she quickly skimmed through the experiment. If one wished to determine the pattern of an oak leaf, one didn't collect elm leaves and hope it led to the same pattern. Had he given her bogus notebooks to try to disguise what he was doing, or was he merely incompetent?

She was reaching for the second notebook when both Sarina and Alexander stiffened and turned to the door. Angel turned, too.

He stood there, his golden hair mussed, his cheeks flushed as if he'd hurried. He looked between Alexander and Sarina, who stood arm in arm, apparently on perfectly cordial terms with their niece. To Angel's fury, the look he turned on her was considerably more fiery.

"Blast it, girl, do you ever stay in your bed after it turns dark?" He stormed inside the room.

Angel slammed the notebook down and surged to her feet. "Only when I'm accompanied by my two lovers. Neither one blond, I might add." Almost, she laughed at his slack-jawed astonishment. When had she become so bold?

Apparently Sarina was less surprised, but far more appreciative. She gave that lilting, feminine laugh that men likened to the music of the ages. "A sally even the Earl of Trelayne cannot top."

The Earl of Trelayne turned on her. "If anyone other than yourself, my dear Lady Blythe, can better *top* the subject of lovers, blond or otherwise, I cannot think whom."

Sarina paled and shrank away as if from a blow.

Making fists, Angel took a couple of steps toward Max. Really, that was most uncalled for. She'd heard the rumors, too, but accounted them exactly that. Rumors perpetrated by other less lovely women.

But before she could take more than two steps, Alexander surged toward the door.

Max stood where he was just inside the room with a "please do" look.

Alexander glanced at Angel and stopped. "Get out of my house, out of my county, and out of my life. It's your last warning, Britton."

"Or what? You'll send another loving assortment of villagers to do your dirty work for you?"

Angel looked closely between the two men. Villagers? She also noted that Alexander looked at her again—sneakily this time.

Max turned from his rival in disgust and offered his arm to Angel. "Come along."

If he'd commanded her in a manner a bit more polite than that he might use for a recalcitrant dog, she might have taken his arm. She was still uneasy about those voices she'd heard and Alexander's defensiveness. And after all, tonight, in the crypt, Max had been quite protective of her.

Before he'd hovered over that poor unfortunate girl with a glitter of unmistakable hunger in his eyes.

Angel looked at Max's arm, flexing with his own strong but shielded emotions. Then she glanced at Sarina.

Sarina's eyes were jewel-bright with tears, pleading. "If you follow him out of this house, you take a step on a pathway from which you will never return." Her soft voice had the air of certainty, more than prediction. As if she knew. As if she'd been there . . .

Angel looked between Alexander's saturnine face and Max's handsome, expressionless one. Unable to choose between Scylla and Charybdis, Angel instead turned to her solace: science. Sitting back down at the table, she picked up the second notebook. She couldn't resist a last peep up, however.

Was it her imagination, or had Max's cheeks gone ashen with pain? A flash of something hot and hurtful and dangerous roiled in those emerald-green eyes, but then he'd shielded them with his lashes.

Having made her choice, she knew she must live with it. She bent her head over her research, wondering why the pages suddenly swam before her gaze.

A slight rustle of clothing, and she knew Max was gone. This hot burning in her throat was merely her reaction to the dust, she told herself.

Alexander took the notebook from her hands and set it back on the shelf. "Enough science for tonight, dear child. I'm quite proud and touched at your trust in us, however. I promise tomorrow morning you can come back down and I shall share with you everything I've learned in my years of research." He caught her arm and helped her to the door.

Numbly, Angel followed. And just as numbly, that night, she lay in bed, staring into the darkness, wondering why she felt as if she'd betrayed someone.

That someone was, at the very least, a dangerous rake. Probably far worse. And while Alexander obviously had his own secrets, he was her kin. Turning on her side, Angel hugged the pillow and told herself over and over she'd made not only the right choice, but the only one.

The trick was believing it. . . .

* * *

In the ensuing days, the choice felt no more palatable. She neither saw nor heard from Max, who had seemed almost her shadow since she'd heard his voice in her head. Now she heard nothing but the whisper of her own foolish regrets. She had a feeling that quite possibly she'd never see him again. Since he made her weak and made her forget why she'd come here, she tried to tell herself that was for the best, too.

She didn't need a bright, bold star that drew her out of her dark obsessions with her own heritage. She didn't need a man whose kisses made her forget who and what he could be behind that brilliant facade.

She needed . . . blood samples. So many people died so needlessly. Once the mystery of blood typing was unlocked, operations could be performed safely, accident victims could be resuscitated.

And vampires, if there was such a thing, could perhaps one day be stopped. If they truly thrived on the blood of humans, then if that blood could be duplicated in the laboratory, they'd have no need to kill.

Angel kept telling herself that this, then, must be why Alexander was also obsessed with the blood composition of humans. What other explanation could there be? A vampire shouldn't care whether a human's blood was the kind that another human could take intravenously; he should care only if it was fresh.

For several days, Angel scarcely left the lab. She'd reviewed all of Alexander's notes and discussed with him what she saw as the flaw in his reasoning. In fact, they'd argued quite heatedly on the matter in a way that was curiously reassuring to Angel concerning his humanity.

"My dear girl, where do you propose we get so many samples?" he expostulated. "My cows shan't complain, aside from a moo here and there if I prod and poke them, but my servants are another matter entirely."

"Have you considered paying them?"

His open mouth closed. "No."

"This is the typical dilemma all scientists face, Uncle. Time or money. You must spend one or the other." Her eyes danced at him as he made a disgruntled snort at her impeccable logic. "You've spent a great deal of time trying to compare cow and human blood. Now I suggest you spend a bit of money to get adequate samples. Only when we compare human blood to human blood will we truly discover the fine chemical differences."

"What with all these rumors flying about the

countryside, I do not wish to be known as the Blythe who pays for blood."

"If you'll supply me the funds, I'll do it, then." He eyed her closely. "I believe you would." She eyed him back evenly.

And so the next day, at a table in a very clean stable stall, she found herself doing a brisk, peculiar sort of barter. The more servants who came and submitted to the controlled bloodletting, the more who seemed to appear from even farther away. As usual, the gossip post was far more efficient than the queen's mail.

"The mad Blythe girl," she heard herself referred to behind her back. "They're all that way, they say."

The growing pile of samples was worth the criticism. And the stack of coins her uncle gave her was dwindling in a quite satisfactory way. Only a few more to go, and they should have enough for a year's worth of research. Angel tightly wrapped the latest sample, keeping it pristine for later viewing under a microscope.

Mad she might be. But she was still methodical. . . .

The next arm offered to her wore a much fancier sleeve. In fact, lace, the old-fashioned kind, flowed freely over a strong wrist and hand far too finely shaped to belong to a servant. She knew before she looked up.

Here he was again. "Max," she whispered.

Those green eyes were unreadable, steady upon her face. She listened for, but didn't hear, his voice in her head. He was shielding his emotions from her.

"Since you seem to enjoy drawing my blood with your verbiage, I decided to see if your needle stings less," he quipped.

She didn't smile. Why had he really come? To prove somehow that he wasn't a vampire? How could she possibly know the composition of the creatures' blood when she still hadn't quite convinced herself they even existed? How did she even know it was different from a human's?

He apparently read the questions in her eyes, for he leaned so close his breath brushed the mussed hair at her earlobe. "Poke me and find out."

Maddening that he could apparently read her mind so easily while shielding his own.

A small, taunting smile stretched those full, tempting lips. He leaned even closer. "Of course, if you prefer, I can poke you."

Heat curled through her at his double entendre, but that only added anger to her perturbation. Grabbing up a needle, she quickly pricked his wrist, catching the copious drops of blood on the glass plate and wrapping them up.

He yelped.

"It's not quite so pleasant when you're the one being drained, is it?" She needled him verbally as well, just for the fun of it.

"You tell me."

A flash of white-hot pain caught her off guard. She looked down, stunned to see he'd poked her with one of her own needles and neatly caught her blood sample on a fresh plate. He had the temerity to use her own wrapping material to keep the sample pristine. He stuck the sample in his pocket.

"You have no right to do this," she began, but a bright coin flipped through the air, end over end, and landed neatly in her lap.

"The going rate, I believe." He rose and walked away, taking her blood with him.

Just like that, leaving her staring after him, mouth agape.

When she blinked back to reality a few seconds later, she looked down at the plate still in her hands. Marking it even more carefully than the others, she vowed to break her own self-imposed banishment from his estate.

If he was conducting blood experiments, too, she had to know why.

But first, if she could somehow get a sample

of Alexander's blood and take it with her, she could compare them. . . .

For the next few days, Angel hunkered down in the lab. She felt in some atavistic sense as if she were doing battle. The unruly combatants were the hardest to defeat: her own emotions, her own fears. Only scientific proof, observable differences in Max's blood, or in Alexander's or, God forbid, in both, would ease her mind.

She compared random samples supplied by the servants throughout the district, making careful, copious notes in the pristine notebooks Alexander supplied her. No matter how she tried, she found little difference in the samples. They looked very similar under the microscope. They separated into similar components when mixed with solution. They appeared to be almost half a watery substance, and almost half a deep, brilliant vermilion.

To her extreme relief, Max's blood sample separated the same and looked the same under the microscope, though it did seem to have more of the bright red component. But not so much more that it was far outside her mean. When tested in the proper solution, it also seemed to have a slightly higher iron content.

On a whim, she even inserted a minute piece of garlic between the plates and looked under the microscope. Max's blood stayed inert. What had she expected, to see the fluid dance away in alarm? Smiling at her own foolishness, she was so relieved he was apparently human after all that she removed the glass plate a bit hastily from its holder.

There was the distinct crack of broken glass, and then Max's precious blood dripped down onto the tabletop. Dismayed, she ran for another plate and a swab, but in the few seconds it took her to return to the table, Max's blood had hardened.

It was dry, crusty, unusable unless she liquified it again, which would change its consistency. She was so angry with her own carelessness that it took a moment for the significance of the hardening to dawn on her.

Blood clotting normally took minutes, not seconds.

Angel took some of the samples she'd already studied and exposed them to air, timing how long it took them to harden. Anywhere from five minutes to ten.

She found a tiny speck of Max's liquid blood in the unbroken part of the plate and dabbed at it with a swab.

It hardened in three seconds flat.

Impossible. Just as she'd always deemed the existence of vampires impossible?

She sat down hard at the table, her head in her hands.

She'd kissed this creature, longed to lie with this creature.

Very well, to put truth upon the matter—she'd lusted for this creature. What did she do now?

That was a much harder verity, for another question had logically followed.

If Max were a vampire, why had he not bitten her when he had the chance? And why did she sense a protectiveness in him, as if he were truly concerned for her well-being?

Vampires weren't supposed to be moral creatures. They didn't have laughing green eyes more in common with sunny meadows than moldy mausoleums.

Or perhaps they did, if they were very old, and very intelligent. The longer one lived, the more defense mechanisms one learned. And by his own admission, he'd known her mother.

Chilled to the marrow, Angel forced herself to go back to her experiments. One thing was incontrovertibly certain now: her wish for a sample of Alexander's blood had become a need.

She had to compare Max's hemoglobin to Alexander's and see if they both clotted so rapidly.

Alexander came often to check on her progress, and always it was on the tip of her tongue to request, purely in the interests of objectivity, of course, that he supply his own blood sample. But she could never quite think of a credible reason to demand one from the master of the household.

Finally, a plan came to her as she handled beakers filled with various solutions she mixed with the blood samples. She stared down at the glass, sparkling in the dim sunlight coming through the high, dirty, leaded casement windows.

She carefully emptied a beaker. She greased it with a clear oil, then set it upon the very edge of the table.

When Alexander entered a few hours later, she was bustling about, sorting bottles and beakers. To her delight, he said, "You seem to be making progress. Can I help, my dear?"

Her arms were full, so she nodded at the beaker on the table. "Can you bring that one to the sink for me?"

He picked it up—or tried to. It slipped from his grip and shattered on the flagstone floor.

The shards flew everywhere but at him. They clattered against the chair leg and flew all the way across the floor toward the door. A few pieces even stuck in the wainscoting. But they left him unscathed.

"Deuced slippery," he remarked, bending to pick up the shards.

But he did so very carefully.

"Careful. I'll help." Angel walked toward him, setting her burden down on the tabletop. As she knelt, she "accidentally" brushed against him while he was picking up pieces.

The shard he held was thrust deeply in his thumb. He yelped.

Making a commiserating sound, Angel jerked a clean cloth off the table above her head and dabbed at the tiny cut.

"Never mind," he said brusquely, rising abruptly. "I'll send a servant down to clean this up. When you reach any valid conclusions, please send for me." And he hurried out, sucking his thumb.

Too late. Angel stared down at the soft cloth. She twisted it and numbly watched hardened flecks of dark blood flake off.

Alexander's blood had hardened in less than three seconds.

Both men were vampires.

Chapter Six

The next night's ball held neither promise of joy nor hope of delight for Angel. Earlier she'd spent the entire day grappling with the consequences of the truth she'd sought with such zeal. She was a reformer, a rebel, a scientist. She should accept even the most unpleasant consequences of her experiments with equanimity.

But objectivity was beyond her now. Her feelings seesawed between terror, sadness, and anger.

The man who'd almost made love to her was a vampire.

The only family she had left in the world was also a vampire.

She'd stumbled upon some sort of ancient grudge match between two creatures of the night. And she was the prize.

Even worse, one of these two beings liked to torture and murder innocent young women. The memory of that girl in the mausoleum was so horrific in light of the new facts that it finally, curiously calmed Angel's torment.

Perhaps that was why fate had sent her across an ocean. Not to find herself, but to find the Beefsteak Killer and save other poor girls with more pride than prosperity.

That night, with unwonted care, she dressed for the ball in the bright blue dress Sarina had lent her for the occasion. This one was as low-cut as the red, the bias seams so long and form-fitting that every enticing curve and hollow of her body glimmered with lustrous blue waves ranging from sea foam to deepest marine blue when she moved.

Angel eyed her own form objectively. She'd always hated her shape, the full bosom, small waist, and flaring hips, for it caused her nothing but problems. Tonight, however, she'd use it to her own advantage.

Pinning sparkling brilliants in her coiffure, Angel decided she was perfectly capable of planning her strategy. Let these two despicable creatures think they used her as their pawn.

Her mother had been a formidable chess player, and she'd passed her skill down to her daughter. The best chess players were methodical, setting up the entire board move by move instead of impulsively striking prematurely with the queen.

Oftimes, the innocuous pawn captured the king.

The ballroom sparkled with the gaiety of laughter, and good food, and good spirits. The gaiety seemed centered around the punch bowl, where ruby wine glowed under the candle sconces. As Angel watched, an old man emptied a cup, dipped up another full one, and drank it thirstily, too. Then, seeming more animated, he bowed in a courtly fashion over a young girl's hand and led her to the dance floor.

Indeed, in this setting, the usual rules of age, social standing, and gender were broken and cast aside in the interests of a good time.

In other circumstances, Angel would have been invigorated by the comity. But when she saw her uncle holding court amidst a circle of sartorially correct and socially corrupt admirers, Angel's resolve almost wavered.

How could she hope to outsmart someone so rich and powerful and wily? He even had a woman as strong and bright as Sarina in his thrall. Angel looked around the room among handsome buck and winsome femme fatale. If her uncle and Max were both vampires, it logically followed that many of these social butterflies showed their true colors only at night. When they flew the countryside on bat wings . . .

"He does like to hold court, does he not?" Sarina locked her arm with Angel's. "Sometimes Alexander reminds me of a peacock, strutting his way through life, tail feathers trailing, assured of his own superiority. Until he opens his mouth and tries to crow." Sarina covered her own mouth, her blue eyes sparkling above her hand. But Angel knew Sarina wasn't in the least contrite for the criticism, as she proved with her audacious whisper: "But you won't tell him I said that, will you?"

Angel smiled at her aunt. Again she wore white. Again she looked about twenty rather than a respectable matron in her forties. "He has much to be proud of. His wife, most of all."

Sarina smiled her pleasure and tapped Angel's cheek. "Tush, you almost make me wish I'd been brave enough to spoil my figure with children. How I wish you were my own daughter in blood as well as in deed. But I shall take equal pride in you nonetheless, even though it was only an accident of marriage that brought you to me. Now, I shall force myself to share you with my guests. Come along."

Touched, Angel let Sarina draw her around the ballroom, introducing her to people who seemed quite normal and quite respectable. One of the eager young men offered to get her a glass of ruby-red wine punch. Angel nodded, but she watched him carefully all the while.

She needed no more spiked libations, this night of all nights. But he merely dipped her up a sizable glass and carried it carefully through the spinning dancers. When he returned, she let him sign her dance card. She held her glass up to the light, admiring the deep vermilion hue and sniffing the pleasing though heavily spiced aroma.

"Cloves?" she asked her aunt.

Sarina nodded. "Alexander's favorite punch recipe. Cinnamon and nutmeg as well."

Angel was about to sip when there was a stir near the door. Angel had her back to the entrance, but she felt him, a tingle on the back of her neck, an itch where she couldn't scratch, before she saw him. She froze, the glass halfway to her mouth. She turned, watching the smooth, powerful way Max walked.

No, he glided, walking so lightly he scarcely seemed to touch the floor. As if the crude physical realities of time and gravity and distance held no sway over him. He was dressed tonight in navy blue, the same old-fashioned coat and fall of ridiculous lace that somehow seemed so right on him.

Ignoring Sarina, Max bowed over Angel's hand and whisked the glass out of it as he did so. Angel jerked her hand back, then reached for the glass. He held it out of reach and then set it on a tray carried by a passing servant.

The young man who'd fetched it for her protested. "I say, that's most rude of you—" One look from those green eyes and Angel's admirer departed with a muttered excuse.

Sarina wasn't as easy to intimidate. She glared at Max. "I suppose you have an invitation this time, too?"

Max reached inside his jacket pocket, but she flounced off before he could hand her . . . a clean white handkerchief. His eyes brimmed with laughter at Angel's expression. "Admit it. You like the bold sort."

"On the contrary. I detest arrogant men."

"Then you must have a veritable hatred of your own uncle."

No, but she was forming one. "Would you please go about your business?"

"I am about my business." *You are my business.* She heard his voice in her head again.

Their gazes locked. She felt the pull of those verdant green depths, sucking her into a sun-dappled pool hidden within a forest, where right and wrong ended at water's edge. Angel felt herself teetering toward him. How luxurious to warm herself in those hypnotic green eyes. They were too bright and bold and beautiful to be evil. If she frolicked there maybe she could plumb the depths of who he really was, vampire or man.

Good or evil.

Curse or blessing . . .

"Tomorrow is a gift, but today a blessing." This time he spoke aloud—again, as if he'd read her thoughts.

She caught her breath. "That was my mother's favorite saying."

"I know. She trusted me, Angel. Why can't you?" He held out his hand to her.

Every particle of her being gravitated toward him. She looked at that perfectly steady, perfectly shaped hand, reaching out to her. It was a simple thing, to take a man's hand. But the feeling behind the handclasp was not simple in the slightest.

Trust. A problematic idea to anyone of her bent and background, even if he were a normal man. But vampire or not, there was nothing ordinary about Maxwell Britton, Earl of Trelayne.

Someone laughed loudly, startling her. She broke eye contact, and that was enough to jolt her back to the reality of the parquet floor beneath her feet and the wavering of her good intentions. Jerkily, she turned toward the refreshment table. "I'm thirsty." Truly, she was parched, and that ruby-red punch looked enticing under the wall sconces.

At the punch bowl, she dipped herself a goodly drink—only to have Max take it and pour it back in. Twice more they repeated the game, but then she got tired of playing. She smacked the back of his hand with the ladle.

He looked so shocked that she was startled into a laugh. "It's obvious you were never disciplined even as a child."

That slow, lazy smile made her light-headed. And she'd had not so much as a sip of punch yet.

"I was always . . . good. Very, very good." He leaned so close his sweet, clean breath, which carried not the least hint of blood or decay, set the brilliants in her hair to dancing. "And now that I'm a man, I'm even better. I should be happy to prove it to you. But it requires a change of venue."

"I enjoy my own bed, thank you very much."

He arched an eyebrow at her. "My, you do have a mind in the gutter. I was referring to the dance floor." And he whisked her away from the punch bowl onto the middle of the gleaming floor.

They danced—country dances quite dissimilar to what she'd learned in America. He had to guide her slowly through the steps. But then came a reel, which she knew, and finally a waltz, which she loved most of all. Angel had always found her enjoyment of dances contingent upon the skill of her partner.

And Max was right, damn him, as usual. He was very, very good.

Angel forgot all about the other young men who'd signed her dance card. She forgot she was supposed to be devising stratagems to trick Max into revealing damaging information about the murders. She even forgot she quite likely held a vampire to her breast.

She saw only the green of eyes that were full of life, not death. She felt only the flexing of muscles that were powerful, but surely not unnaturally so. He looked like a man; he felt like a man; he smelled like a man.

"I am, you know."

Her step faltered. "I beg your pardon?"

"Only a man."

Her heart skipped a beat but she managed

153

to keep her voice even. "A man who can read minds."

"It's not such an unusual skill, you know. If you think back, you'll realize your own mother could do it, too."

Angel's gaze went dim as she remembered all the stories she'd heard about how her mother had had an uncanny sense of what people would do and say even before they knew themselves. "Then why do I not have it?"

"You do. You just haven't figured out how to use it yet."

Could that be true? There were times when she could almost predict what people would say, but Angel had always credited that to her instinctive reading of human nature, not some mystical gift. Angel concentrated, hard, on the spot right between his golden eyebrows, her own brow crinkling with the effort. She'd give a fortune to be able to read *this* man's thoughts.

His chest shook with soft laughter. He released her hand to smooth her frown away with a teasing, gentle fingertip. "One does the trick with thought. Not by staring a hole into the desired repository of knowledge." He gently mimicked her exact way of speaking.

She blinked. "Do I really sound so pompous?"

"At times. It's the unfortunate consequence of having a vocabulary few can rival, much less understand." He bent his forehead to hers, rubbing gently from side to side. Only then did she realize he'd brought them to a halt, barely moving their bodies from side to side, too. She heard the supple whisper of silk against silk, and then he was holding her shockingly close. The warmth of their bodies melded, a precursor to the melding of their minds.

"Can you read my thoughts, Angel mine?"

Images blazed into her brain: the two of them, naked upon his bed. Writhing in a bonding that had no beginning and knew no end. Vermilion velvet spread, baronial fireplace, passion crackling in the vast room louder than the roaring fire . . . Angel sagged against him, her feet barely moving. She felt the hardness at his loins and knew the images were not one-sided. She blinked up at him.

The green eyes weren't laughing anymore. They'd caught flames from the sconces. They blazed a trail through her brain right to every sinew and impulse of her body. And she yearned to give in; oh, yes, she did. A moment, a night . . .

A lifetime . . .

Eternity.

If she let him, this man who was most probably a vampire would invade not just her body, but her soul. She knew the stories. Vampires were created by other vampires. The thought of having to consume human blood to survive nauseated her. She would hate to become a creature so powerful, so ruthless, that innocent young women like that poor unfortunate in the mausoleum became not just easy prey but chattel. Inferior, put on Earth to be fed on by stronger, older beings.

Her eyes finally coasted to his face, skirting that gaze that did such strange things to her. But it was apparently enough for him to yet again read her thoughts in his unnerving way. He rested his cheek against her hair, still swaying them from side to side. He hesitated, then said softly, "All vampires aren't ruthless, Angel. Some find the affliction . . . a necessary evil."

Was this an admission on his part? Almost. But not quite. "Are you speaking hypothetically or empirically?"

He pulled back and looked at her again, his perfectly shaped mouth lifted in a rueful smile. "You are without a doubt the most logical woman I've ever met. Perhaps that explains your unnatural . . . equanimity in situations that should quite overset most innocent young women."

"You presuppose I'm innocent. How do you

know?" She stared boldly into his eyes.

His hand coasted from her waist up her side to the tender underarm flesh no one but he had ever touched. She caught his hand and placed it firmly back at her waist.

The laughter was back in his mellow voice, like golden sunshine warming honey. "Ah, I have just empirically proved that you don't allow most men to touch you so."

"You've all but admitted you're not a normal man." This was indubitably the oddest ballroom conversation she'd ever had. And quite the most enjoyable verbal skirmish she'd ever dared.

"I admit nothing save that I find you powerfully attractive." There was a rueful note in his voice that made her laugh.

"You make me sound like an ailment."

His eyes went forest green. Fascinated, unable to look away, she watched his pupils expand until they consumed the color, consumed her composure, her breath.

Her being.

"You are exactly that, Angelina Blythe. A fever, a hunger, an itch. A dream I take into sleep and bring back into day to haunt me there, too." He pulled her lower body tightly to his own. She felt the thrust of what felt like a quite normal male into her abdomen. "Come home with me, Angel. Cure us both."

She should be terrified he could read her so well. He'd neatly described her own symptoms where he was concerned, too. But his "cure" could lead to a far deadlier sickness. If he was the Beefsteak Killer, what would stop him from doing to her as she'd almost seen him doing to that poor girl?

Stopping even her pretense of swaying to the soft tempo of the waltz, Angel pushed him away. She ached as she did so, but she knew she had no choice. She wanted this man—no, this being, for only a creature of the night could be so magnetic and yet so charming, reading her thoughts and dreams before she knew them herself. She was alone, she was afraid, but suddenly she knew that no matter what this man was, she had to share with him a bit of her soul. By choice, not because he demanded it.

"No," she said simply. "Home is something I've wanted all my life. But I can't find it in anyone's arms until I find it within myself."

On some dim level, Angel realized the music had stopped and that the other guests were staring at them. From the corner of her eye, she saw Sarina start toward them. Alexander caught his wife's arm and pulled her back. She was, yet again, causing a scandal for her uncle, but for the moment she didn't care.

"And where is home, Angel? Blythe Hall? America? Or somewhere else far away? Somewhere else where you can escape the truth you claim to seek?" He bent until his green eyes bored into not just her mind, but her heart, where it hurt. Those secret places she could scarcely bear to touch, much less allow others to trespass upon. Her mother, her loneliness, her own fear of what she'd find when she learned why her mother had left England.

"Is it the Beefsteak Killer you seek? Or is he just a distraction to give you an excuse not to look where truth darkens instead of illuminates?"

His words hurt because they were true. Her hand had flown out to strike him before she realized it. She saw his head jerk to one side, she saw her hand imprint appear redly on his cheek. And for an instant, when he bared his teeth at her, she saw fangs. . . .

But then he whirled and stalked out onto the balcony, his steps as soundless as usual. He climbed onto the rail, his arms extended like a giant bird, and leaped into the night. He was gone.

But he burned in her consciousness as surely as the sun he often reminded her of.

Jerkily, her eyes bright with tears she refused to shed, Angel skirted the staring looks and whispers, making her way to the door. Sarina, bless her, clapped her hands.

"La, are we such a dull lot as to be voyeurs? Dance, my dears. Dance!" The orchestra struck up a lively country dance and the floor was soon filled.

Outside, on the landing, Angel looked at the stairs leading to her room, but with a will of their own, her feet started down, not up. Beakers, that was what she needed. Solutions, formulas, boring notes. Tangible reality instead of amorphous feelings.

Some hours later, that was the way Sarina found her: still in her lovely blue ball gown, though she'd donned an apron, mixing a beaker in which she'd isolated yet another blood sample.

Sarina set down a tray of meat, cheese, bread, and fruit and handed Angel one of two glasses of ruby-red punch. "Red and blue don't go well together."

"Which is why I'm wearing a white apron, Sarina. I shan't get blood on your frock."

"Are you never lost for a response?"

"It seems to be a family trait."

"Not this night. Alexander is sleeping it off as we speak."

Angel continued her mixing.

"If you're going to be dull and choose research over revelry, at least get tipsy while you're at it." Sarina took a hearty swallow of wine from her own glass, taking her own advice, as Angel could clearly see.

Strange. She'd never seen Sarina tipsy before. Angel eyed the glass Sarina offered, but turned back to inscribe another note. "I need to keep a clear head."

"Why? Your clear head seems to be getting you into more trouble than behaving impulsively."

Angel tossed her pencil down. "I came to Oxford with a clear head. Or so I thought."

"Do you regret that?" Sarina's blue eyes were so kind, so sympathetic, that they brought a lump to Angel's throat.

"No. You've been nothing but kind to me."

"Unlike the men of the area?"

Looking industrious, Angel picked her pencil up again. How did one tell one's aunt that she was quite likely married to a vampire? One didn't.

"One way or the other, I'm going to teach you that frivolous pursuits quite often lead to serious progress." Laughing, Sarina poured some of the ruby-red punch into a beaker.

Angel smiled reluctantly at the ridiculous

sight. "I hope you rinsed it first." But she accepted the beaker Sarina offered.

"I took a clean one from the cabinet. To progress. Of the heart and mind." Sarina clinked her crystal goblet against the pedestrian beaker.

Angel could hardly refuse to drink, so she sipped. Surprised, she licked her lips and sipped again. "This is very good. Normally I don't like such concoctions."

"It's a very old recipe rumored to have started in Alexander's family with a Crusader."

Angel was too busy drinking to pay much mind to the explanation.

Sarina smiled and took the empty beaker. "Would you like some more?"

Tempted, Angel forced herself to shake her head. "I have too much work to do."

"Can I help?" Sarina looked around, unable to disguise her little grimace of distaste. "I can . . . sweep. Or dust. I'm sorry for the filth, but Alexander rarely allows the servants down here."

Angel hid a grin in her notebook. She tried to picture Sarina using a broom. The mind boggled. "I shall contrive, thank you. But if you'll excuse me, I really need to concentrate."

Sarina propped her knuckles on her hips. "Are you saying I talk too much?" At Angel's speaking look, Sarina smiled reluctantly and let her hands drop. "Oh, all right. Really, you and Alexander are of a piece. You can both be frightful bores where your work is concerned." She walked to the door. "But I'll send a servant down with more punch for you." She left, satisfied she had had the last word.

Somehow epiphanies and punch went together. Over her third glass, Angel realized that she could test these prosaic samples until Judgment Day, trying to figure out—and prove—that the composition of a vampire's blood was different from that of a human. And progress not at all toward her goal.

Holding her beaker filled with lovely red liquid up to the candlelight, Angel squinted through a rosy reality. As usual, Sarina had been right. Progress was sometimes made through frivolous pursuits. Angel lowered the beaker and glanced around her drab surroundings. She was looking in the wrong place.

If there was a mystery to be solved surrounding blood research in the Oxford area, where she had every reason to believe vampires were as thick as thieves, she didn't need to know what a human looked for in blood composition; she needed to know what a vampire looked for.

Why had Max taken a sample of her blood?

Angel drained the last of her punch, the tiredness she'd finally begun to feel magically washing away. She should feel fear at what she contemplated. At the very least, she should feel cautious.

She felt neither. Strangely enough, save for that moment when he'd bent over the girl's blood-drained corpse, Angel had felt no fear of Max. He threatened her virtue, her sleep, her independence, but not, at least to date, her life. Whipping off the apron, Angel blew out the sconces. This time her eyes didn't even need to adjust to the total darkness. She could see. Instantly. Not just shadowy outlines of chairs and tables, but the brown wood and spindly legs of the stool next to the wall.

Feeling, finally, as if she knew her way around and truth was guiding her, Angel left the lab, locking the door behind her. She made her way upstairs. Rustling silk was not the thing to wear when one invaded a vampire's lair.

Somewhere in her things she still had a boy's garments, remnants of her tomboyish childhood. She only hoped they still fit. As for the wisdom of what she was about to do . . . well, perhaps the wine had made her overly bold, but at least if he discovered her, she had an excuse. One he'd given her this very night.

He'd invited her to his home, hadn't he?

* * *

From an upstairs balcony, the Beefsteak Killer watched as Angel rode out of the stables. She was dressed in such tight-fitting garments that any respectable man would have a difficult time resisting her. The girl had no idea of her own power over men, Max in particular. She really was a sweet child, that delightful rational streak almost enough to counterbalance the darkness of her own nature.

Almost.

But soon enough, the heritage she couldn't escape would evidence itself as the changes she was undergoing would in all likelihood be completed in Max's bed.

All was going according to plan . . . tonight was truly the beginning of the end for Maximillian Britton, the last of the tenacious Trelaynes. He'd be trapped, finally, in a lure even his almighty self-righteousness wouldn't be able to resist.

Once he had sexual congress with Eileen's daughter, he would be a vampire in deed as well as name. That righteous, flaming sword he carried would be turned upon him when he finally forsook the vows he'd made when he became a Watch Bearer.

Finally, he'd be weak enough to kill.

The killer heard footsteps approaching and

quickly dissolved into mist, filtering over the balcony into the night.

As Angel rode through the gates some time later, the clouds gathering in black mourning over the Trelayne estate parted before a gush of wind. They emitted an eerie fog that had no form or substance.

But as the clouds drifted over the crenellated roof of Max's estate, the white mist took form. Scabby fingers clawed through the heavy underbellies of the clouds and began to reach for the ground.

There they took amorphous shape again, became harmless mist dripping on leaves and windowpanes at ground level.

Waiting. For the invitation that had been inevitable the moment Angel set foot on English shores.

Thinking there was no spring like an English spring, Angel stepped right through the heavy mist that had collected before the doors and windows of Max's home. She tried numerous lower floor windows but they were all locked. Finally she picked up a rock, wrapped it in her kerchief, and used it to break a casement window. The crunch of glass sounded devastatingly loud, even muffled by the mist as it was.

She looked around guiltily, but saw nothing stirring. Protecting her hand from the glass with the kerchief, she reached inside and opened the window. Automatically she locked it behind her again, though the precaution was ridiculous, since she was the invader.

Her night vision was so strong now that she caught every pattern and shade in the tasteful room. For a vampire, Max had a surprising taste for light and airy decor. One of many odd things about him—but not as odd as the sight that met her eyes.

She stopped, surprised to see a large cross on the wall. But then, she had no idea what decor a bona fide vampire preferred.

Visions of black velvet and scarlet silk adorning a bat-winged bed danced in her vivid imagination. She tried to picture Max in such a suite.

He wouldn't be caught dead in such a place. Perhaps undead . . .

A nervous giggle escaped her. She clapped her hand over her mouth, wishing she hadn't had so many glasses of that strangely delicious wine.

She made her way to the door as quietly as she could.

Now where would he situate his lab?

* * *

Awakening from a sound sleep, Max sat upright in bed, feeling her more than seeing her. Even in his dreams, she was a powerful presence.

She was here.

As expected. From the moment he'd seen her face when he took her blood sample, he'd known she'd have to investigate his motives for herself. He tossed back his covers, wondering what to wear for the strange meeting to come.

He hadn't been able to talk her into visiting his home since that night in his carriage, nor lure her here, or even tempt her here. But give her a logical reason to come . . .

Grinning, he decided to wear only his most frivolous silk robe, a fine old Italian emerald-green silk embroidered with dragons that had reputedly belonged to Casanova. He'd have the proper excuse that he'd dressed hastily to investigate the strange noises. Another thump came from downstairs.

She really didn't have the art of silent movement down yet. But that was just as well. When she fully realized her powers, his own would be in imminent danger. While she was still human, he could safely bed her. Once she was under his spell, he'd be able to control her, stop her conversion.

Help her as he hadn't been able to help Eileen.

As a vampire, Angel could threaten all the good he'd tried to do for the last hundred years. Max walked downstairs to meet her, thankful yet again that he'd managed to stop her from drinking Alexander's old family-recipe punch. The secret ingredient that gave it that lovely crimson hue was human blood. The iron reputedly offered a silky, slightly salty taste that was pleasing to human and vampire palate alike.

It was an elixir concocted in a lab by a vampire researching human blood. Not to aid in the mysteries of blood transfusion, which was the tale Alexander put about. His research was far more insidious than that. On the face of it, his studies were harmless, merely an attempt to investigate the components of various types of human blood.

But they were not so harmless when one learned the reason behind his research. He hoped to learn which type of human blood offered the greatest strength to those of the vampire persuasion. Only vampires knew that, just as humans addicted to alcohol were often more susceptible to a particular type of spirit, vampires also formed a preference for a particular type of human blood. It varied with the vampire's own body chemistry.

But, as Alexander had discovered, there was one type of human blood that every vampire enjoyed and thrived on. A universal type, as it were. That type was mixed with wine, spices, and fruit juice, and then served at the balls. It was rumored to empower even the weakest vampires.

And it was deadlier than poison to vampires fighting their urges, even more lethal to latent vampires who didn't know their own power. Max knew he must continue to be vigilant and ensure that Angel never drank it, or the battle he helped her fight against her vampire half would be over before it began.

There was no time to waste.

Max pushed open the salon door.

Two harsh realities hit him immediately. Angel had broken into his home, leaving a large hole in the glass of a window.

And right outside, perilously near that hole, hovered a mist that had no form.

But it had a name.

The Beefsteak Killer.

Max felt his fangs forming in a reflex action, but he took a deep breath and forced himself to regain his calm. Fangs would do him no good against such a menace. He stuffed two divan pillows into the hole, but that would only slow the killer down, not stop it. As mist, it could invade the tiniest nook or cranny.

Then Max stalked back to the door, knowing that Angel was the key to the battle begun over a hundred years ago. The Beefsteak Killer wanted her all vampire; Max wanted her all human.

But in either form, Angel could offer the killer the one thing necessary to every vampire, even the oldest, deadliest ones—they couldn't enter hallowed ground unless invited. Max stalked straight past the cross prominent on his wall and made for the door.

It shouldn't be difficult to keep Angel too busy for such niceties as social invitations to undesirable guests. He'd meet the killer on his own terms, in his own time, when he was strongest.

When Angel was safe and he'd fulfilled his sacred promise to Eileen that no matter what it cost him, he would protect her daughter.

Below stairs, Angel tried every door she came across. She found pantries, storage areas, even an ancient armory filled with weapons that looked more rusty than lethal.

But there was no trace of a modern scientific lab.

Could he perform such dirty work in his master quarters?

Coming back out on the landing, Angel gulped and looked up the stairs. There was only one way to find out. She'd been trying to avoid this, she told herself. But that new boldness she'd felt since drinking the punch wouldn't allow for such weak denial.

She wanted to see him. Wanted to confront him in his own chamber. To see for herself if he slept in a crypt on soil, or in an ordinary bed.

She wanted to see him. Period.

Her cheeks heating, Angel climbed the stairs toward his quarters.

Max was four steps behind her, smiling as he watched her try to be quiet.

And outside, the mist swirled inchoately, formless, but not faceless. Twin red, glowing eyes glittered with both hunger and hatred.

Chapter Seven

She'd reached his half-open door when she finally seemed to sense his presence. He was further reassured that she was still more human than vampire, for surely she'd have felt him earlier if her dull human senses of smell and hearing were not still predominant. However, her sight was powerful enough. Glowing in the near dark, those lovely brown eyes widened, and he was gratified by her frightened gasp. Her gaze ran over his exposed muscular chest which was dusted with a smattering of golden hair.

Pleased at the flare of lust she couldn't hide, he gave her his brightest smile. "I've always known you were resourceful, but I didn't think to add trespassing and property damage to your list of accomplishments. Should I fetch the constable?"

He had to admire the speed with which she recovered her composure. She leaned casually against the wall beside his door, crossing one shapely leg over the other. "You invited me here."

Blood rushed to his loins. Her movement made the already tight breeches she wore stretch until he saw every supple outline of her legs—and where they joined. "I did n—"

She smiled not so demurely back at him, her eyes glowing even brighter, but now with laughter.

He admitted ruefully, "I'm a dolt. I did, didn't I? This very night at the ball. But that doesn't give you leave to damage my home."

"It was more fun than knocking."

This wasn't going quite as he'd expected. He was supposed to be the one in control. She seemed . . . different. Bolder. Stronger.

Maybe it was the clothes. Again, his gaze ran up and down her form in the tight breeches and the shirt that strained over her breasts. "You're dressed for the occasion, I see. I admire your tailor."

"Henry Tynes chooses only the finest attire available in Brooklyn, New York." She brushed off her tattered sleeve as if it were the finest silk. "Or so he yelled after me when I . . ."

". . . stole them off his wash line," they said in unison.

Her smile faded. "I really wish you wouldn't do that."

"Do what, Angel mine?" He grew tired of the game and decided it was time to reach for the prize. He placed both his palms flat beside her head, trapping her in the warm circle of his arms. "Reading your mind is so much safer for both of us than obeying my instincts."

"Perhaps I prefer you to obey your instincts."

He cupped her cheeks in his hands, his mouth unsmiling as he whispered, "That would take the decision out of your hands, wouldn't it? How easy for you if I were to whisk you away to my crypt and mesmerize you into my padded coffin." He kissed her hairline, his lips soft and tender upon her warm, flushed skin.

She felt good.

She tasted good.

She smelled good.

Good enough to make him wish that she were fully human, so he could take her and enjoy her without the duality of this dangerous game he played.

But if she were less dangerous, she wouldn't taste so sweet. . . . Before he'd finished the thought, his lips had coasted down the side of her face to her neck. He buried them in the throbbing hollow of her throat, scenting the rich smell of the blood that pulsed so close beneath her skin. His fangs grew at the thought even as another part of his anatomy swelled with a different hunger.

He set her firmly back against the wall, his teeth clenched, and forced his fangs to recede back into their sheaths. But his erection remained, that part of him a bit less governable, even for a vampire who'd survived by his wits these last hundred years. "I shan't tempt you, Angel. If you come to me, it will be because you choose to."

Setting her gently aside, he walked into his bedroom. His heart thumped with nervousness as he turned up the gas lamps. Would his bluff work?

He almost sagged with relief when her quiet steps followed his. He turned to see her curiously appraising his domain. She walked to his well. He automatically moved to stop her, but then he froze. It was time she knew the truth.

Before he bedded her.

She pulled on the rope and lifted one of his bottles of sustenance. She held it up to the light. He expected her to drop it in disgust, to cower from him or run screaming from the

176

room at this proof he was a vampire who drank blood.

To his astonishment, she merely twirled the bottle around, noting its dark red color. She said judiciously, "It must not taste very appealing," and let the rope drop back into the well. And she had the audacity to lift an eyebrow at him, as if daring him to disagree.

He threw back his head and laughed. He laughed so hard he had to wipe tears from his eyes. "Pity the poor man who wins you to wife. He will never, ever get the last word."

"Then it's good you're not a man, isn't it?"

His laughter faded. "You knew?"

She nodded. "The evidence was there, but when I exposed your blood sample to air, it coagulated immediately. As did Alexander's."

Slowly he began to close the gap between them. "And still you came. Why?"

She bypassed him and walked over to his bed. He stopped, knowing her evasion was as much of her own feelings as of him. A smile tugged at his mouth again when he read her obvious disappointment as she stared at his bed. So much for his concern she'd fear him when she discovered he was a vampire.

"I thought you slept in a crypt," she said, running her hand over his soft spread.

"I was merely playing to your fantasies. But

I can have one fetched if you prefer. It would be quite cramped, however." Not to mention off-putting to his own still-manly instincts in the art of love. Lovemaking was a thing of joy and creation, and it had no place in a dark repository of death.

She wandered the room, too curious to mind his gentle needling. As she approached the sitting area where his coat of arms was prominent above a chest, he decided she'd done enough exploring. He quickly caught her hand and kissed it. "Why did you change your mind and come to me, dressed so . . . seductively?"

This was a test, too. To see if she'd tell the truth. He knew she'd ostensibly come to look for his lab, denying even to herself the real reason.

She wanted him, too.

And not because he'd mesmerized her. In this, at least, he wanted to be nothing but a normal man, though as a virtuous vampire, he must have her in his bed before he could safely have her in his life. Nothing was more dangerous to a Watch Bearer than falling in love with a female vampire. Hence his urgency to use whatever means necessary to keep her human.

He unbuttoned her sleeve and let his lips coast up as far as he could go before the fabric stopped him. The moment he touched her, the barriers she'd tried to erect in her mind began to waver.

She shivered, and he felt the mental bond between them growing stronger. He used that bond to his advantage, but still left the choice firmly hers. *Come to my bed, Angel. Not because I seduce you. Because you want to. Freely. Passionately. Because you knew we were meant to be lovers from the moment we met.*

She weakly struggled to pull her arm away. "No. I only came for the blood."

Planting a small love bite in the delicate hollow of her arm, he lifted his head to pinion her with his eyes. "Mine? Or yours?" He watched her closely. If she knew the truth of her heritage now, she was already dangerous to him.

Her astonishment blazed into his brain. "I already have your blood sample, but why do I have the feeling you're talking about something else?"

"Feelings can betray you, Angel. You're quite right to listen to your head more than your heart."

"Very well then . . . my head wants to know why you took my blood and what you plan to do with it."

"Your head would be wiser to ask those questions of Alexander Blythe."

"I have."

"And were you satisfied with his answers?" He could see that she was not by the hasty way she turned from him. He searched her mind, and softened at her genuine confusion and frustration. No pretense there. "Why do you think Alexander is studying blood?"

"To further science." She turned back to face him, lifting that indomitable chin.

"Alexander Blythe has no love of science. He has no love of anything but himself."

"He adores Sarina."

"He only uses her, too." As his familiar. "He's using you also, Angel."

"As are you. But confound you both . . . *why?*"

Almost, he wanted to tell her the truth. But she wasn't ready for that. And she wouldn't be until he'd finished his own research and found a way to stop her transformation from human to vampire. Since she belonged to both species, her blood, and only her blood, would provide the last clues he needed to finish his formula. He needed another sample from her this night.

For a hundred years he'd been strong. He'd swilled cold, almost congealed blood from icy bottles instead of sipping the thick, warm, salty elixir from a throbbing vein as a typical vampire was meant to do. But he was not a typical vampire.

He was born of the night, but never restful in it. Like an avenging angel, he was put on Earth to rid it of predators and protect the innocent, but the cost of his quest had been high. No home for him, no true love, no surcease. So it must be until he trapped and killed the one who could not be killed. He'd lost count of how many vampires he'd put out of their misery over the years, but his most dangerous foe was still at large.

Luckily, the killer thought he didn't know Angel was half-vampire.

Max's eyes strayed to Eileen's picture beside his bed. He remembered the last time he'd seen her, pleading, those lovely eyes—so like Angel's—wet with tears. Reaching to him from her casket. The same casket he later shipped to England.

Angel's eyes widened. "Mother," she whispered.

Immediately Max cast a veil over his tormented memories. This mental bond he shared with Angel was a two-way road. Time to distract her.

Brushing his hip accidentally against the table beside his bed, he knocked Eileen's small portrait over facedown. Then he caught Angel in the circle of his arms. "I'm using you for my own base ends, I admit." He traced a light but searing trail down her arm, past the winsome curve of her small waist, to the fulsome poetry of her hip. He caught her hand and placed it flat against his chest inside the vee of his dressing gown.

"No, I . . ." She trailed off, her fingers curling at the warm contact with his skin. He felt the titanic struggle in her mind between sensuality and rationality.

"But that's the beauty of this particular task. It takes two to complete it." He lowered his mouth until his lips hovered above hers. "Use me, Angel. Well and long, right into tomorrow."

Even without his entrée into her mind, he would have felt the moment of her capitulation. She went limp against him, pressing her cheek shyly to his chest hair. She rubbed her cheek around and the sensation was both sweet and sharp at the same time. But her words were even sharper and sweeter.

"My mother was right. Tomorrow is a gift, but today a blessing. I came here because of that." She looked up at him with eyes that didn't ask, or demand, or plead. Eyes that gave. And this time it was she who hypnotically, wordlessly transmitted to him. *Vampire or not, I want you. I'll let you into my heart and my body, but please be kind.*

He stared down at her, his eyes the same shade as his flamboyant robe.

The trust she placed in him should have made Max Britton feel guilty, because he suspected she was a virgin. Guilty enough, perhaps, to let her go. But Maximillian, the last of the Earls of Trelayne, couldn't afford such weakness. Reminding himself of that poor girl in the crypt and that he was the last line of defense against the Beefsteak Killer, Max the vampire quelled the scruples of Max the human. He swept Eileen's daughter into his arms to carry her to his huge bed.

Her hair spread around her shoulders in a silken fan. The contrast with her boyish clothes made him long to rip them off to reveal the curves of this magnificently feminine creature.

Because he wanted so badly to take her, he forced himself to be patient. He appraised her through half-lowered lids, wondering what she saw in his eyes. Her own had widened as she stared up at him.

He traced the lush, sensual curve of her mouth. "You don't look like a dangerous woman." But she was—dangerous to all his plans, dangerous to his very life if she made him weak when he must be strong. Never drinking of a vampire's blood was the first of many cardinal rules a Watch Bearer disobeyed at his peril.

Yet if the Beefsteak Killer had come into the room at this very moment and told him to take her, be glad in her, that all was going according to plan, he could not have stopped. Every remnant of the human and every sinew of the vampire wanted to bond with this woman sent across an ocean to him—and only to him. A violent wave of possessiveness almost overcame him. He stared down at the pulse in her neck, longing to stamp her with his mark.

One little bite couldn't hurt. . . .

She wasn't afraid. She smiled up at him and cupped his face in one hand. "You look like a dangerous man," she replied softly. She lifted her arms to him and clasped his strong shoulders, bringing him down to her level. "But I've always had a taste for dangerous things." And just like that, she kissed him.

And just like that, she crept into his heart, too.

Before, kisses had always been a means to an end. Excite a woman's mouth and win her for a night. That had been enough for him.

But Angel's shy, awkward movements, her lips gentle upon his, her quickened breathing a soft, feminine promise in his mouth, shamed him. This was not just a kiss. It was a bond, a beginning.

An end . . . of his lonely searching for a human female to be his helpmate, not just his bedmate. It was up to him to keep her human. For the life of a vampire was not life; it was eternal death. And if his research was successful, after he obeyed the blood oath he'd made to his last brother and killed the Beefsteak Killer, he'd forsake the life of a vampire, too.

But for now, the first step in keeping her safe was to own her, possess her, mark her. That he would do, with every primitive instinct clamoring in him for release.

He unbuttoned her shirt, surprised to find his hands shaking. The buttons gave up their purchase with little pings of gladness, revealing soft, scented skin in a low-cut chemise. He buried his mouth in her revealed cleavage. The lurch of her heart against his lips made the last of the wide world outside recede.

He unlaced her chemise with his teeth, feeling his fangs lengthen at the luxurious brush of her soft skin. She smelled so good. New life, new hope. No tinge of death or decay, as he'd so often scented in vampires.

One of the silken threads tangled. He patiently worked to unknot it at first, but he grew frustrated seeing the lovely rounded flesh only half exposed. He ripped the ribbon loose, fabric tearing.

She laughed. "Ah, finally you act true to type. The rake, or the vampire?"

He didn't smile back. Her breasts had tumbled free, ripe and round and tasty, pouting for his attention.

Bending his proud golden head, he accepted the invitation. Her eyes widened at the touch of his mouth. She squirmed at the first contact, her hands restless upon the back of his head, trying to bring his mouth down more firmly. But he resisted her wordless demand, refusing to suckle her nipple. His nimble tongue did a dance of desire around the areola instead, laving her skin, then barely scraping with his fangs in the same path.

She threw her head back, a live thing of desire beneath him. Finally he gave her what she asked for and suckled the point of her pebbly nipple. Her muffled groan of pleasure made him look up to see her face while he suckled.

He saw only the long arched neck, the pulsing carotid vein that carried the life he longed to share with her. She could drink of him, then he'd drink of her . . .

He scrambled to the side of the bed, his hands clasped between his knees. Why was the urge so strong? Usually in the early stages of lovemaking he had little trouble controlling himself.

"Don't stop." Soft arms snaked around him from behind. Her small hands reached to his waist and unfastened his robe.

He made a token effort to stop her, but her hands were faster. They reached down and fastened on the proof of his desire.

It was his turn to groan. He sank back against her shoulder as she caressed him. She was a novice in the art, but the touch was still bliss. He covered her hands with his, showing her how to slow and fondle. His voice was rough with laughter. "I'm not a cow with an udder."

"But I can milk you."

Shocked, he turned to look at her.

She blushed. "Females talk, too."

He ripped off the remnants of her shirt and chemise, leaving her bare to the waist. He clasped both her breasts in his hands. "What else do females say?"

"To avoid blond rakes..." When he kneaded her, firm and fecund in his palms, she gasped.

"And I should avoid dark vixens who have no idea of their power over men." He calmly began unbuttoning her breeches. "I guess this means we're both idiots." He pulled her breeches down her long legs. When the dark vee of hair at her thighs was revealed, he closed his eyes in pain, feeling his manhood and fangs ache with longing.

She kicked her breeches off and stretched, luxuriating in her nakedness before him. "We're only idiots if we walk away." She reached up to him, her smile sultry, her eyes glowing with a tiny tinge of red even in the candlelight. "And your bed is much too comfortable for that."

He stared down at her, alarm bells ringing in his brain, but his body didn't want to listen. She was quite bold for a virgin. Ergo, maybe she wasn't one. That would certainly make things easier. He swept his gaze over her again.

The tiny warning bells went dead quiet as his manhood leaped in response.

With extreme effort, he mastered his instincts and made do with a complete caress, up one side of her lush, sensual body and down the other, instead of spreading her legs as he longed to. He'd never wanted a woman so much, but then he'd never lain with a woman who had vampire blood, either.

He licked his lips, unaware his fangs were on display until she touched the tip of one. He gasped and drew back, but she followed, pressing harder until a tiny dot of her blood appeared on her fingertip.

No power on heaven or earth could have stopped him then. He licked the delicious drop away. His eyes fluttered closed as ecstasy exploded in his mouth.

Warm. Salty. Smooth. Angel was as delicious as she looked. A groan of pleasure escaped him. He shuddered.

She looked at the tiny pinprick, then back at him. "Why do I feel no fear?" she whispered, her fingertip resting on the glistening point. Harder and harder she pressed. A bigger drop landed on his famished tongue.

Some remnant of sanity gave him strength enough to pull away. "No!"

"But it's only a taste. You want it. And I don't mind."

He flung off his robe. "A taste isn't enough. I want"—he pushed her knees apart—"all of you." He knelt between her opened legs and touched the sweet center of her. She opened before him further like a rose to sunshine, unfurling for the warmth and heat that would bring her life anew. Still, he mastered the desire drumming in his temples and made himself go slowly.

He inserted the hard tip of his sex into the mouth of her womanhood. That tiny contact made him shudder with a feeling of rightness. Belonging.

A bond of body, mind, and soul he'd never felt before. He badly wanted to complete their melding, but still her humanity remained present to him, precious to him, despite the violent vampire instincts urging him to give her no second chances.

He poised there, feeling her moist and ready, and ran his fingertips through her hair, brushing the silken tresses away from her temples. Staring down into her eyes, he probed as deeply into her mind as he would probe into her body. *This is your last chance to say no, Angel mine. In a few moments you will belong to me utterly. Always. By your own choice and deed.*

She reached up to trace his features with the fingertip still showing a dot of her own blood. Gently she trailed her finger over his brows, his bold nose, his sculpted cheekbones and wide, generous mouth. This was a tenderness Max hadn't felt since his own human mother had died.

His heart lurched at this intimacy. She looked deeply into his eyes, her fingertip resting on one fang. "You're the dream I had on awakening, the reward for the good deeds I've done, and my blessing for today. There is no death about you, Maximillian, Earl of Trelayne. Only life."

Max was humbled, he who'd never been humbled by anything since the day he became a Watch Bearer. And he felt guilty, for he was using her in his battle against the killer.

She went on. "I know little of men, but this one thing I'm sure of . . . you are a good man. Vampire or not. And I trust you. With my body and my life." She tucked her hands at the base of his skull and pulled him down atop her.

The movement made him slide inside a bit. They groaned at the ineffable pleasure. Both went very still.

Each knew they had to make this stolen moment last. For if the darkness gathering outside, unseen but felt, had its way, this time could never come again.

Max flexed his muscles at the exquisitely sensitive gate to her body, feeling himself harden and relax in tempo with that mysterious rhythm every female seemed to instinctively know. She answered every tiny pressure with an inward tightening that began drawing him in, inch by inch. He tried to resist, truly he did, pulling back slightly, but her hands were on his buttocks urging him on. Pulling him forward.

Even that he might have resisted, but then she was in his mind, too. *Come to me, creature of the night. Teach me how to be strong, like you.* Her words sent up a roaring flame that consumed his thoughts, his fears, and even his concern for her. She had no fear of him, even knowing what he was. It was the most arousing experience of his long life.

The heaviness in his loins had one end now. Surcease could be found only in this one female.

"Angel . . ."

Saying her name aloud and in his thoughts, like the blessing she was to him, Max plunged deep. He sipped the sweet cry of pain from her lips and went still, hurting for her pain even in his male exhilaration at the moment. But she writhed beneath him, trying to adjust her own silken sheath around his male encroachment. The movement tightened her around him. Sweat broke out on his brow.

He forced himself to be still, letting her stretch to accommodate him.

When he felt her relax slightly, he bent his proud golden head and nibbled a hungry path from one breast to another. "You don't need to move, Angel. Just be still and look at me."

He barely flexed his hips into her, aiming high on the upstroke. She gasped at first as she took him fully, her eyes closing. She was so tight, so womanly, that it was all he could do to master his urge to thrust, uncaring for her pleasure, like the wild rake she'd at first thought him.

He set up a rhythm, thrust and retreat, the dance as old as time, but new as every sunrise. At first she followed his lead, pushing gently back every time he inserted himself, but her response made his mastery of the moment expendable. He'd learned long ago that in bed there was no conqueror and no slave.

Only two spirits free enough to go where the wind of passion took them.

Her pleasure in this first time became more important than his own completion. For what seemed like hours but was only minutes, he let her set the pace. Her eager upthrusts were matched with a down tempo, timed exactly to her pace, not one beat faster or slower. The melding below was made all the more powerful by the way he felt her own consciousness falling away, leaving nothing but a primitive urge to bond with her mate in every way.

When she went wild, bucking her hips up into him, he thrust back, plunging full length now, letting her feel.

And feel.

And feel . . . He knew the moment of her pleasure before she did. Inserted to the hilt, he pressed slightly deeper, reaching for the tip of her womb. He felt her throbbing upon his length and withdrew a final time, aching with the fluids of her fulfillment and his. He pressed deep, reaching high, high, pressing against the hard nubbin of her womanhood to bring her to completion at the same time.

Only when she arched beneath him, crying out as she opened and closed around him, did he let her milk him as she'd promised. He arched his back and erupted, spilling into her the essence of life she'd brought to fruition.

And as they both pulsed in the little death, new life beckoned to them. If they were strong enough, and brave enough, to accept the blessing of today. A few moments later, he slumped against her, panting, still loath to withdraw from the melding. He traced the lush curves of her mouth with a fingertip.

"You belong to me. Say it."

"You belong to me." Her eyes opened. And they glowed with more than a tinge of red.

Startled, he pulled away. The sight of her blood on him, the scent of it mingled with the scent of sex, made him look at the one place on her body he'd avoided with eyes, mouth, and teeth: her neck, throbbing now in the aftermath of passion.

His head dipped until he could smell her. His tongue traced the tender vein. She arched her neck for him. "Yes."

With a guttural cry of pain, he rolled away and leaped out of bed so fast he stubbed his toe. He scarcely felt the pain. Angel sat up, reaching down to feel her own blood. She turned her hand from side to side, appraising the reddish tint in the light.

She sniffed her hand. Then . . .

"No!"

He felt her urge before she realized it herself. Before she could lick her own blood, he dipped her hand in a pitcher of water, rinsing temptation away.

Resentment shone in her eyes as she looked up at him. "Why did you do that?"

He read the hunger in her gaze. A hunger he recognized with a sinking heart. A hunger too strong for food.

Tonight was theirs alone, he told himself, loath to spoil the moment. But he had no choice. It was time to tell her the truth, so she could help him fight her own transformation.

"Angel," he whispered, drying her hand. "Did you drink any of the punch tonight at the ball?"

The carnal glow dimmed somewhat. "No."

He sagged with relief, then tensed again as she added, "But after the ball Sarina brought me some down to the lab while I worked."

"How much did you drink?"

195

"I don't remember. Two glasses. No, perhaps three."

He bolted up, throwing on his robe. "How long ago?" Perhaps he could mix something, make her throw up before it got into her system.

"Hours." She sat up, too, and stared at him. "Why are you so concerned about a few glasses of watered-down punch?"

"The primary ingredient isn't wine."

She stared at him. He saw recognition and repugnance flare in her eyes. She turned her face away, staring stubbornly at the wall. "No."

"Yes. Alexander's special family recipe is probably half blood. Why do you think he's been conducting all that research? He's looking for the perfect type of human blood that will give vampires even more unnatural strength. Vampires come from five counties just to drink at his punch bowl."

She went green and caught her stomach. "Why did they give it to me?"

"I think you know."

He didn't have to mix anything; she leaned over the side of his bed and retched.

He sat down with her head against his shoulder. He wiped her face and offered her some water; then he rocked her back and forth. Thanks be to heaven, she was still more human than vampire. If the sickness had taken over she wouldn't be disgusted at the thought of drinking blood.

She'd be fascinated.

He'd caught her in time. Tossing off his robe, he pulled her back into his arms. "Sleep, Angel mine."

Tears still trickling from her eyes, she buried her face in his chest hair. He stroked her hair, soothing her with his strength, until she drifted off.

Just a moment, I'll rest, he told himself. But he was exhausted. He hadn't slept well in some time, planning, aching, for this apogee of his love life. Never had he known, or given, such pleasure. If he'd doubted the strong emotional bond he'd sensed with Angel from the beginning, he doubted it no longer.

He fell asleep vowing to keep her safe.

An hour later, Angel awoke from a sound sleep with the voice in her head again.

It wasn't Max's voice, but in its own way it was equally seductive.

Arise, sweet darling. Come to me.

She looked at Max, sleeping soundly beside her. She'd heard the voice only once—before that night in the crypt.

She hadn't trusted it then, and she trusted it

even less now. Tears came to her eyes as she finally understood why she was so susceptible to this strange telepathy her scientific instincts had never put any stock in.

She could commune with vampires because she was half vampire herself. Max had all but confirmed it for her, and the knowledge explained so much.

Her mother's dislike of daylight, her odd way of reading minds. Even her mother's wish to be buried in the soil of her homeland.

But why hadn't she wanted her daughter to visit that home that had once meant so much to her? Angel had no time to puzzle through the facts. The voice was too insistent.

He's using you, Angel. Before the night is over he'll ask for more of your blood.

"Go away!" She buried her head in the pillow.

Let me in and I'll prove it to you. I'll help you find his lab.

Angel clenched her hands in the coverlet, which was still warm with their passion. This night had proved one thing to her complete satisfaction: Max was a reluctant vampire. He'd initiated her gently, using none of his vampire powers of seduction.

And thus seduced her utterly. There was nothing more arousing than strength controlled. Only the totally secure man was strong enough to allow a woman control when he wanted her so badly. She looked down at his strong, uncompromising mouth, his bold nose and perfect features. Max wasn't capable of killing, much less of mutilating an innocent young girl.

Angel stood and went to the window, where she sensed the source of the voice lurked. She started to throw the casement open, thought better of it, and said, "You hate him. Why should I trust anything you say when you're afraid to show yourself?"

A brief moment of silence, then: *Invite me in, if you think yourself so brave. I fear nothing.*

Somehow Angel knew that was a lie, too. The owner of this voice not only feared Max; it hated him. Angel drew the curtains over the window and went back to bed, steadfastly ignoring the insinuating voice. Angel nestled against his warm hardness, enjoying the touch of skin against skin.

Max held a much more powerful allure.

The voice got the last word. *You can't trust him. Look around his room. Carefully. He knew your mother.*

"I know that. He told me himself."

Did he tell you he killed her?

"No!" Angel insisted.

She bolted out of bed, staring at Max.

No, he was too fine. He could never do something like that.

Ask him. Ask him why he became a Watch Bearer. What he does with that kit of golden spikes he keeps beneath his bed.

Then the insinuating voice was silent. The presence she'd felt was gone.

Angel backed away from the bed, but she had to know. Before she could change her mind, she knelt and reached under his vast bed. She felt a wooden case and pulled it out.

She opened it.

A golden hammer. Golden-handled yew spikes. Various foul-smelling herbs. Crosses. Small vials of what looked like water.

Angel's dull eyes went from the case to the golden-haired man sleeping in the bed. How easily he'd fooled her. He looked like a golden god, a man of morality and honor. He'd treated her tenderly, courted her.

Lied to her. He'd admitted he'd known her mother. But how well? And if he'd killed her, why? Was it simply because he hated his own existence as a vampire so much that he systematically wiped out anyone with vampire blood?

But if that were the case, he wouldn't be bedding her, and helping her face the facts of her own heritage.

Unless . . . He meant to catch her off guard. Enjoy her before he dispatched her as efficiently as he had the rest.

Revolted, she closed the case and shoved it back under the bed.

Then, being as quiet as possible, she began to search his room. If he'd really known her mother, perhaps he had some memento, some proof that he'd cared for her. She longed to wake him and ask him, but this was something she had to learn for herself.

She'd opened herself to this man in every way. Trusted him with her heart, her mind, her body, even knowing he was a vampire. But if he'd killed her mother . . .

It took only a few minutes for her to find it: the coat of arms above his dresser.

The motto blazed into her brain. *Tomorrow is a gift, but today—*

"A blessing." Max's voice came over her shoulder, all too close. "Your mother's favorite saying because she always loved my family motto."

Angel spun to face him. Only then did she see the small picture in his hand.

"If you must search my room, at least be thorough."

Numbly, Angel accepted the miniature. She looked down. At first she thought she saw her own face, but then she recognized the subtle differences. This was a portrait of her mother.

"What was she to you?" Angel asked, thrusting the picture back.

"The woman I loved but could not touch."

Angel wanted to believe him; she really did. Tears were gathering inside, enough to last her a lifetime, and somehow she knew his answer before he gave it. "Did you kill her?" She stared into those emerald-green eyes. *Say no. Tell me no.* She probed with her mind and found a stone wall where he'd once been so open. Then came flashing images.

Pain. Resolve. Love of family. Love of home. And loss. Terrible, aching loss. Finally, rage. Hatred. Vengeance. His steps, firm and unwavering, entering too many crypts to count.

Death and decay. The life he'd chosen. But then he emerged, his hands bloody, and looked up at a clear sky.

Always, he had hope for today . . .

"Max," she whispered. He'd sent her the visual images, trying to make her understand. But when he reached for her, she shrank away.

For an instant she felt the full menace he was capable of but had never shown her. He took one tiny step toward her, fangs bared; then he

202

stopped. What might have been pain flashed over his perfect, cold features, but then he enunciated, "Keep your suppositions to warm you at night. I'll have my coachman take you back to what you obviously consider to be your home. I'd wish you joy in it, but you'll find only despair."

Tossing her clothes at her, he stormed out.

Angel looked between the coat of arms and her mother's picture. And she sank to the floor where she stood, clasping her clothes for warmth and comfort.

They gave her neither.

Chapter Eight

Outside, the mist had thickened with the dawn. It coated the trees with a moisture so thick and shiny it resembled mucus. Then, in a slow cohesion, it gathered like spit upon the windowpanes of the upstairs bedroom, the droplets casting back images of the man and woman locked in combat.

For an instant, glowing red eyes formed out of the mist, smiling as the girl sank to the floor with her clothes in her hands and despair in her heart. The man stormed out.

The mist fed on that despair, thickening to an impenetrable curtain. As the girl ran out half dressed, the mist curled into a hand, reaching for the back of the carriage that a yawning coachman waited to drive.

As the girl threw herself inside, the hand pulled back, startled, for something it had never encountered before stood between it and the coach.

The night stared back, but not with vampire eyes.

Two green orbs pierced the darkness, searing into glowing red. Pale green, slanted, and—strangest of all—unafraid.

The hand curled into a defensive claw.

What adversary was this? Not human. Not vampire. Yet another creature so comfortable in the night that it had approached undetected.

The hand paused and then darted forward, reaching to close into a fist.

The green eyes seared through the mist, forming into the grimace of an enormous wolf. The wolf leaped to meet the hand, claws bared, slashing repeatedly. The mist scattered into a million harmless droplets. They sprinkled like rain upon the ground.

For an instant, limned against a full moon, the wolf stood triumphant as the coach rattled away. But drop by drop, the mist began collecting again, diaphanous this time. Stealthy. A thin skein of menace with no form or substance and thus impossible to fight.

"Who are you?" came the harsh demand from the mist surrounding the wolf.

A feral growl was the only answer. For a moment, the mist hung motionless while the red eyes confronted a strength and hatred almost as strong as their own.

The wolf clawed in every direction. This time the mist parted, a silver sigh upon the wind.

Then, as the wolf fought harder still, the haze thickened around the creature's nostrils and mouth. The wolf coughed and wheezed, choking. The wolf shook its head, but the mist was in its throat.

The glowing green eyes began to dim. The wolf staggered, shaking its head one last time.

Green eyes met menacing red, and then . . . there was a searing splash that was cold yet hot. The mist was diluted, swept aside, defeated by its only enemy—water like itself. But a pure water against which it had no defense. Swept into a million particles, the mist dissipated with what might have been a hoarse scream of pain. But the acrid stench of something old and evil and full of hatred, lingered.

The wolf collapsed, panting. The great head lifted and clear green eyes looked up at Max Britton.

His fangs still bared, his golden head of hair

gleaming under the full moon, he looked magnificent in a red cape. He held a large, empty glass bottle that he tossed carelessly aside. "I'd offer you my hand, Miss Holmes, if I can be assured you won't bite it off."

The werewolf stood, careful to move several safe steps away, and shook herself. The droplets didn't hit him. "Holy water, I presume?"

He nodded gravely. "Does it burn you, too?"

"Slightly. But it's much more pleasant than choking." Shelly licked a paw clean. "And Angel?" Shelly looked around for the coach.

"Gone."

The one word was simple, yet full of pain. He turned aside from her gaze.

It was odd feeling sympathy for a vampire. "Would you care to talk about it?" She sat on her haunches.

He turned back to look at her, and now a smile played about his mouth. His fangs retracted fully, and he was just another ungodly handsome man.

"All we need is a tea table and scones and we shall be quite cozy. Though I should love to see my parlor maid's expression at the guest's choice of delicacy—meat. Rare."

"Oh, I prefer it raw these days." If she'd expected to disconcert him, she failed.

His smile deepened. "I knew you were a redoubtable . . . creature the first time I saw you. Forgive me if I seem a bit overset, but it's not every day, you see, that I share my deepest, darkest secrets with a werewolf."

"It's not every day I converse with a vampire half the district believes to be the Beefsteak Killer. But since you just saved my life, I admit a bit of partiality toward you."

"And what do you believe?"

"I admit I suspected you at first, but no longer. Please, this conversation is most interesting, but I prefer to conduct it as a human. Merely to invite your confidence, you understand."

"I quite like talking to canines. Women, however . . ."

"Have better uses. I know. A common refrain from those of your sex, vampire, werewolf, or man." Shelly retreated to the bushes and transformed, her rear paws turning into feet, her forefeet into arms. The transformation was so quick and easy, a matter of will for her now, that she was dressed and facing him before three minutes had passed. She finished with an arch look, "It's somewhat reassuring to know that vampires take the basic human virtues and flaws into eternity with them: lust, envy, jealousy . . . love."

His gaze flickered, a brief tinge of redness

staining the green, but that was his only indication that she'd struck past his barriers. "Ah, finally you are wrong about something. Most vampires have no concept of love. They know only possession. Power."

"You are not most vampires. You, my dear Earl of Trelayne, are a Watch Bearer."

This time his fangs showed as he automatically pulled out his watch, as if she'd purloined not only his secret but the proof of his voluntary mantle of sorrow. He flipped it open and a strange blue glow emanated from the face. It was snuffed out when he closed the watch with a snap and put it back.

She had to admire how quickly his composure returned.

"The crest tipped you off, I assume?"

She nodded gravely. "It took many hours at the Bodleian Library for me to track down a most obscure illustrated manuscript, written many years ago by a monk from Transylvania."

"And what did your little investigation reveal?"

"Oh, only that you became a vampire willingly, not because you had no morals, but because you had too many. Yours was a decision many would find reprehensible, no doubt, but one I find intriguing." A smile played about her generous mouth. "The concepts of revenge and justice are ones that, shall we say, get to the meat of the matter for a werewolf."

"And what revenge do you think I seek? You cannot tell me that was revealed in your pretty book."

"No, that will take more extensive digging. In your own quarters." She knew her words were a direct challenge, but to get his help, she had to prove she could be a formidable ally. Which meant he had to respect her.

This time, when his fangs appeared, he made no effort to retract them. In fact, in one bound he was standing over her, his finely crafted, noble hand about her finely crafted but proudly plebeian throat. "In one way I am very much a vampire, proprietary about things that belong to me."

She met his eyes, her own taking on a surreal glow. She let her voice lower to a growl. "And I am proprietary about innocent young girls, half vampire though they may be. I will not see Angel abused."

The hand retracted, as did the fangs. The man looked back for a moment, genuinely wounded at the accusation. "I have not abused her."

"Then I apprehend when she left here she was as . . . intact as when she arrived?"

The telltale color splashing his cheekbones

was answer enough. "She begged for it."

"Of course she did. Because of the wine. Or more accurately, the blood in the wine."

"Long ago, I would have found your summary dismissal of my own attractions insulting, but for now, a more pressing point needs answering—if you knew her wine was poisoned, why didn't you stop it?"

"I only found out after the fact, when I saw the tray in the kitchen. Why do you think I came here? I knew if she'd had that foul concoction, her own blood would be . . . stirred."

"And why didn't you burst in to rescue her if you are the savior of innocent young girls? You intervened once before."

Ruefully she had to admit she was playing a dangerous game. He'd undoubtedly been astute as a mere mortal. As a vampire who hunted other vampires, he'd become resourceful and shrewd even beyond her capabilities. They'd danced around each other long enough. It was time for the bald truth. "Because she has to face what she is to overcome it." *As do you,* she thought.

As do I . . .

Shelly sighed softly. She'd become so comfortable in her rough, hairy skin that she wasn't certain she wanted to overcome it anymore. But she wished for a better fate for Angel, and for Max. She had her own suspicions as to why he was doing blood research too.

She looked him straight in the eye. "Killing the Beefsteak Killer may cost you Angel."

"I did not bring her here, or use her as a pawn. In fact, I did my best when I first met her to get her to leave. As for last night . . . we had an interlude, nothing more. I lay with her to make her mine and fully human—"

"Ah, so you are a protector of young innocents, too."

"—but I did not know she'd had the tainted wine. I fear she is firmly under Alexander's spell by now. She does not trust me, even after—" He bit back the rest.

"Are you so certain it is Alexander?"

"If I were fully certain, he'd be dead."

"Or you would." He did not argue, but he showed an indifference to that possible fate that she found chilling. She asked, "Would you like to tell me how the last Earl of Trelayne became a vampire hunter sworn by blood oath to kill the oldest, most evil vampire ever to wander English shores?"

"I thought you said you knew only about the Watch Bearers."

"I've an ear for rumors. Rumors that most dismiss, but I heed due to bitter experience that only the least likely myth can sometimes explain the unexplainable. For instance, I heard it was decreed that each Earl of Trelayne's grisly inheritance was to attempt what the previous one had failed. I do not know why, or how you undertook this task. Or the rules that govern your role as a Watch Bearer. Would you care to elucidate?"

"You are the curious, inquiring sort, my dear Miss Holmes. I fear you must continue to wonder."

And with that, he turned in that graceful, silent way of his and glided around the hedges lining his estate, back toward his house.

Shelly was left alone to contemplate her strategy. She'd thought her frankness would disarm him, but instead it seemed to have made him more guarded. She'd hoped that, as allies, they'd have a better chance of catching the killer together than individually. She shivered as she recalled that slimy monstrosity that had filled her throat and nostrils.

It would take both of them at their strongest to defeat something so powerful and remorseless. Shelly disappeared into the darkness, thankful that at least for the moment, Angel was safe. Her self-appointed role of guardian would be even more challenging now.

At all costs, Shelly had to be sure the girl drank no more of that tainted wine.

*   *   *

Angel found the next few days almost unbearable. The slightest sensory impulse brought a flood of memories back—a bright guinea recalled the color of his hair, green grass the color of his eyes, or even the scent of sweat from her mare the scent of their union. No doubt now he thought the wine had been responsible for her driving need to mate with him, but deep inside she knew that was wrong.

For once in her life, she'd acted without worry for tomorrow, or fear for today. Because she wanted him. In a way, she'd been following the motto of his family. She regretted it now. His way of using her was far subtler than her uncle's. And far more devastating.

The motto she'd so loved as a child had been passed down to her mother by a vampire. The bitter irony of the homily didn't escape her, either. A vampire couldn't possibly understand the value of a single day when it had an eternity to choose from. What other secrets did he hide?

Hoping to outrun her demons, Angel reined her mount sharply away from the hall and struck out for the open road. Even the experiments held no appeal for her. Her world had never been stable, but now it was shifting sand under her feet. The knowledge that she was half vampire, that her own mother had been as unnatural as the creatures using her for their own advantage . . . her stomach roiled. Would she be like them soon? Ruthless, using anyone and everyone like a toy?

Finally, for the first time since she'd bedded him, Angel let her defenses down enough to ask the question that really haunted her: Had Max killed her mother?

Blackness descended like a curtain over her eyes. Pulling the mare to a stop, she dismounted and removed the bundle that held her luncheon. Shelly had mysteriously been appearing during most of her repasts in the last few days, distracting her from the wine served with every meal.

She needn't have bothered. Angel knew now what gave that wine punch its lovely deep red color, and she wanted no part of it. She restricted herself to the brisk black tea Sarina had informed her they'd imported from China.

Angel spread her cold meats, cheeses, and fruits out on the blanket. The repast looked appetizing, but it tasted like sawdust in her mouth. She washed it down with Cook's good, strong tea, which was increasingly delicious.

But the roast beef. . . . Cook had cut a particularly rare piece for her. The red juices tasted like ambrosia in her mouth. Famished suddenly, she wolfed down the roast and left the fruit and cheese. But even when she'd finished, she was still hungry.

She stared down at the pink juices on her fingers. For some odd reason, she suddenly had a vision of Max's neck. The vein pulsing in the hollow of his throat looked so good, smelled so good. How would it taste?

Gagging, Angel got up and ran, knowing, deep inside, that the truth about her heritage was far more terrifying than anything she'd imagined. Her skin that never tanned, her dislike of bright sunlight, her love of rare meats, her strange ability to see into other people's minds—she was her mother's daughter, now that she stood on the land that had birthed her.

She was becoming a vampire.

And she had no idea how to stop it. Had that night with Max accelerated her transition somehow? She'd had no more of the tainted wine, that much she knew. Or was her fate inevitable? Angel ran and ran, stumbling over dead logs, tripping over piles of detritus until her clothes were ripped and her legs stung with scratches.

Finally, exhaustion helped her panic subside. She looked around. She was in a small copse of woods not far from the hall. She longed to collapse in tears and never get up, for the future, which had seemed bleak before, now stretched endlessly dark.

Maybe she should ask Max to take that bright golden hammer that matched his bright golden hair and release her from her misery. But finally, as the sun began to lower in the sky, she realized she had a long walk back to fetch her poor mare, tied to a tree. As she turned to make her way back, her foot struck something metal.

She looked down. A handle poked up, barely visible beneath a pile of leaves. She brushed the leaves away to reveal a trapdoor. Curious, glad to find anything to distract her from her thoughts, she tried to open the door. It was locked. From the look of the keyhole, it would require a very large, very ornate key.

Angel sat back on her haunches, wondering why there was a heavy metal trapdoor in the middle of nowhere. She looked toward the hall. The answer was, it wasn't in the middle of nowhere. This was obviously a tunnel opening.

Brushing leaves away with her feet as she went, Angel noted a very slight rise in the ground, a minute difference in the texture of the earth. Here it felt a bit spongy, there solid. After five feet or so of careful exploration, she looked to see where the tunnel would lead if she followed a straight trajectory.

It led to the rear of the hall into a walled garden not far from the laboratory.

Swiveling on her heel with a purpose that banished some of her fear, she walked back to fetch her mare. Maybe this would help her find the Beefsteak Killer. And maybe if she helped capture the Beefsteak Killer, somehow this terrible sickness taking over her blood could be stopped, too. For somehow, she didn't know how, their fates were linked, the three of them: the Earl of Trelayne, an ancient, evil vampire, and an American orphan whose biggest crime was a need to learn who she was.

She'd barely taken two steps before she came face-to-face with a man in a dark cloak. She froze, a scream caught in her throat, but when he flipped the hood back, she was relieved to see only Gustav.

"Why be ye here, girl? All alone?" He looked around suspiciously, as if suspecting her of some tryst.

"I was . . . enjoying the day."

They both looked at the waning sun fast disappearing over the horizon.

"Alone? Ye got rocks for brains, me girl? Ye know what's been happening to innocent young ladies what be alone in these parts."

Indeed she did. Angel sidled slightly away from him. There was something about this man that made her uneasy. Everyone in this district seemed to have a secret, but she sensed in the head groom a mind far keener than he let on. She was tempted to try out her new mind-reading abilities, but if he was a vampire, as she suspected, his skills would doubtless be far stronger than her nascent ones.

Well aware of that trapdoor lurking behind her, she decided it was far smarter to play dumb. She simpered, "La, my good man, I'm a colonial. Up to a small scamper through the woods. I but lost track of time. Now if you'll excuse me, I have to get back to my poor mare."

Pretending not to feel his suspicious glare following her, she trekked back through the heavy brush, making as much noise as she could. When she was safely in the cover of a leafy canopy of trees, she went very still, trying to teach herself to glide like Max.

It was surprisingly easy to slip out, soundless, from behind the tree. She could just see Gustav's dark outline hovering as if he debated following her; then, as she suspected, he pulled a huge key from his cloak, unlocked the trapdoor, and let the earth swallow him up. He tried to close the door quietly, but the clang was like a warning bell to Angel.

Behind that door vampires met. She was

convinced now that the voices she'd heard that night outside the lab had been some sort of conference of the local vampires. As to who led it . . . she was quite certain that person—no, that unnatural being—had a crooked tooth.

Angel went back to her mare, vowing to search high and low for a key into that tunnel.

For some reason she couldn't define, she knew that if the killer won its ancient battle with Max, Angel would lose. And Max would die.

The desolation she felt at that thought was so great that she knew she'd risk anything, even her own death, to save him. Melding with him that night had increased the bond she felt with him, but it had also exacerbated her fear.

What if, when she plumbed the secrets of that cave, she learned Max was the one with the crooked tooth?

Such a simple thing as a huge key should have been easy to find. It was much too large and unwieldy for Alexander to keep on his person. That it remained elusive despite her thorough search was all the more proof of its importance.

Over the next few days, Angel spent as much time poking about the hall as she could disguise with subtle excuses. To the maid who found her rattling through drawers in the study she said, "I need some stationery." The maid supplied it from a bureau, along with a pen and wax.

To Alexander, who found her pulling drawers from the long cases against the laboratory wall and searching behind them, she said, "I misplaced a blood sample." He gallantly offered to help her look.

When every drawer had been pulled out, every cabinet ransacked, she pushed her bedraggled hair out of her face with a dusty hand. "I must have accidentally swept it into the trash."

She turned to find him reading her notes.

"You find no similarity so far between various types?"

She longed to answer, *Yes, between yours and Max's*. She shook her head.

He asked far too casually, "And have you compared your own blood to the others? Purely in the interests of science, you understand."

Angel stared at him. "No."

"Would you object if I do so?"

Yes. But what excuse could she give to refuse him?

Angel sat still for the poke of the needle, but

221

after he took three samples, she protested, "I need a few pints left for such inessential things as breathing."

He had the grace to look embarrassed. But it did not escape her notice that he bundled up the samples as if they were precious—and took them with him. "I'll compare them later if you don't mind. Sometimes scientific advancements rest on pure happenstance."

As she watched him leave, she cynically reflected that sometimes they rested on careful planning. It was now apparent to Angel that, for some peculiar reason, both Max and Alexander prized her blood, and not just to drink. They wanted to study it. As if it were the key to the battle between them.

How?

That night, as Angel tossed and turned in her bed, belittling her own skills as a detective, she heard the voices again. Muffled, secretive, far below her feet. Audible only because her hearing had become incredibly sensitive of late. There was another conference this night behind that wall that she'd not been able to breach.

While the vampires were meeting, she should be able to search the master quarters undetected.

Throwing on a night robe, Angel didn't even bother with slippers. She eased into the master suite on silent feet. The sitting room between the bedrooms was dark. Quiet. But her eyes adjusted very quickly, and she was able to search Sarina's bureau without lighting the lamps. She found only the usual feminine toiletries, except ... she pulled out a box of wrapped candy.

Turkish delight. A delicacy lately the rage in high society. She unwrapped a piece and sampled it, almost gagging as she spit it out, for she immediately recognized the taste. Cloyingly sweet, yet with a tinge of salt, too. Angel lit a gas lamp and wasn't surprised to find the candy bloodred.

Either Sarina was a vampire, which was hardly surprising, since she was wedded to one, or she kept her husband's candy in her own bureau. Angel searched Alexander's bureau, but she found no similar box. However, she did find her own blood samples. She was tempted, mightily tempted, to take them back, but she knew if she did, he'd suspect her. Would she be able to sneak into the lab and fetch substitutes before she was caught?

"I wouldn't try it if I were you. You've not yet learned the subterfuge any self-respecting vampire must master."

She jumped and would have dropped the glass plates if Max hadn't steadied her. He looked down at them, back at her, and she knew he'd already read her mind and figured out they were her own. She half expected him to grab them, but he didn't.

Irritably, she turned to him, trying to hide the sudden pounding of the pulse at her throat by turning up the collar of her night robe. Her movement had the opposite effect. Max's green eyes locked on the hollow of her throat with a hunger that made her skin tingle. But somehow, with extreme effort, she kept her gaze away from his own throat and rejoined, "Walking into their quarters, bold as you please, is hardly subtle."

"It's subtle enough if they're occupied for a goodly time. We seek the same evidence, I expect. Some clue as to where Alexander hides his casket."

Angel frowned. "But if he was born here, he already sleeps on the soil of his birth."

"If he was not, then he needs a casket."

"But the vampires hereabouts don't seem to be subject to the mythical weaknesses. They go about in daylight—"

"Only the strongest, and that immunity is dependent upon consistent consumption of Alexander's punch. But all must occasionally sleep upon the land of their ancestors or they grow weak."

"You never drink the punch, yet you go about as you please, whenever you please."

A bitter little smile curled his lips. "Concerned? The way you left the other night, I should think my well-being was the least of your worries."

She nibbled her lip, then stopped when his eyes, beginning to glow in the darkness, followed her movement.

"Or do you seek my vulnerabilities?"

She felt him probing her mind again, and she blushed. She'd just been remembering the feel of his skin on hers, his eager thrust into the secret depths of her body.

His voice took on a husky note. "Ah, so you do remember. Very well, Angel mine. You opened yourself to me, so I shall show you the same courtesy."

He flipped open his watch. The room immediately filled with an eerie blue luminescence that centered around him in a protective glow. When he closed the watch, the blue glow faded, yet if she narrowed her eyes just so, she sensed it still around him in an invisible aura.

"If you lose the watch, are you vulnerable then to sunlight?"

He nodded gravely. "I have shared with you

a secret no being on Earth knows." He waited, hoping she'd reciprocate by admitting the plates in her hand contained her own blood.

She wanted to believe his protective posture toward her was genuine; she truly did. But what if this was another ruse? She seemed surrounded on all sides by people she should be able to trust implicitly—her mother's brother, her lover. Yet trust was not a birthright; it had to be earned and then freely given.

At her long hesitation, he turned away from her, but not before she saw the pain in his gaze. She nibbled her own lip so hard that blood spurted from a cut on the inside of her mouth.

Nostrils flaring, he whirled and gathered his powerful muscles to leap. He caught himself just in time. They stared, each aware of the bed behind them and the chasm between them. It took only a step to bridge, but that step took more courage than she could muster, and more compassion than he could apparently offer.

Almost unaware, she licked the inside of her mouth, the tip of her tongue luxuriating in the taste of her own blood. He saw it, felt it, tasted it, through that strange emotional and mental linkage that had become stronger since their coupling. His hands clenched and she felt the supreme effort of will it took for him to master his own driving need to taste of her, too.

Finally he grated out, "What have you been drinking, Angel?"

"I haven't touched a drop of wine in a week."

"What else?"

"Nothing but tea and water."

He eyed her; then to her shock, he bridged that chasm between them in one step, pulling his own shirt collar down to bare his jugular vein to her. He leaned down to her level, his eyes, those green eyes that were verdant and alive, filling her own vision. Eden-sent, hell-bent to tempt her. "Prove it."

The faint scent of clean male and forbidden delight exuded from him. Both inextricably entwined somehow with who he was, who he'd been, and who he might yet become. And she wanted all of that complex, dangerous being. The tip of her tongue slipped out to dart against his warm skin. He tasted so good, so normal.

Not dangerous at all.

What could be harmful in something so natural it called to every feminine impulse in her? The thought scarcely left her before she felt her own teeth sinking into the side of his neck. For one forbidden instant, ambrosia dotted the tip of her tongue, but then he'd jerked her away. So quickly, so powerfully did he move her that one minute they were twined together in the center of the room and the next, standing before a long cheval mirror.

"Look."

She looked. She went so weak at the knees she would have fallen if his grip hadn't held her up.

Just visible between her half-open lips were fangs. Nascent, pearly white, barely pointed, but fangs nonetheless. "Tell me how to stop it."

"Go. Run as far and as fast as you can. Don't look back; admit no regrets." He stepped away.

She swayed where she stood, but managed to stay on her feet. No regrets? He might as well tell her to close her eyes and wish herself back to America, an innocent in every way. Alone in her grimy little flat, living a hand-to-mouth existence. But there she'd been blissfully ignorant of the painful facts she was still grappling to face.

Most painful of all was the belief that if she left him, he'd die facing the killer. Alone, as he'd always been. Leaving her alone for the rest of her life, as she'd always been.

There had to be a better way.

"There is no better way," he said dully. "Your transformation has already gone too far. If you stay here, nothing will stop it." He watched her expression in the mirror, and somehow she knew that when he looked at her, he saw her mother.

Would her mother's fate also be hers? "But blood . . . if I don't drink of it—"

"Somehow they're getting it into your food or drink. They must have been poisoning your tea." He gave her a little push. "Go now, while they're occupied."

She resisted, almost dropping the plates she still held in one hand. She whirled on him, following, at last, her instincts instead of her intellect. Intellect said he was not to be trusted, but instinct warned her to take a chance.

Perhaps the last chance. For both of them.

Gravely, Angel held out her hand, offering him the blood samples. "And these? They must be important since both you and Alexander want them so badly."

He went very still. His eyes probed hers, past her thoughts, into her mind, into her still-guarded but hopeful heart. "What do you think I want to do with them?"

"I don't know. But I'm hoping you'll tell me."

"You don't know and you offer them anyway?"

Her hand remained outstretched. A plethora of emotions flooded from him to her—joy, relief, and then, strangely, sadness. Despair. As if

229

he knew that this tiny bit of trust would not be enough.

Still, to her mingled relief and fear, he took them—only to put them back in Alexander's bureau. "It's best he not find them missing." Then, taking her hand, he led her straight to Alexander's window. Lifting her into his arms, he leaped outside with her, landing lightly and then crossing the grass in that gliding way of his straight to his coachman and carriage lurking behind some trees.

When they were safely ensconced on the plush squabs, he lifted her hand and kissed it. Turning it over, he trailed kisses from her palm, having her with his tongue as he went, and stopped at the blue vein pulsing in her wrist. With the barest flick, he let her feel his own driving need to meld with her in that way, too. Blood to blood, in the way of vampires.

She closed her eyes and offered herself to him, but with a strangled curse, he pulled away to his side of the carriage. "I cannot. You are temptation unbearable to me, Angel, but the more vampire you become, the more dangerous you are to my life and my sacred vow."

And no matter how much she asked and pleaded, he would tell her no more. "I've shared with you one of my fatal flaws this night.

Allow a self-respecting vampire a secret or two."

"Where are we going?" Her heart skipped a beat. She hoped, she needed . . .

She got something most unexpected.

"To my laboratory. Where you will give me fresh blood samples and I will show you, my dear little scientist, why your blood may be the key to defeating the Beefsteak Killer. And his key to defeating me."

Chapter Nine

Of all the answers she'd expected, this was the least likely. Angel was flabbergasted. How could that be? Her own blood some magical elixir that offered life or death?

He threw back his golden head and laughed. It was the hearty laughter of a man who'd once known joy and contentment—before he became a vampire with a mission.

"You expected me to say I was taking you to bed, did you not?" He leaned across to her and whispered, "Or hoped I would."

She blushed, hoping, indeed, that the darkness hid her embarrassment. She should have known better.

"That may yet come. If we both work hard enough."

"Pray tell, which is the reward and which the task?" she asked tartly. "I've never been equated with a laboratory experiment before, and I'm not sure I like the notion."

He laughed louder, his rich chuckles as aristocratic as his fine hands and perfect face and form. "Why, that depends upon the level of your own enthusiasm." He raked her with that sparkling green gaze. "A female such as yourself can be a formidable conquest, even for a vampire. Do you wish me to worship your mind or your body?"

Angel scowled at his teasing.

Softly, he kissed her brow. "Angel, you are delicious." And with that, as the carriage drew to a stop before his mansion, he assisted her down.

"Does that mean you want to kiss me or eat me?"

He grinned. "Both." He led her to his front door, unlocked it, and ushered her inside. He lit gas lamps as they went. She expected him to lead her down, but as usual, he did the unexpected.

He led her up.

Her heart rate accelerated as they approached his bedchamber, but he walked right past it, straight to what appeared to be a leaded glass window high on the blank wall at the end of the corridor. Beneath the window was a small parson's table that held a vase, a clock, and a candelabra.

Making no effort to hide his movements, he unscrewed the base of the candelabra, revealing a strange knob that somewhat resembled a key. He stuck the knob into the back of the ornate clock, which she could see now was bolted to the table. He turned the knob. There was a metallic clang, and the table swung smoothly away from the wall, revealing a recess with steps leading down.

He turned to face her, smiling as he saw her stunned expression. "You never would have found it, you know."

So he knew she'd wanted to look. "Why did you show it to me?"

He cradled her face in his hands. *Trust is an elusive gift. If you grab it, it becomes sand in your hands. But if you give it, it's mortar that survives the ages.* Angel heard the words so clearly, she thought he'd spoken them, but then she realized he was too busy using his mouth for other, more tempting things.

Like kissing her temple, her brow, her cheek, and then barely brushing her mouth. He'd used that strange mind meld that was becoming as much a bond between them as the tangible physical link their bodies had instinctively formed.

Trust me. Such simple little words. So difficult in the execution. After the events of the last few weeks, Angel didn't trust anyone.

Least of all her own judgment.

He clouded her mind and seduced her body. Why he was showing her the secret research he'd obviously shared with no one, she couldn't say, but she still wasn't convinced he didn't have some base motivation.

She pulled away, trying to shield her thoughts from his probing. "I'm going with you into the bowels of your home where no one would hear me scream, am I not?"

He read her response for what it was: withdrawal. Refusal to trust him. Immediately, his mind closed her out. His expression was blank, but she sensed she'd hurt him. He hesitated, looking between her face and the dark steps. Then he swept a hand before him. "After you."

Why he made that choice, she didn't know. She'd scarcely have blamed him if he'd ushered her to the front door. But she proceeded down into the darkness, her eyes adjusting quickly to the black cavity.

The walls were smooth stone, and she realized the reason the laboratory was so well hidden was that it was not part of the house but carved deeply into the hillside upon which the house stood. The smell of moist earth and strong chemicals assailed her nostrils as they reached the bottom. They faced yet another heavy, barred door.

He twisted the door handle several times and the bars smoothly slid open. Lighting candles as he went, he led her into his laboratory.

Angel went still, delighted. Alexander's lab was serviceable, but this . . .

Glass-fronted cases held a huge assortment of scientific equipment—protractors, an abacus, scales, various surgical instruments, beakers, innumerable chemicals, burners, funnels.

On several spotless tables stood the most sophisticated microscopes she'd ever beheld. She looked through one. The optics were so fine that there was not the slightest distortion, even when she turned the instrument to its fullest power. "German?"

He nodded.

Angel wandered, seeing the long wall of books covering every conceivable category of science: biology, chemistry, anatomy, astronomy, and of course virtually every respected book written on blood in the past twenty years, including the one she'd helped edit. He even had a signed copy of that subversive book that had the entire scientific community in an uproar: *The Origin of Species* by Charles Darwin.

Angel said sincerely, "I am most impressed. I had no idea you were of such a scientific bent."

"I wanted to be a scientist before . . . I became the last Trelayne heir. And took up the mantle of my inheritance."

Angel knew he was speaking of more than estates and assets. He always talked of his inheritance as if it were a curse. "Why did all your brothers die?"

Max swallowed harshly. "One by one, they were killed trying to catch the Beefsteak Killer. The first victim that I know of on English shores was my only sister."

Angel gasped. This explained so much.

His good humor had apparently returned. "I should have realized the best way to seduce you was not with jewels or furs but with microscopes and books."

She was too busy operating the largest microscope to heed him. The magnification was so good that she could define individual corpuscles in the blood sample on the slide.

"I want to show you something, Angel. May I?" He lifted her finger and pricked it with a pin. For a long moment, he stared down at the bright red dot of healthy, welling blood. His breathing quickened. He licked his lips. He started to bring her finger to his mouth, but because she wanted to feel the touch of his mouth sucking her blood so badly, she knew she didn't dare allow it. She was acutely aware of how alone they were. It was the middle of the night, no one knew she was here, and she still wanted him desperately. She was struggling enough against the spell he'd woven about her mind and body without letting him form a blood link, too.

She jerked away, wrapped the tiny prick in her kerchief, and stuck her hand in her pocket.

Out of temptation's reach.

Seeming to recall himself to cool scientific study, he removed the plate from the microscope and separated the two glass slides. He held his hand out for her own.

Reluctantly, she gave it to him. He pressed the tiny cut, which had already coagulated, and forced a small bead of blood on top of the other sample. Then he took a stopper out of a small vial and dripped some strange glowing solution on top of both blood samples.

"What is that?"

"A formulation that isolates the components of your blood into discrete elements. If my theory is correct, your blood will now interact with this sample." He put the glass slides back together and inserted them again in the instrument. "Look, Angel."

Angel pressed her eyes to the viewing piece and carefully focused. As she looked, the brighter, fresher blood—her own—seemed to seethe and foam, separating into clear serum and bright red corpuscles. To her astonishment, as she watched, her blood began to well around the paler hemoglobin, surrounding it, and then . . .

. . . consuming it. With amazing rapidity, the paler sample was absorbed by her own bright red proof of life. One moment it was there, full of vitality, the next . . . gone. Stunned, Angel looked up at him. "Whose blood is this?"

"Mine." Ignoring her expression, he proceeded to draw a small vial of her blood from her wrist, licking his lips as he did so, but stoppering it before it had time to coagulate.

Numbly, Angel looked down at the blood on her wrist, then back at the deep red vial. "But I don't understand."

"You are my one weakness, Angel. I suspect the killer knows this and was somehow instrumental in bringing you to England. And the more vampire you become, the more dangerous you are to me."

Angel leaped up. "But how? It's you, the

vampire, who are a danger to me, surely."

He removed his pocket watch, absently rubbing the gold case over and over with his thumb. "When I became a Watch Bearer, I was warned that although I would have most of the strengths and few of the weaknesses of the vampire, I had one fatal flaw: because I accepted the conversion willingly, and my abilities rest partly upon my devotion to my vow, I cannot drink of fresh human blood. Human blood will weaken me."

He tilted her neck up and finished his sentence against her throbbing jugular vein. He whispered, "And most dangerous of all to me is blood from someone half human and half vampire. It is not I who threaten your existence, Angel. It is you who threaten mine."

He finished the words on a groan, and she felt the brush of his teeth, the trembling in his body as the blood lust took him. He wanted to sink his teeth into her, to share with her the great intimacy of his kind.

Whether to protect him or herself, Angel didn't know, but she twisted away and backed toward the door. "Why are you telling me this?"

Why was he baring himself to her this way? She'd surely given him no more reason to trust her than she had to trust him. She inhaled sharply as she felt his answer in her mind.

Because you are mine, Angel. By the blood of your mother, whom I loved and could not save no matter how hard I tried, you are a fulfillment of my motto and hers: a blessing sent to me for today.

Tears came to Angel's eyes as this bright, bold being, the best of vampire and the best of man, bared himself to her. She felt unworthy, she felt shamed, but most of all, she felt exalted.

The touch of him in her mind became so sweet, a tender caress, that she walked straight into his opening arms. And softly he finished, with both his lips and his mind, *"No matter how the killer tempts you, I cannot believe you will betray either my confidence or my faith that the blood you carry of your mother calls to the blood that made me vampire. And yet there is much of the human left in each of us, and that, too, cements our bond. We are both unique, yet two of a kind. Meant to be together. If I have to risk my very existence to keep you safe as I could not keep her, then so be it. I give you this knowledge to do with as you will."*

As she willed. Angel wished for only one thing at this moment: to meld with him in body as they had in mind and, though she feared their joining still, meld perhaps even in their unique souls, part vampire, part human.

She pulled his head down to her level and kissed him full on the mouth, a flaming kiss that held little of the innocent she'd been but much of the temptress she was becoming. His reaction was immediate and tangible: the root of his masculinity swelled into her abdomen. His mouth teased hers open for the intimate caress that presaged that complete immersion of souls that allowed no barriers and no denials.

When he swept his notebooks and even a small microscope off his table, Angel could no longer doubt that part of his declaration, at least, was true. He wanted her, as he'd wanted her mother. Badly. As both vampire and man.

The microscope fell with a clatter, its fine optics shattering. Angel felt the sting of glass enter the side of her knee, but the physical pain only made the pleasure of what he was doing to her with tongue and teeth all the more puissant. He'd been gentle the other time, easing her into the powerful sensual delights so many virgins found overwhelming.

This time he suckled her mouth so hard that he sucked her lips between his teeth. For a long moment he tasted the gentle softness, his wildest instincts urging him to bite. She felt it in the trembling of his body, saw the image in the fiery connection between their minds.

"Bite me," she begged into his mouth, not knowing or caring where the urge came from. But it was as deeply ingrained in her as the emptiness in her womb that begged to be filled.

For an instant, she felt the graze of his fangs, but then with a queer little half sob, half groan, he pulled away, caught his hands in the neck of her high night rail and robe, and ripped downward with all his unnatural strength.

The sturdy garments fell in shreds to her feet. It was chilly so far beneath the hillside, but she was burning. Burning at the look in his eyes, the touch of his hands, the sensual promise in his smile. His pupils expanded, leaving only a bright rim of green that beckoned her like hope.

His hands started at her collarbones and coasted downward, barely brushing, but leaving a trail of molten desire that made her emptiness expand. She felt as if her entire body were a receptacle, craving the fluid of their mutual fulfillment. She knew now the pleasures of sin, and she was so lost to him that it seemed good and right that she revel in them again.

Making the same queer sound, she wrenched open the front of his pants. Buttons went flying. She scarcely noticed, for he sprang free into her hands. The first time she'd hesitated, but now she explored him without reserve. Were all men so magnificent? He was velvet without flaccidity, iron without hardness, wildness without threat.

Man, at his most mesmerizing.

He was all the more bewitching because he quelled his own vast strength to let her know him in this most intimate of caresses. The veins on his neck stood out with effort when she glanced up at him through slumbrous, half-closed lids. His neck was thrown back, open and vulnerable to her. She felt her own fangs growing, and not heaven or earth or fear of hell itself could have stopped her natural urge.

She sank her fangs into him and sucked with tongue and teeth. As she drew his essence into her mouth, the emptiness in her midsection began a primitive aching that bordered on the edge of pain. The taste of him, the blood so thick and sweet and warm, made the power of what she held that much more mind shattering. She pulled at his manhood, milking him with her hands as she knew she soon would with her body. The tactic made his strong legs almost buckle, weakening him so that his feeble efforts to get away from her bite were aborted.

For an instant more he tried to resist. "No, Angel, stop. If you drink my blood, it will make your transition go faster."

Greek, Swahili, Hottentot, his words made no sense.

She had to taste of him, to know him, to sustain her femininity on the masculinity pulsing above and below.

She fed on him, the consummation of joining with his blood making her sexual frenzy all the greater. Then she was rubbing the hard, hot head of his sex against her flushed lower belly, lifting one leg to slide him into the moist vee between her legs. His greater height interfered.

Her mouth still full of his blood, she begged, "Lower, put it in me—"

He took the plea from her mouth, kissing her deeply, insatiably, tasting his own blood on the sweetness of her lips and tongue. The shared intimacy made their passions soar out of control. With a fierce strength that made her feel invincible because she knew she, and she alone, had incited this storm, he lifted her hips to the table, pressed her legs widely open with his knees, and thrust deeply home.

He impaled her, but this golden stake filled her, fulfilled her, and made her yearn for more. Harder. Faster. Further. She squirmed on him, around him, filled to the brim, but it still wasn't enough.

She didn't say the words, but she didn't have to. He heard them in his head, felt them in that wordless communication of their kind. Lifting her legs over his shoulders, he cupped himself in the intimate cradle of her body, giving her no respite, and no quarter.

She asked for neither. The wildness took her.

Instinctively she lifted her hips to try to force him deeper, though in this position she felt him pulsing at the very lip of her womb. They touched everywhere; there was no space, no reserve.

No tomorrow. Not even today. Only the . . .

Now.

This moment snatched from the evil forces trying to pull them apart would link their fates as it linked their bodies. And fortify them for the time yet to come. Pausing with his strength pulsing high between her legs, he turned his head to kiss her leg. She felt him stiffen as he scented her blood. He pulled the bit of glass out of her knee and watched delicious, bright red blood well up to fill the tiny hole. Still nestled moistly in the welcoming clasp of her body, he licked at her wound. He used just the tip of his tongue at first, the tiny dab of moisture and heat so slight she scarcely felt it.

"Angel," he said in a groan. His fangs baring with a grimace of desire and pain, he ringed the tiny hole with his teeth and bit into her flesh at the same time that he pressed to his fullest extent into her body.

In the most erotic experience she'd ever known, he suckled the fluid of her life and gave her his own at the same time. Her head fell back over the edge of the table, her long hair falling to the floor as she exulted in the violence of his release. She welcomed it with her own dewy convulsions, breaking apart in the undertow of murky half-truths, doubts, and fears. As she shook with ecstasy, she felt as if she were climbing out, complete again, on an unknown shore where truth, at last, was hers for the reaching.

As she sagged under him, the world forming again into a cold, hard table and cold, hard reality, one verity was still emblazoned in her mind: this moment had been destined the moment she set foot in that cemetery where her mother lay buried and saw him standing sentinel over her grave. Whether Max was friend or foe, whether he'd killed her mother or not, she had no regrets for the virgin blood she'd given him. In return, he'd endowed her with the natural strength that was her heritage.

As the sensations faded and the roaring in her ears abated, she finally realized he was still drinking insatiably at her leg. She welcomed this final consummation, feeling her own fangs growing. She sank her teeth into his neck and drank deeply.

Forbidden sustenance, but she had neither strength nor will to deny him—or herself. It was right that they bond this way, too.

He collapsed on top of her, kissing her still, her lips, her eyes where tears seeped out, inspired by the powerful emotions consuming her.

But then, to her shock, she felt him sway, still standing between her legs. Even as his knees buckled, he latched more firmly onto her leg again, suckling, drinking . . . and weakening himself.

Appalled, remembering his earlier words about his weakness as a Watch Bearer, Angel pulled her leg away from his mouth. He tried to hold on to her and bite her again, but she shoved hard with her free foot against his chest. He went sprawling.

The last little twinges of glory faded all too quickly to shame as she saw what her blood did to him. Even as he licked the last morsel from his lips, he slipped sideways to the ground, his breeches around his knees, his eyes cloudy. She felt the mind link with him break and knew only that he was alone now, in some faraway dream or nightmare she could not fathom. As she watched, his fangs receded back into his mouth.

Unmindful of her nakedness, Angel knelt over him, patting his cheeks. "Max! Max, wake up."

For several more wrenching moments he remained in a near fetal position, but when her hot tears of anguish welled up and fell onto his face, he blinked back to awareness. Huskily, his voice still weak, he said, "Do you see now why I brought you here?"

Angel pulled her tattered robe over herself before she could frame an answer. "I . . . hurt you. You make me strong, and I make you weak."

Hearing the awful truth in her own shaky voice was more than she could bear. Oh, yes, she understood. He'd risked everything in an effort to get her to trust him, revealing his worst weakness to the one woman who could emasculate his powers as a vampire and leave him helpless to the killer.

And she could not bear it.

Fleet of foot now, more fleet than ever before, she ran out, bounding up the long staircase in two strides and opening the casement window at the top to leap to the ground. Unhurt, she ran and ran, her heart bursting in her chest.

But not with exertion. What terrible blood right was this? This man who made her long to share everything with him, heart, soul, and deepest truth of who she was, could lose his very life in the melding that should have made them each whole. The sexual congress between them made their urge to share their blood well nigh uncontrollable.

He wasn't dangerous to her.

She was dangerous to him.

And somehow the killer knew it and had lured her here to use her to get to Max.

A few minutes later, still weak but able to move, Max forced himself up off the cold floor, but he knew Angel was long gone. He'd brought her here to risk everything in the bold gamble that the natural kindness of her nature would overcome her vampire instincts if he only showed her how vulnerable she made him. And it might have worked if passion hadn't swept him away, too. If he hadn't broken the microscope in his haste to take her. If he hadn't smelled her blood. If . . .

Despite himself, he licked the inside of his mouth, still reveling in the forbidden taste of her. His body was sated but his mind was tormented.

For he knew that neither his sacred vows nor

the luminous glow of the watch that had always been his talisman would fortify him against this powerful lure. No matter how many of his brothers had died, passing the blood oath from heir to heir, no matter that he was the last earl who could fulfill the grisly Trelayne inheritance, if he was given the chance, he'd drink of Angel again.

She was meant to be his. Every instinct in him demanded he brand her as such. Again and again, until the exchange of bodily fluids linked them irrevocably.

The fact that the exchange could make him easy prey for the killer wouldn't stop them.

Bowing his head in his hands, he despaired. Then he realized how ridiculous he looked and rose to fasten his breeches. As he did so, his foot struck a piece of the microscope. He stared down at it.

Science had led him to the Watch Bearers. Science had led Angel to England.

Perhaps it could yet save them both.

Pulling out his watch, he let the radiance give him strength for the night, and then he set back to work. No matter how long it took, or how many calculations and serum separations he had to make, he'd find a way to turn Angel's miraculous, powerful blood into a weapon equally devastating to the Beefsteak Killer. And then, his quest ended, he could give up this half existence and share with Angel a natural life span.

As a man.

By the time she reached Blythe Hall, Angel's feet were raw. Dawn colored the sky with red fingers of warning. She saw the hall silhouetted, a dark, dangerous heap, against the bright red dawn and knew, in the desolate recesses of the soul she feared for, that she witnessed a harbinger of what was to come.

Blackness and bloody conflict.

For an instant she rested her head against the gate, wondering if she shouldn't just get in the first available coach and flee back to America. Her lips twisted bitterly as she looked down at the tatters that revealed far too much of her skin.

She would not make it far.

Besides, there was one quality Angel the innocent and Angel the vampire shared: neither of them was craven. Whether Max had killed her mother or not, she now knew Max was not the Beefsteak Killer. No defiler of innocents would dare show her his one fatal flaw and then love her so passionately to prove it to her.

No. Someone in this hulking monstrosity was the killer.

A vampire had to refresh itself upon the soil of its birth.

She had to gain entrance to that tunnel.

For several days, life seemed to regain some semblance of normalcy. Though she ached for Max and longed to talk to him about the strange rapture-regret they'd shared, she knew it was best to leave the subject alone for now. Somehow she knew the killer had lured her to England precisely because she was half vampire and half human, Max's only weakness.

Until she found the killer, she didn't dare tempt either Max or herself to experience again that odd bonding that was so satisfying yet so perilous.

When she saw them at dinner the next day, Sarina and Alexander noticed her scratches and sore feet, but they accepted Angel's excuse. "My mare rode under branches with me and knocked me out of my saddle, and I got blisters walking back."

"Indeed, you look as though you've had a particularly wild ride," Alexander said blandly.

Angel didn't like the look in his eyes or his implication. How could he possibly know she'd been intimate with his enemy? Making some excuse, she left the table early. She let the maid prepare her for bed, but as soon as the girl was gone, she put on her boy's attire.

She was observant, too. Alexander had not been dressed for dinner. He wore tall boots and tough breeches, as if he had a rough outing of his own to make that night. And since he wasn't the rough-and-tumble type, she had to assume he had a mission.

A mission to kill his next victim?

Hoping her nascent vampire skills were enough to disguise her attempts to track him, Angel cracked her door to listen for footsteps. She heard loud voices from the master suite, a slamming door, and then she felt him more than heard him, for he moved with the same skill that Max had perfected to an art. Almost soundlessly, he glided down the hallway toward the curving staircase.

Angel was about to go after him when she saw movement at the end of the hallway. She ducked back in time to see Gustav pass, his movements stealthy as if he, too, followed his master and didn't want to be seen. What was the head groom doing in the family living quarters?

Giving them quite a lot of space, Angel counted to eight and then sneaked out her door. She saw no trace of either Gustav or Alexander. She was halfway down the stairs when she sensed someone watching her.

Shrinking against the wall, Angel waited, her heart pounding at her ribs. She used all her strong senses to seek through the darkness for the source of her unease, but she saw nothing, heard nothing.

Only felt—a menace so ancient and evil that she couldn't fathom it.

Telling herself she was just nervous, Angel continued down the stairs and eased open the front door in time to see Alexander get on his stallion and ride away. Had he sensed her watching him and somehow projected that menace to scare her off?

Angel was about to bolt toward the stables for her mare, but a tearful voice said right behind her, "He's going to his mistress again, the rotten bastard."

Angel whirled. Sarina stood in her white night rail like a ghost against the darkness. Her fair skin was streaked with tears. "I forget if this is number five . . . no, I believe it's number six."

With a last regretful look at Alexander disappearing into the night, Angel lit a gas lamp and led Sarina to a settee. Her aunt by marriage had been very kind to her, and Angel couldn't leave her in such despair while she went on what was not only likely a fool's errand, but a highly dangerous errand at that.

Going to the liquor tray on a sideboard, Angel poured a glass of brandy and brought it back to Sarina.

Sarina made a face. "I detest the stuff. I prefer punch."

Angel looked at the ever-present decanter full of deep red wine. Biting back the urge to warn Sarina what else was in the punch, Angel poured a glass and offered it. Sarina sipped. "Won't you join me?"

"The brandy suits me," Angel said, taking the tiniest taste. She actually detested the stuff, too, but at least she could see from the pale golden color that it held no blood.

Sarina eyed Angel's attire. "You look as if you had an assignation of your own planned. Where were you off to, Angel?"

"Just a late ride. I've . . . been having a difficult time sleeping." That, certainly, was true.

Sarina obviously didn't believe her, but she didn't press the issue. She swirled the liquid in her glass, staring down at it as if mesmerized. "Don't ever fall in love, Angel."

A lump appeared in Angel's throat. She remembered the look on Max's face as he thrust into her and knew, deep inside, that the warning came too late. But she wasn't ready yet to admit that truth even to herself, much less to anyone else. "Surely mutual love is the greatest happiness any man and woman can know."

"Mutual slavery, more like."

"Alexander loves you, Sarina."

"Does he? Then he'd be faithful, would he not?" Sarina's troubled blue eyes probed Angel's. "And dismiss the notion that he's getting even with me. Despite what rumors you hear to the contrary, I have always been faithful to him."

Angel stared down into her own glass, wondering how Sarina had read her mind. It was true that Angel had occasionally doubted Sarina's morality. She was so sensual, so lovely, so popular at the balls, perhaps some of the rumors were true. But seeing Sarina's genuine pain, Angel believed her. Alexander was the unfaithful one.

And yet . . . he'd not been dressed like a man going to a mistress.

Sarina finished her drink and poured another. Then she paced, her long golden hair floating around her hips, her white gown barely shielding her lush curves.

Not for the first time, especially now that she knew the ingredients in that concoction Sarina so loved, Angel wondered why Sarina showed no vampire characteristics. Surely, as Alexander's wife, he'd converted her long ago. Perhaps she was ashamed and hid her nature.

Sarina whirled on Angel. "Tell me, my dear,

where you went last night so late? And please, don't use the excuse that your mare unseated you. You forget I've seen you ride."

Angel smiled weakly. "Do you do a bed check every night?"

Sarina didn't smile back. "Please do not consider this an interrogation. It is more in the way of concern for you. You live under my roof, and you are dear to me. I only fear for your well-being."

Shamed, Angel admitted, "I went to Max's. He . . . showed me some of his experiments."

Sarina's eyes narrowed slightly. "He showed you his lab?"

Angel hesitated, but finally nodded.

"Every blood researcher in the country has begged for entrance to that lab and he's refused them all."

The tide of color that swept Angel from head to toe was all the explanation Sarina apparently needed. Setting her glass aside, she came forward to clasp Angel's hands. "We're two of a kind, sweet Angel. Both mooning over men who claim to care for us but use us in their own tawdry battles."

Tawdry? That was hardly the term Angel would have used for the search for the Beefsteak Killer.

Sarina took a deep breath and squeezed Angel's hands. "Very well, Angel, since I cannot prove my concern for you any other way . . . It's time I admit that your suspicions of your uncle are true. Alexander is a vampire." Sarina saw the question in Angel's eyes and her voice went soft with shame. "And so am I. Though a very weak one, which is why I drink so much of the fortifying punch. It's the only way I can go about in daylight, and even then, you see how fair my skin remains."

Angel longed to ask, but the words wouldn't come.

Fiercely, Sarina squeezed Angel's hands, as if Sarina, too, struggled against the question Angel couldn't ask. "No. While I admit we do both sometimes partake of human blood, to my knowledge Alexander has never killed a living being. He is not the Beefsteak Killer."

"Then who is?"

"Why do you care so much to find out? Surely you know how dangerous your search is, not just for you but for everyone in this household."

"Girls are dying." *And Max is in danger, too.* "I cannot escape the feeling that the killer lured me here, Sarina. And I will not be a tool in such an evil enterprise. My life might not mean much to him, but it means a lot to me, and if I cannot determine my own fate, then I don't want to live at all."

An admiring light softening her blue eyes in the candleglow, Sarina squeezed Angel's hands a final time and then let her go. "You remind me so much of myself at your age. I think it was my fearlessness that first tempted Alexander to make a dancer his wife." Sarina cocked her head. "You do not look shocked at my horrid secret."

"I adore dancing."

Sarina dimpled, but then she sighed. "What a stubborn child you are. But you are quite right. You have a unique value to those of us who are creatures of the night." With a last glare after her miscreant husband, Sarina marched toward the stairs. "Alexander has deliberately kept this from you, fearing you'll run, but I believe you're made of sterner stuff. Men are such tiresome creatures, thinking that because we are soft, and generous, and nurturing, that we are weak. Well, Alexander and Max have manipulated us for their own ends long enough. You wish to know why you were brought here, do you not?"

Angel nodded vigorously.

"And I wish to prove to my wayward husband that he may be the stronger one in our relationship, but I still have a brain and a loyalty to my gender. Weak women indeed!" With what might have been a genteel snort, Sarina marched down the first level of stairs. "Come along."

Angel followed. "Where are we going?"

"To the laboratory and the one secret you have not yet uncovered." Sarina looked over her shoulder at Angel, her blue eyes earnest. "Most important, you need to learn why Maximillian Britton is not the friend he claims to be, but your most natural, bitter enemy."

Sarina led the way down the stairs into the bowels of the estate.

Chapter Ten

After the wonders of Max's lab, Alexander's seemed dreary. Angel watched Sarina light lamps, the illumination limning her aunt's magnificent face and form. How could Alexander even look at another woman when he was married to one so gorgeous? And vampire or not, Sarina's physical beauty seemed matched by an inner loveliness, for she was unfailingly gracious to everyone, noble and servant alike.

Yet she had waylaid Angel a bit too neatly tonight. No doubt Sarina's ultimate loyalty was to Alexander, as it should be, so perhaps she'd been distracting her niece to give her husband time to ride off.

Angel was a bit ashamed of her suspicions,

but after the events of the last few weeks, she wasn't sure whom to trust, if anyone. Again, she remembered the way Alexander was dressed.

Like someone on assignment, not assignation.

But Angel could see tear streaks on those fair cheeks. They, at least, were genuine. Deciding to take Sarina's offer at face value, Angel walked straight to the microscope, which still had a sample inserted.

"It's my blood you all want," Angel said, sitting down before the microscope.

Sarina froze on her way to a cabinet. "Max told you?" She seemed shocked.

No, Max showed me. With devastating effect. Trying not to remember how weak she'd left him, Angel looked through the microscope. "Whose sample is this?" But somehow she knew.

"It's the sample you gave to my husband of your own blood. Alexander has been studying it for days."

"To what end?"

"After much experimentation, Alexander has proved that your blood is the perfect food for us, Angel. The human components give us sustenance, but the vampire components strengthen us." Sarina seemed disappointed

263

when her revelation brought little reaction from Angel. "You knew?"

"It's logical." Max had not told her this, but it only made sense that if she weakened a reluctant, self-converted vampire who still retained many of his human traits, she would strengthen true vampires who were wholly creatures of the night.

"And you know also that your blood is dangerous to those like Max?"

How much did they really know about Max? "Those like Max? How is he different?"

Sarina gave her a look. "Prevarication is not your long suit. Every vampire in the district knows Max is a Watch Bearer. He hates himself, and he hates us. A sentiment we return in full."

You all fear him, too, Angel reflected.

"There is no one more debased than one who kills his own kind for sport." Sarina wrapped her arms about herself, and suddenly she looked fragile. As if she were deeply afraid of Max, too.

Angel frowned. "For sport? He kills to stop the killing of innocent human lives."

Sarina shook her head. "So he would have you believe. In actuality, he kills because he enjoys it."

Half-numb, Angel didn't know what to believe anymore. But one thing was clear—she was tired of being used. By either side. "This revelation is supposed to bring me comfort?" Angel burst out. "I feel like a cow who needs milking! And my supply is finite!"

Sarina laughed. "You should take to the stage, dear child." Gently pushing Angel back into the chair before the microscope, Sarina went to a supply cabinet and took out a gleaming scalpel. "Since you doubt me, I can prove what I say is true. We shall mix my blood sample with yours."

"But we only need a pin to pierce your finger." Angel tried to take the scalpel, but Sarina pulled it back out of the way. There was something erratic and strange about her behavior. Was she truly so angry with her husband that she would endanger her own life? Her cheeks were flushed, her blue eyes brilliant. Angel felt uneasy for the first time since entering the lab. She glanced at the door, then back at her aunt.

Moving to stand over Angel's table, Sarina readied a clean slide. Then she lifted the blade, the edge uncomfortably close to Angel's face.

The hair on the back of Angel's neck stood on end. Instinctively, Angel leaped up and out of the way. "Sarina, what are you—"

Her movements awkward, Sarina sliced downward, not toward Angel, but into her own wrist. She winced and her blood spurted outward in a starburst pattern. She stared stupidly down at the stream that pulsed with the rhythmic ebb and flow of her heartbeat. "I didn't mean to cut so deeply," she whispered, groping for a chair. Her blood continued to spurt, onto her clothes, seeping onto the floor with a hypnotic *drip, drip, drip.*

Angel leaped up and went for bandages. She knelt in front of her aunt, unwrapping the clean cotton. But the moment she touched Sarina's bloody wrist, every nerve in Angel's body went on tingling alert. Her nostrils flared at the rich, coppery scent.

The pulsing flow was slowing because Sarina was already coagulating, but her blood, the deepest, darkest crimson Angel had ever seen, was dripping down Sarina's arm into a pool on the floor.

All Angel could think was, What a waste.

Sarina thrust her wrist under Angel's nose. "Help me, Angel. It hurts. Lick it and the cut will start to close."

Angel stared down stupidly at the bandages in her hand, then back at the crimson stream of life. *Don't, Angel,* her human half begged. But the vampire half, the strong half, was tempted beyond bearing.

Bending her head, Angel suckled at Sarina's

vein. Ambrosia. Sarina tasted wonderful, even better than Max. She suckled harder, the blood oozing into her mouth.

Gently, Sarina stroked Angel's hair as she watched the girl feed.

And she smiled.

In his lab, Max had just nodded off, his face buried in his own notes, but he snapped awake under the influence of that powerful mental bond that he'd seldom felt with anyone other than Eileen. For a moment he was disoriented, wondering what had awakened him. He stared into the darkness and saw Alexander's laboratory form in the shadows of his mind. Angel was kneeling before Sarina, who wore only a white night rail.

A night rail spattered with blood.

Angel was feeding on that thin wrist! Max ran up the steps, intending to transform into a bat, but he'd almost leaped out the window before he realized he was still too weak to transform. Poised on the transom, he swung his weight back inside barely in time.

Cursing his own weakness, he ran down the hallway and descended the stairs, calling for his horse as he went. He knew it would be too late by the time he got there. Angel would be lost in the blood lust. So lost he might not be able to coax her back.

As he rode like the wind, he feared Angel was already perilously close to the point of no return. Sarina was Alexander's familiar, a vampire herself. Her blood, if Angel drank enough of it, could seduce the last of Angel's humanity into the immortal but dark world of living death.

Max had straddled both worlds for more years than he cared to remember. As a vampire, he'd laughed at death, drinking cold blood to survive, not because he wanted to live forever but because he needed the strength of the night to defeat his bitter enemy. He'd played the Grim Reaper himself for so many misbegotten souls, he could scarcely remember their faces. And somewhere, in the pitiless march of time, his own long life had become wearisome to him, one gray day stretching into another black night.

Angel had changed all that.

She made him long for the things he'd once taken for granted those many years ago when he was human: hearth, home, hope. Joy and daylight, not pain and mausoleums. Angel was no more suited to eternal night than her mother had been. If she lost her humanity, she would lose all that made her unique. She'd be miserable.

No matter the cost to his own soul, he could not bear to see Angel become one of those pallid, insatiable creatures feeding on the weak. The price of eternity for a vampire was measured in the cost of human lives.

Until ultimately, the oldest vampires became ruthless, evil, without conscience or remorse.

He'd do anything necessary to save Angel from that fate.

Anything.

Angel had scarcely begun to suckle before something enormous, rough with dark hair, leaped from the doorway in a single bound. The creature's full weight landed between Angel and Sarina, knocking them apart. Angel sprawled to the floor, but Sarina nimbly side-stepped and flew to the door. Angel lay still, supine on the ground, licking the last luscious drops from her lips.

She heard the patter of retreating steps, and then a cold nose stuck itself into Angel's neck and snuffled. The moist breath brought Angel back from an icy place by warm degrees. Angel opened her eyes and looked up. She drew breath to scream but had the presence of mind to clap her hands over her mouth. That would only incite the creature.

Angel glanced around for Sarina and realized her aunt had run. Angel couldn't really blame her, but still it stung that she'd been left to face this terrible beast alone. Angel scooted away from it, expecting it to lunge at her. But it was still.

As if it appraised her.

The enormous wolf had pale green eyes that glowed brightly. It had a thick ruff of hair standing up from a muscular neck, a powerful chest, and huge paws, larger than Angel's hands, that ended in sharp, curving claws.

And the teeth. Angel swallowed. The wolf was panting slightly, so Angel saw the canines gleaming in the light. One bite from those massive jaws—

"Have you a peppermint?"

Angel blinked and looked around the room. It couldn't be . . .

That sounded like Shelly Holmes.

The wolf sat back on its haunches, licking its lips. "After raw rabbit I always finish off with a peppermint, and my own store is exhausted."

Astounded, Angel peered up at the wolf that talked. The wolf that talked with Shelly's voice and used Shelly's mannerisms, right down to the curious tilt of the head, the direct stare, the wry expression of the generous mouth.

Angel cleared her throat. "Shelly?"

"Forgive me for startling you, but I should hate to see you become one of these loathsome creatures."

So weary that she felt beyond shock, Angel rubbed her forehead. "I should have become a practitioner of the dark arts rather than a scientist." She stood. "Science can certainly not explain the phenomena I've witnessed since coming to one of the oldest repositories of knowledge in the known world."

That generous smile seemed to widen. "Ironic indeed. Still, it has always been the unknown world that is most intriguing. That is why you study blood. That is why you are fascinated by Max. And that is why"—the generous mouth went straight—"you shall shortly have to choose between two worlds."

Angel turned away. The sweet taste of Sarina's blood now had a tinge as bitter as the truth Shelly had just stated. Already Angel felt the feverish need to feed again.

And again. It was as if she were addicted to poison. A poison that would kill Angel Corbett and leave Angelina Blythe, part-time resident of the family mausoleum. Angel hurried toward the door, knowing she couldn't escape that choice for much longer, but that she had to try. She froze, feeling him before she saw him.

Max was there, his dark green eyes somber. He stared at a tiny dot of blood on her lip, but she felt the probe of his mind and knew he'd figured out she'd scarcely begun to drink when Shelly had burst in.

He looked past her to Shelly. "It seems I once again owe you my thanks, Miss Holmes." But he didn't sound gracious.

Shelly nodded her fearsome head as if she were in a drawing room. "You are quite welcome, but I didn't do it for you."

Max looked at Angel. "Have you seen Alexander? And why are you dressed like that?"

"To follow him. He was also dressed in country attire when he rode off. But Sarina waylaid me."

The wolf and the vampire exchanged a look. Was he hunting? And if he were, could they catch him red-handed?

Angel scowled. "I am not a child. If either of you know what's going on, please apprise me."

Max caught Angel's arm and led her to the door. "I'll take you back to your room. You need sleep."

Angel planted her feet. "I only have bad dreams. I'm going with you."

She saw him debate lying to her, but her own

mind powers were growing stronger. *We can look for Alexander together, or we can look for him separately,* she informed him in that powerful, wordless communication.

Shelly glanced between them, her wide mouth slanting upward again.

Max looked on the verge of exploding with rage, but then he bared his fangs at Angel. "You might not like what I have to do."

She bared her own nascent fangs back. "And you might find me capable of more than you think when my own life is in danger."

Max stomped out, his footsteps for once not soundless. Angel stomped after him.

The sound a werewolf made when it laughed, Angel reflected as she followed Max, was quite a strange one. Husky howls, not quite human but not quite wolf, either, chased them upstairs. And somehow, they warmed Angel for what she suspected would be a long, cold night.

Gustav stood toe-to-toe with Alexander. They were of a height, but Gustav was stockier. "No! I'm tired of doing your bidding, your ruddy worship," Gustav bit off. "I planted the servant girl in the mausoleum—when I didn't even get a taste of her, I might add—I stirred up the villagers against Britton. I've even followed your niece for you. She's smarter than you give her credit for, I'll tell you that."

Alexander wrapped his long hand about Gustav's throat and squeezed delicately, his nails barely making an impression on Gustav's thick skin. "You knew the price when you, an unknown, joined our covenant. You have to prove yourself."

"I have!"

"Not to our satisfaction. We've been wondering about you since our last conference," Alexander said conversationally. "You claimed to come from Wales, but we've checked our Wales connections and none of the converted ones there have ever heard of you."

Trying and failing to knock Alexander's hand away, Gustav said in a snarl, "I was only recently initiated. Besides, there are so few vampires in that remote area, they can hardly keep up with everyone."

Alexander only squeezed harder. "Since your loyalty is obviously in question, other doubts arise. The killings of virgins in Oxford coincided with your arrival, for example."

Gustav had difficulty responding, but he managed with wheezing breaths, "You say . . . I'm incompetent, and then you call me the . . . killer in the next breath?"

That long hand closed a bit tighter. "I cannot

imagine a better concealment for the oldest, most dangerous of our kind than acting the bumbling servant."

Viciously, Gustav kneed Alexander in his privates. With a grunt of pain, Alexander stumbled back, but collected himself for a lunge. He froze where he stood when Gustav brandished a sharp, pointed stake he whipped from his cloak.

Gustav said huskily, his throat still red with Alexander's fingerprints, "And I cannot imagine a better concealment for the Beefsteak Killer than a rich lord who used to be a respected professor at Oxford."

Grudging respect flared in Alexander's dark eyes. "You make a valid point. Very well, then, I'll give you an opportunity to prove you are genuinely new to the art, but one of us. Transform."

This time, Gustav looked a bit embarrassed. "I've . . . only managed a . . . rabbit."

"Show me," Alexander said, stepping back with a skeptical look.

Gustav took a deep breath, closed his eyes, and hunched down into his cloak. Lower and lower he sank until only the top of his head was visible, and then, suddenly—the cloak fell to the ground, limp and shapeless. Something squirmed inside it, and then out hopped a rabbit.

Alexander relaxed. "You can come back now."

The rabbit hopped behind a tree and Gustav stepped out a second later. "Satisfied?"

"For the moment. If you'll do this last task, then I promise you may sit in on the next meeting."

"How will I get close enough?"

"Use the girl. Threaten her, and you won't have to worry about getting too close to Max Britton. He'll get all too close to you."

Gustav swallowed, his ruddy face going a bit sickly. But he nodded and accepted the watch Alexander handed him. It was heavy, and gold, and looked like Max's watch.

But it wasn't.

Angel kicked her mare after Max's stallion. She was beginning to think he was deliberately leading her in circles. After riding for several hours in the direction in which Alexander had departed, they'd found no trace of him. Angel drew her tired mare even with Max's horse. "I cannot believe, the way you see in the darkness, that you cannot track Alexander's horse better than this."

He reined his mount sharply to a stop. "Nor-

mally I'd fly as a bat and cover the territory
much faster. But I have a certain amount of . . .
baggage at the moment."

Angel glared at him. His goading smile only
made her angrier.

"Would you like to try, Angel mine?"

Debating, Angel crossed her arms over her
saddle. Finally she nodded. She urged her
mare into a trot, not even looking at the
ground. To her delight, Max seemed nonplussed at her behavior. But he followed read-
ily enough.

She wasn't even trying to track Alexander's
horse; she was acting on instinct. And she
knew exactly where she was going.

It took only a few moments for them to reach
that strangely quiet place in the woods behind
the hall. It looked different in the dark, but Angel remembered the odd shape of that half-
dead tree, limned now against the moonlight.
She dismounted and knelt, feeling for the trapdoor. To her delight, this time when she
tugged, it opened. A gaping hole yawned, leading down rough steps.

She gave Max a triumphant look. "Do you
still think I'm baggage?"

He dismounted, too, tying up their mounts,
and grabbed her arm when she started to de-
scend into that hole. "What is this place?"

"I don't know, but whatever it is, it leads to the hall."

Max stiffened, his eyes glowing as he traced the small rise of ground to the rear of the hall. Without another word, he kissed her. "This could be it, Angel. You're brilliant, you're beautiful"—his voice hardened to a command—"and you will stay put."

Her glare bounced off his hard green eyes.

"If this place contains what I think it does, it's very dangerous." He removed the vampire-killing kit from his mount and stepped down into the darkness.

He gave her a last minatory look. "I mean it. Stay here, or ride back to the hall." The trap-door clanged shut behind him.

Counting to ten, Angel gave him a few minutes' head start before she lifted the door and followed.

Wearing a clean white dress, Sarina clung to Alexander, uncaring for once of his dirty garments. "It was huge and horrid, and it stopped me from finishing Angel's conversion. I'm ... sorry I failed you, Alexander."

He patted her back, feeling her trembling. "Are you sure it wasn't one of us?"

"I've never seen one of us transform into a wolf so large." She thought back, but then she

278

shook her head resolutely. "No, I'm sure its eyes glowed green, not red."

"Could it possibly be...do you think it might be a werewolf?"

Sarina debated. "There was a strange intelligence I could feel about it. And I'm almost certain it was protective of Angel. I heard no scream after I ran." She peeped guiltily up at Alexander. "I should have been brave enough to stay."

"Never mind, my dear. Your skills are not strong enough yet to face down such a beast. The question is, Who is this creature and why does it wish to protect Angel?"

"I'm not even sure Angel is still here. I think I sensed Max right before I left."

"We'll check, shall we?"

They went to her room and found Angel's bed undisturbed.

Alexander's eyes narrowed. "This battle over the girl grows tiresome. If I didn't need her blood, I'd let Max have her. The more he hungers for her, the less he'll be able to resist her. Just as we planned." He licked his lips, his fangs growing to glistening points. "But if she's with Max on one of his nocturnal wanderings ... this is the chance I've been waiting for. I'm hungry. It's time we celebrated with the ultimate intimacy, sweet. I've had enough does, fawns, and punch. I need to hunt." He caught her hands. "Are you brave enough to follow and sup alongside me?"

Sarina swallowed, but then she nodded bravely. "It's time I became your wife in every way."

He kissed her forehead and started toward the window.

She caught his arm. "Alexander . . . tell me true. Are you the Beefsteak Killer?"

His smile faded. "Will you love me more or less if I say yes?"

She nibbled her lip indecisively.

"My only response is that I am powerful, and becoming more so. And once Max Britton is dead, no one will stop us from becoming rulers of every covenant in England." He led her to the window and transformed into a huge, glistening raven. He flapped away on the breeze, blending with the night. She followed, transforming into a dove, her wings luminous in the moonlight.

Choosing white even as a bird.

They both flew toward the village, searching for prey.

In the night, the smithy's fire burned hot. A pretty young girl exited his shop, her face glowing with beauty and innocence, carrying the remains of his supper. She walked down the dark village road, unafraid. She heard the swoop of wings and looked up, peering at the strange sight of a raven and a dove sharing the same branch.

But then she walked on. The attack, when it came, was totally unexpected. Strong hands ending in long nails caught her about the throat, cutting off her scream.

By the time they dragged her into the darkness, they'd already begun to feed.

It was almost dawn. Max felt the light creeping along the walls after him through cracks in the tunnel. For reassurance, as usual, he touched the watch in his pocket. He almost missed the side chamber, but when he turned back, he came face-to-face with Angel.

He gaped at her, stunned not so much because she'd disobeyed him but because she'd followed so silently, blocking both the sound of her movements and her presence from him. Indeed, as he watched, she shied away from the weak light filtering down around her.

Angel, go back, he commanded silently.

"No," she whispered fiercely. "I found this place and I . . . need to help you."

He gave her a little push toward the entrance. "Doesn't it tell you something that the door was unlocked?"

281

"Yes. It's a trap. And I'd rather die still part human than exist in this twilight world for all eternity."

That, he could not argue with.

Shielding her behind him, Max silently made his way into the side chamber. He wasn't surprised to see it filled with empty coffins. Impossible to tell who rested here on the soil of what land. He looked up again at the grayish light.

However, they shouldn't have to wait long.

If the Beefsteak Killer rested here, as he suspected, he'd kill every single vampire in this chamber if he had to.

If he was strong enough. He glanced at Angel, who had her head cocked as she listened tensely. He shoved her back into the shadows beneath the stairs, wishing she were strong enough, and he were experienced enough, to transform into mist.

He opened his rosewood case and stuck all four of his stakes in his pockets, holding his golden hammer firmly in his hand.

Angel swallowed as she saw the gleam of gold, and he felt her abrupt fear.

"Go, while you still can. You won't enjoy this."

"No." She wrapped her arms about herself, as if she felt cold.

Then they heard a slight rustling in the corridor.

From both ends.

Max gripped his hammer more tightly.

The attack came from all sides at once. Stepping in front of Angel, Max struck wildly with his hammer, driving a stake deeply into a broad chest. The creature in front fell, but it was all too soon replaced by another.

And another.

Max had experienced similar attacks when he'd been green and too eager, but he'd always managed to escape by transforming.

This time he couldn't transform or he'd have to leave Angel behind. They had only one hope.

Using all his unnatural strength, Max kicked, and slashed with his nails, feeling skin slicing open to bone everywhere he struck. With his other hand he pounded with the hammer, but all he did was keep them at bay. They seemed to multiply, and the ferocity of their hatred made them even stronger than most of his prey.

Then, to his shock, Angel was fighting alongside him, using all her puny skills to force the hissing vampires a bare half step farther away. Max redoubled his own efforts, and slowly the creatures gave ground until there was a gap between them.

It wasn't much, but it was enough.

They had just enough space for Max to pull Angel under his arm and jerk out his pocket watch. He flipped it open, whispering the incantation he'd learned by heart at the feet of a monk in the Transylvania highlands. The invisible glow brightened to a pale blue, iridescent and as lovely as an aurora borealis.

But deadly to vampires.

The pasty-faced creatures fell back again.

The glow brightened as Max held the watch high into a pale glimmer of sunlight. Suddenly light flashed in a white hot beacon from the crystal, radiating in every direction.

There was a sizzle, the scent of burning flesh, several unearthly screams, and then the creatures ran, some of them with blackened flesh falling in burned flakes to leave the grisly mark of their passing.

Max held Angel firmly in one arm, the watch raised in his other, as he dragged them both, still caught in the protective circle of light, toward the entrance.

He felt some of the more powerful creatures striking at them. Most of them were devotees of Alexander's balls and punch, but even they feared the extreme purity of the radiance surrounding Max and Angel.

Backing up the steps, Angel limp at his side,

Max made his way into the dawn, the watch still their only protection. He slammed the trapdoor shut with his foot and hurried them to their mounts. He spared a moment of regret for his killing kit.

Finally, he looked at Angel, intending to compliment her for her bravery.

The words died stillborn on his lips.

She was unconscious, her fair skin as bright as a beet. The radiance that had protected them had burned her. She was not a Watch Bearer, with his immunity to the light.

This was the last proof he needed that she was dangerously close to full conversion.

Slamming the watch back in his pocket, Max cradled her before him on his stallion and galloped like the wind toward his estate. Questions tormented him. Why hadn't he made her go back? Why hadn't he realized the same light that saved them would inevitably harm her?

Because he'd been frantic for her safety, thinking only of getting them out of there. So he had used the only powerful weapon he had left.

Angel moaned, writhing in pain at the touch of the wind on her face, and Max slowed their wild pace slightly.

He had a potion that would help heal her skin.

But was it too late for her spirit?

Chapter Eleven

Max saw the glow outside his estate and at first thought the dawn had tipped the trees with fire. But it was a strangely mobile glow, if so.

He drew his mount to an abrupt stop, still hidden in the trees, and listened with his acute senses. Without the noise his stallion made, he realized there were voices outside his ancestral home.

Many voices. Angry voices.

Someone had stirred the villagers up against him again.

Agonized, Max looked down at the girl in his arms. He'd covered her with his cloak to protect her from the rising sun, but when he moved the thick material aside to peek at her, she didn't move. Mercifully, she'd fallen unconscious.

What should he do? His medicines, his own research, the rest of his weapons, all were in his home. But he didn't have to be able to read the Beefsteak Killer's mind to know that the creature had struck back by planting something incriminating now in his own home.

Perhaps even in his own bed.

With one last indecisive look between his home and the open road, Max wheeled his mount and chose the lesser of two evils. As he rode wildly away, he prayed: *Dear God, don't condemn me for a sinner, because I've always tried to follow the path of truth and justice, even if I had to kill to do it. Protect Angel and I swear not another innocent life will be lost in my quest for vengeance. Even if I have to die myself.*

Outside Max's estate, Gustav fanned the flames of hatred and torchlight, berating the villagers even as he waved his own torch around to make it burn hotter. "Let's not wait any longer. We'll go on in and see what terrible secrets the bastard be hiding. He's a killer, he is. He'll steal your daughters from their beds and drain them of their blood and he'll convert your sons to unholy monsters, unfit to walk the earth with decent folk."

The smithy shook his beefy fist. "Aye, remember the girl we found not two seconds after he appeared from the same filthy hole. He's a vampire, he is."

The prelate, still in his tight collar and robe, carried a stake. "It's past time we took back our village and made it safe for decent folk to go about at night."

With the prelate's blessing, the smithy led the way, storming the heavy front door. He banged on it with a cudgel. He was quickly joined by other men eager to regain their self-respect. Between the heavy beating of cudgel, stick, and even, from a carpenter, an ax, the locked door quickly fell, shattered into splinters.

The mob stormed inside.

A few screams sounded. Max's servants ran out into the woods. A few minutes later, a tiny puff of smoke, a slither on the wind, escaped the gaping front door. Then a bright flame appeared at a window curtain in the ground-floor salon. A blaze crackled merrily upstairs.

Soon the entire estate, built by Max's ancestors in the time of Henry VIII, was ablaze. The villagers came back out, some carrying the spoils of war, and watched with satisfaction as the ancient timbers caught fire from the blazing furnishings, priceless paintings, and tapestries.

The smithy came out last, stumbling down the stairs, carrying something. Something far heavier than gold coins, but something far more precious to him.

General satisfaction gave way to horror as the others saw what he carried. The prelate made an abortive move forward to help the limp girl in the smithy's strong arms, but they all knew, from one look made all the more horrific by the gory dance of red flames on her ripped throat, that it was too late.

The telltale mark of the crooked tooth was everywhere on her neck and upper torso.

Tears streaked through the soot on the smithy's face. He stared at the Trelayne estate with a hatred that went far beyond mere mob violence.

For the girl he carried in his arms was his own lovely, virginal daughter.

"You'll die for this, Maximillian Britton, Earl of Trelayne. I care not how much money ye have or how far ye run, I'll find ye and kill ye."

His face frozen in a grimace of rage and grief, he stalked away from the conflagration that burned no hotter than the fiery rage in his heart.

As the fire took over and the villagers walked

away, three witnesses watched the last tower collapse.

Gustav watched blankly from a distance, with less satisfaction than one might expect from a rival vampire.

And high in a tree lurked two birds. They sat silently, the brilliant flames reflecting in their beady eyes. Watching. Enjoying.

A raven and a dove.

Shelly Holmes looked severely at her stable-boy. "What do you mean, you don't know where he is? I expect my second in command to make his whereabouts plain to me at all times."

"I don't know, ma'am, truly I don't." And the lad scurried off to muck out the stalls.

Shelly went in to check on a mare about to deliver, pulling on clean gloves. It amazed her that horse doctors couldn't figure out, as human doctors finally had, that sterility in a birthing chamber was as critical as calm. As she had to gently labor to turn the foal by herself, for the poor mare was about to deliver a breach birth, Shelly debated the mystery of Gustav.

Blast the fellow's impudence!

There'd been something different, something too bold and too secretive about Gustav, from the very beginning. This wasn't the first time he'd disappeared without notice, sometimes at night, sometimes early in the morning, like now, when she really needed his help with a fractious mare.

In fact, Shelly had her own suspicions about the fellow who played the crude groom with a bit too much felicity to be believable. With vampires thick as the nightly mist on the ground, she'd even watched him closely at night, looking for that telltale tinge of red she'd noticed in every vampire's eyes. Even Angel's.

And just last night, when she went down to the toolshed late, she'd seen him conceal something bright and gleaming gold in his pocket. It looked almost like a watch, a large watch similar to Max's, but she hadn't caught a close look at it. He'd dropped the tiny engraving tool he held and hurried out with a muttered excuse.

Very well, she could hardly fire the fellow for sneaking around with an engraving tool on his own time. And he showed no vulnerability to daylight, he was visible in mirrors, and he even seemed to have a taste for garlic. But then Alexander shared all those qualities, too, and he was quite obviously a vampire.

Shelly was frustrated beyond bearing that she'd found no clue as to who Gustav really was, even when she'd searched his tiny quarters off the tack room. But the insolent gleam he sometimes sported was definitely distasteful to her. If he wasn't a vampire, what was the purpose of his nocturnal wanderings? Or could it be that he was a vampire, just such an old and evil one that he'd learned to mask every sign that would give away his identity?

"Here, let me help you." Gustav suddenly appeared. He looked exhausted. No, he looked beyond tired. He looked distraught.

Shelly took in the soot on his face and the dirt on his hands and slapped him away. "Wash up!" While he did so, she made the mare as comfortable as she could and followed him out. "Where have you been?"

"A . . . village meeting."

Shelly's eyes narrowed. "What sort of meeting?"

He dried his hands without answering, his face twisting with guilt. He hurried back into the stall and made gentle clucking noises to the mare. He truly was good with horses. If he hadn't been, Shelly would have fired him long ago just to see his reaction. Unsettled, for it was the rare man who could throw her off balance, Shelly knelt beside him.

For the next few minutes they were too busy with the mare to talk, but when one stableboy ran to the stable door, then another, and another, and an excited buzz ensued, Shelly looked up. One of the lads ran back.

"There be a fearsome fire at the Trelayne estate, miss! Should we form a fire brigade?"

Shelly leaped up, about to say yes, but she was interrupted.

Gustav said flatly, "It's too late for that. Since the mare's settled for the nonce, I'll be about my other business." And he automatically reached as if for a hat to tip toward Shelly's astounded countenance. But he wasn't wearing one.

Lost for words for one of the few times in her life, Shelly watched him walk off. What a cavalier way to dismiss a calamity like that. And the mere fact that he'd said it was too late was proof enough that he must have been there when the fire started.

Poor Max.

Shelly peered down at the boy. "Do you think you can follow Gustav at a distance and be sure he doesn't see you?"

The boy nodded eagerly, obviously anxious to avoid his usual unpleasant chores. Smiling affectionately, Shelly ruffled his hair. "Good lad. If he spots you, immediately turn around and come home. And when he reaches his destination, return and tell me where it is. There will be a quid for you in it if you do your task well."

More inspired than ever, the budding detective tiptoed after his quarry.

Shelly was about to turn back to the mare when she heard the voice. *Please, Miss Holmes, help us.*

It was so clear, she looked around for Maximillian Britton before she realized she'd heard him only in her head. Damn his powers that were, in many ways, so much more useful than her own. *Where are you?* she responded silently.

In your quarters above the stable. Bring a burn salve.

For once obeying a male's bidding without argument, Shelly grabbed a pot from a shelf and snapped at a hand, "See I'm not disturbed!" She ran up the side stairs to her own room and burst inside. She froze in horror.

Writhing in pain, Angel reclined upon her bed, Max gently holding her chapped hands in a cool bowl of water. Angel's face was patchy with red splotches in places, and peeling skin in others. She even had a few blisters on the end of her nose.

Shelly didn't waste time asking what had happened. She rinsed her own hands and immediately applied the salve to Angel's face. Angel stiffened at the additional pain, but then the oil of peppermint Shelly had personally mixed with aloe and other medicinals in her own powerful burn concoction began to numb the pain. She relaxed slightly as Shelly treated her arms and hands.

"Anywhere else?" Shelly asked. Angel shook her head.

When the girl was eased, Shelly scowled at Max. But his face was full of torment, and Shelly's questions died stillborn. "You were battling vampires and somehow Angel got caught in the cross fire because she refused to let you go alone."

Max turned away from Shelly's acute gaze, but Angel's troubled dark eyes filled with tears. "He used his watch, Shelly. It emits a bright radiance different from anything I've ever seen. And it . . . he didn't know . . . I didn't know I would be hurt by it, too." Angel subsided back against the pillows.

Sympathetically, Shelly looked at Max's broad back, turned away from them both. He'd pulled the curtains tight over the daylight to shield Angel, but still he stared as if into a far distance.

A far distance he could not see or hope to reach.

As sorry as she felt for Angel's pain, Shelly

felt more deeply for Max; she knew he blamed himself.

"It's not your fault," Angel whispered. "You were only trying to protect us both."

Max whirled on her. "It's my fault for starting you onto this path. If I hadn't initiated you that night, if I hadn't taught you the need to feed, then you'd not be in danger of far more than a few burns. Your soul, your humanity, your ability to love will be forfeit if the killer has its way. Don't you understand? They're using you. They're using me. They're using the attraction between us not just to drive us apart, but to kill our spirits first and then our bodies."

Angel's voice was very small and very bleak. "Then we shouldn't see each other again."

"They'll find a way to finish converting you whether I'm around to tempt you or not. No, together we stay. For whatever time we have left." Max turned back to the window.

Shelly reached out with her mind and found only a black wall of pain. She glanced at Angel. Angel's eyes were closed, and tears rolled down her temples, dotting the pillow under her head.

Max was blocking Angel out, too. "And now," he said hoarsely, "my last hope is destroyed. My research burned. My other weapons cinders. My home, my refuge, annihilated."

With my head groom's help, Shelly thought bitterly.

Max's green eyes cut into her face. "Gustav?"

Shelly nodded.

Frowning, Max considered this news. "Could it be . . . ?"

This time Shelly shook her head. "No, I don't think he's the killer. I think he's a gentleman pretending to be a groom so he can infiltrate the Oxford covenant."

"Are you saying you don't believe he's a vampire?" Max asked incredulously. "Impossible. He'd never get near them."

Angel interjected, "I overheard him in that meeting."

Max said, "About what time?"

Angel rubbed her forehead. "It was late."

"Their covenant meetings last for hours and begin at sunset."

"So he was only allowed in when all the important matters had been settled," Angel concluded for all of them. They exchanged a look.

"And that means they don't trust him," Shelly pointed out with her usual irrefutable logic.

"They trusted him to start a riot that would destroy my home."

"Perhaps he was forced to do it," Shelly said. "He seemed a bit . . . distraught when he returned a few minutes ago."

"Where is he now?"

"He left, but I had one of my boys follow him."

Max debated with himself. They both saw some of the guilt and grief fade from that strong face, leaving only iron-hard resolve in its stead. A very dangerous resolve, for it was part Trelayne earl, and part Watch Bearer. "Take her back to the hall," Max ordered. "Just see that only you supply her food and drink and I think she'll be safe enough. They're not ready to kill her."

Yet. They'll use her to corner me.

Both women understood what he did not say aloud.

Angel sat up, wobbling as if she were obviously still in pain, but she managed, "But you said we wouldn't be separated."

"I have to figure out who the killer is, Angel. How can we battle an enemy we can't identify? I'll return very soon, I promise, and we'll find somewhere to hide."

"But . . . I'm afraid." Her small voice petered out on the last word as if she were ashamed of the admission.

Tenderness softening his granite-hard green eyes, Max knelt next to Angel. He started to take her hands, noted their condition, then started to kiss her cheek and noted its redness.

298

"Damn me, you've always been a prickly wench, and now you're slippery as well!"

Angel laughed, as he had meant her to. And then she winced as the wide smile stretched her sore face. He ran his fingertips through her hair very gently, framing her face but not touching any of her burns. A kiss landed on her lips, light as thistledown, and so tender that Shelly, redoubtable realist that she was, had to turn away to disguise her sniff.

But she heard well enough.

"We're linked now, Angel. That's the only advantage to your conversion. If you need me, only think of me. And I'll come."

If Shelly had needed proof that Max was a most unusual vampire, he'd just provided it. He showed true empathy for Angel's feelings; he was not just manipulating her for his own ends. Maximillian Trelayne was the most unique creature on the face of the Earth: he combined the best of man and the best of vampire. And he was using all his skills to save Angel from the fate of her mother.

Then he was gone in that soundless way of his, his footsteps silent even on the wooden stairs. Angel's head dropped back onto the pillow. "Can I stay with you, Shelly?"

Shelly hesitated, but shook her head. "They'll grow suspicious."

"They're already suspicious."

"I agree with Max, my dear. It's smartest to let them think they've won. Pretend you were disgusted at what you saw Max do."

Angel shivered. "I don't need to pretend." Her eyes closed tightly. "Oh, Shelly, I cannot get the image out of my head. What if he killed my mother with one of those gold-handled stakes and that golden hammer?"

"And if he did?"

"I'll never be able to forgive him."

For this, even Shelly's formidable brain could find no rationalization or offer of comfort. Helping Angel up, Shelly escorted her down the stairs and across the grounds to the hall. And deep inside the most private, tender heart she shared with no one, Shelly, the agnostic, was so troubled that she also silently recited a few rusty prayers from her childhood.

As she came back outside after making Angel comfortable in her room, Shelly sniffed the air and caught a whiff of smoke. And she knew, deep in that same secret heart, that what she smelled might as well be a brimstone portent of the hell to come.

Other than her lupine skills, Shelly had one secret weapon to contribute to the coming battle, a weapon neither Max nor Angel knew about. Unlocking several heavy padlocks,

Shelly went into the tiny cubbyhole closet off her room and closed the door, vowing to work until midnight if necessary to complete her research.

Max had regained enough strength to transform into a wolf, needing his sensitive nose to track not Gustav, but the boy, who'd obviously recently mucked out a stable. His ground-eating lopes soon covered the distance, and he found the stable lad hiding behind a tree watching Gustav enter the tunnel.

When the boy turned, he found himself face-to-face with an enormous wolf with green eyes. Screaming, he backed up so fast he tripped and fell over a log. Obviously fearing he was about to have his throat ripped out, he cradled his elbows over his face and neck.

Ignoring him, Max padded toward the trapdoor. He heard the boy scramble up and run, guessing Shelly would soon get an earful of the lad's adventures.

But Max had bigger worries than scaring the poor lad. Again the open trapdoor bothered him, just as it had, rightly, last time. Either Gustav had forgotten to lock it behind him . . . or he'd deliberately left it open because he knew he was being followed. Max looked down into that gaping hole, feeling the unwelcome presence of more than one vampire.

Warily, Max re-formed into his more practical human shape, dressing quickly in the garments he'd worn tied around his neck and feeling for the heavy comfort of his watch. Then he descended alone, as he had many times in the last hundred years, into the crypt of a vampire.

As Shelly recommended, Angel tried to sleep, but it was impossible. Every time she closed her eyes she saw Max: alone, facing things no being should have to face by himself. Even a Watch Bearer who was endowed with unusual powers.

A knock sounded at the door. "Come in." Angel sighed, knowing it had to be either Sarina or Alexander. She'd have to face them soon enough, but she dreaded it. How would she ever hide her disgust of what her uncle had incited? She hadn't seen him set a torch to Max's estate, but he'd manipulated those weaker than himself as surely as if he'd started the fire.

Angel was relieved when only Sarina entered. Angel pulled the covers up to her chin and let Sarina fuss over her wounds. After Sarina had daubed a bit more of Shelly's salve onto the splotches, Angel sat up with the pillows behind her. Sarina sat next to her on the bed.

"I regret more than I can say that you were hurt in this awful tug-of-war between Alexander and Max."

Tug-of-war? What a mundane term for the fearsome battle of wills that had affected everyone in the district.

"Max's hideous watch emits the only light I know of that can burn so badly," Sarina explained at Angel's questioning look.

"He had to use it to protect me."

"Protect you? My dear child, don't you see that Max Britton is obsessed with killing all of us? Me, Alexander, all the interesting people who have feted you at my balls."

Angel knew for a fact that Max had gone into that tunnel to try to find the Beefsteak Killer's resting place, not to kill. He'd been forced into protecting himself. And yet the image of him wielding that golden hammer with such ease and ferocity was burned forever on the backs of her eyelids. Angel felt a pang as she realized Max had to leave his kit behind when he carried her to safety.

For once, Sarina's lovely blue eyes were not alight with bright mirth. They were moon blue and somber. "Do you finally see, Angel? Max hates us because he hates himself. He'll never stop killing, never stop using you and anyone else who gets in the way of his vengeance. Even . . . those he cares about. Like you."

"So you believe he cares for me?"

"As much as he's able to. But the more vampire you become, the more dangerous you are to him and the more ruthless he will be."

"Sarina, why did you marry Alexander? Did you know he was . . . what he is?"

Sarina rose and paced Angel's room, in a rare state of agitation Angel had never seen before. Angel sensed her need to lie, but finally she whirled, lifted her chin, and admitted, "Yes. But I loved him. And by then . . ." She turned to stare out the window.

"By then he'd started to convert you, too." Angel shoved her covers back and rose. She dabbed more of Shelly's concoction on her face and hands, glad to see that her burn was already fading. When she looked in the mirror, Angel gave a little scream of terror and dropped the pot. It shattered at her feet.

Angel saw only a ghostly outline where her own reflection should be.

Sarina came up behind her and clasped Angel's shoulders. Her hands looked huge and corporeal in comparison to Angel's faint outline. "In time, with frequent infusions of the punch, you will be able to control such things as your image and your vulnerability to sunlight."

Sarina pulled a small flask from her pocket and offered it to Angel.

With one sniff, Angel knew what it was. Cloves. Nutmeg. It was the wonderful ruby wine punch with a base of human blood.

Repelled, Angel shoved the flask away.

Sarina only moved it back, not forcing Angel to drink, but making her smell its heady scent. "You need its strength, Angel. Not just for your burns, but for what's to come."

Angel still resisted.

"One sip. One sip and see what it does to your reflection in the mirror."

Angel looked from that ghastly barely visible outline to the flask. Before she could have second thoughts, she grabbed the flask and took a deep swallow. She shut her eyes, and when she looked into the mirror again a few moments later, she saw a stronger outline. She still wasn't fully visible, but the terrifying thought of literally seeing her own self disappear was less frightening.

Angel turned from the mirror to bury her face in Sarina's soft shoulder. "Oh, Sarina, I cannot bear what's happening to me."

Tilting Angel's chin up so she could beam a

warm smile of comfort into the girl's sorrowful face, Sarina said, "You asked me why I married Alexander. Yes, I knew what he was and what he was helping me become. At first I felt as you do, hating the very thought of having to consume human blood for all eternity. But Angel, you've let Max's hatred poison you to the good things about our existence. With long life comes great responsibility. Have you not observed the way, at parties, we help one another? The young girls assisting old men, the young men helping old women to the punch bowl. And art. And music. And literature. Some of the greatest artists ever known were vampires."

Angel nibbled her lip. "Max said the older a vampire becomes, the more evil and ruthless he is, because he loses all respect for humanity. People become expendable, inferior beings. Only a food source."

Emphatically, Sarina shook her head. "That's not true! He's saying anything, doing anything, to win you to his side away from where your true loyalty should lie—toward your only remaining family." Sarina's voice softened. "Toward your mother. You are her blood, Angel. You are Alexander's blood. And that is the one credo of our kind that decent vampires never break—loyalty to one's blood. I don't care what Max has told you. He hated your mother. And I think perhaps I can prove it to you if you'll come with me to the cemetery."

Angel turned aside. "I'm still too weak."

"We'll go in the carriage."

"I need to work on my research." Angel tried to go to the door, but Sarina blocked it.

"You mean you're afraid to face the truth."

Angel lifted her chin. "Very well then, I'll agree, if you'll tell me the truth—is Alexander, my uncle, your husband, the Beefsteak Killer?"

From the corner of his eye, Max caught sleeping forms in the many caskets and deemed himself safe enough for the moment. He also greatly doubted that the Beefsteak Killer would keep its casket in a communal crypt, so he could turn his full attention to Gustav, the cowardly bastard. If he could make the groom talk, so much the better. But one way or the other, he'd die for what he'd done.

Deep inside, Max mourned for the life he could feel rapidly slipping away. His home was gone, his research ashes, his way to bring Angel back to the world of the living greatly in peril. But he could still fight. One vampire at a time, if he had to, Max would hunt down every vampire in the district and hope that somewhere along the way he got the killer by sheer happenstance.

It didn't take long for him to find Gustav. He was climbing into one of the caskets in a side room Max had not had time to search before. Max leaped over him in a single bound and caught the groom's throat in his long hand.

His nails forming at his whim, Max squeezed hard enough to leave imprints in Gustav's thick neck. "For a man who enjoys playing with fire, you like dark spaces."

Gustav went very still. "I had no choice. He would have killed me."

"Now I'll kill you instead." Max looked around for a stake, frustrated that he'd lost his kit that night in this very crypt, but he didn't see it. "In wiping out my research, you've sealed my doom and quite possibly Angel's as well. For that, you deserve to die. I'm only doing you a favor, actually. I assure you I'll be more mercifully quick than Alexander will be when you're no longer of use to him. Have you seen yet what a vampire looks like when it's totally drained of blood and left in the sunlight?"

Gustav clambered out of his casket and ran for the door, but with insulting ease, Max beat him there.

Since he didn't have his kit, Max would have to use his watch, but he preferred that, anyway.

The light would destroy the other sleeping vampires in the room, too.

Flipping open his watch, Max began his incantation. Gustav had stopped. He watched and listened analytically. As if fascinated. Not afraid.

On one level, Max recognized that, but anger had made his fervent ardor for his mission all the more intense. He spoke quickly, and the pale blue glimmer brightened to the brilliant light that radiated in all directions.

Max expected Gustav to fall back.

He didn't.

Max expected the other sleeping vampires in their caskets to begin frying.

They didn't.

Instead, they rose up in one motion, their voices guttural with rage and hatred. Immune to the bright light, only blocking their eyes, they descended on Max en masse. And Gustav was in the lead, the light falling most powerfully on him. His stolid face bore no trace of vampirism. He didn't burn, he didn't grimace, and he didn't hiss.

In fact, in that instant he had an analytical air that Shelly might have sported.

Gustav was as clever as a vampire, but he was fully human.

Too late, Max realized how neatly he'd been

trapped. All the vampires sleeping in this crypt were, in fact, human. Villagers in fancy dress. Max shut his watch and turned to run, but a net dropped on him from above.

The worst attack came from behind. The smithy used one of his hammers to beat Max repeatedly about the head and shoulders. Max was very strong, but his hands were caught in the net as he tried to fight back. Even as he let his claws grow and tried to slash through the heavy hemp weaving, he felt a blow to the head that knocked him to his knees. One more, and then he passed out, slumping to the dirt floor.

The smithy kept beating him, and it took all of Gustav's strength and that of several other villagers to pull him aside. His chest heaving, he finally looked at his hammer.

Blood dripped off it. Bright red vampire blood. The smithy wiped the hammer off on Max's pristine silk jacket.

Outside, the stableboy had started back home but had seen the village smithy, his face black with rage, sneak along the path with such stealth that he obviously didn't want to be seen. Remembering Shelly's promise of a quid if he performed his task well, the boy crept along after the smithy, knowing there was interesting information to be had if he stayed.

The smithy went straight past the trapdoor the wolf had entered, unburied a spot farther along that slight rise of earth, and then disappeared into the ground.

The stableboy was a former London street urchin who'd been on his own for years. He'd had to use his wits and, more important, his instincts, to survive. Something evil was afoot, something unnatural that would affect the entire district.

And blimey, now his own curiosity was aroused. He was about to find out personally if all those tales of strange goings-on were true.

Climbing up into the safety of a tree, the stableboy waited. And watched.

He didn't have to wait long.

A strange radiance came from the trapdoor opening and then he heard voices raised in hoarse anger. Sounds of a fearsome battle, and then—the Earl of Trelayne was carried out, head and shoulders first, still caught in a net, by several villagers. And the silent rage they exhibited chilled the stableboy almost as much as if they'd been vampires.

The smithy and Gustav brought up the rear. The smithy carried a bloody hammer.

Gustav paused, letting the others go ahead, and looked down at two objects in his hand.

He turned them over, back, and then over again, as if debating what to do with them.

Both gleamed gold, and though the boy couldn't see them well, he'd heard the rumors about Max's magical watch. From the looks of it, there were two of the strange things, just alike. As Gustav stared down at them, a raven flapped out of the crypt and perched on the tree, staring at Gustav with beady eyes. Gustav stared back, recoiling as if he felt terrible menace from so small a creature.

Then, nodding, he put both watches back in his pocket and stalked after the villagers.

The boy stayed still and quiet as he watched them all leave. So still and quiet that when the raven flapped right over his head, it didn't look down at the small figure in brown blending into the tree branches. It apparently didn't see him.

The boy shaded his eyes, looking up at the creature. It was coal black in the sunshine, shining with a blue luster that should have been beautiful, but wasn't. The boy saw it flap away, but eerily, the wings made no noise.

Chilled by all he'd seen, in broad daylight no less, the boy shinnied down and ran back to Blythe Hall.

"It fair gave me the willies," the stableboy said between huge gulps of Shelly's strong, bracing tea an hour later. "I gots no love for the gentry, especially the gentry like that earl, who is a bloodsucker sure as I stand here. But they beat him up good, they did."

"And Gustav? You're sure you saw the bright light, but when he came out, he was not burned?"

"Still fair as a baby's bottom, miss." He blushed and took a deeper sip. "Pardon."

"Nonsense, lad." Shelly gave him another quid. "You've done very well. And this bird you saw—it was a raven?"

"Aye, miss. Big, and dark, and evil. Even if it were broad daylight."

"Thank you. You may take the rest of the day off."

After he left, Shelly carefully locked up her research. She was almost, but not quite, finished mixing the formula. She could hardly admit it to Max, but she'd stolen into his lab one day while he was out and copied down his notes.

He'd done an admirable job of isolating the unique components of Angel's blood. But he was on the wrong track, his logic flawed. Angel's blood could never be used as a weapon against the vampires. Angel's blood, as Alexander had proved by mixing a very small sample with his wine punch and consuming it himself, made vampires stronger.

Max was looking in the wrong place for the weapon the Watch Bearers had been seeking for five hundred years.

It was, quite literally, right under their noses.

Their own blood would be as poisonous to a vampire as Angel's was to Max.

Pocketing a pistol and the kit she'd found lying in the crypt after Max carried Angel to safety, Shelly dressed for battle. Somehow, she had to get Max out of jail. She debated telling Angel, but knew her young friend was still too weak to bear more anxiety.

Shelly hurried out, hoping against hope that she came across Gustav. He'd had his fill of vampires, so perhaps it was time he experienced something new and exciting.

Such as the power of a werewolf.

Chapter Twelve

As she faced Sarina, Angel was beginning to feel strong again. The curtains might be pulled, but there was no wool over her eyes. Whether from the tiny sip of wine, or her loyalty to Max, Angel knew that Sarina was not being fully truthful with her. Of course, Sarina's ultimate loyalty lay with her husband.

Brown eyes met blue. "Tell me the truth, Sarina. Is your husband the erudite, cultured vampire you claim him to be, or a killer of young innocents?"

Sarina jerked away. "I don't know!" She turned away, but not before Angel saw tears in those lovely blue eyes.

Angel was ashamed that her suspicions

should so overset Sarina when she was already devastated by her husband's infidelity. Angel's genuine respect and liking for Sarina made the choice facing her that much more difficult.

A knock sounded at the door.

At Sarina's command, the butler entered. "My lady, there is a message for Miss Corbett from Miss Holmes."

Sarina frowned. "Why would my stable manager be sending a message to my niece?" She reached for it, but Angel was faster.

Angel noted the butler looked straight ahead as he offered the note, and he'd always been friendly to her before. Angel had never seen Shelly's handwriting, but the flowing, spidery script seemed somehow atypical. She glanced up at Sarina and surprised a fleeting look of . . . craftiness in her friend's gaze that disturbed her. But then she read the missive and all other thoughts flew from her head. Angel went white and swayed.

Sarina had to help her to a chair. "What is it, my dear?"

"Max . . . he's been beaten and imprisoned. I have to go to him."

"What possible loyalty do you owe the man who probably killed your mother?"

"You don't know that!"

"I've offered to prove it to you and you won't allow me to."

Jumping up, Angel went to her armoire and scrabbled through it for a thick cloak. Giving a scared look at the sunshine glimmering through the thick curtains, she lifted the hood over her face.

Sarina sighed. "That won't be enough. You won't be able to go out into the sunlight, Angel. Unless . . ." Sarina unbuttoned her sleeve and offered her own fair wrist. The blue vein pulsing there was the most delicious looking thing Angel had ever seen.

Angel's stomach growled. She tried to remember how long it had been since she'd eaten. Too long. But it wasn't food she was hungry for. Jerkily, she turned away. "No."

"It will give you strength, for my blood is of the universal vampire kind, too. For all our sakes, we must have an end to this fruitless vengeance. Max kills one of us; we attack him. It's gone on long enough." Sarina stroked Angel's hair. "Angel, there has always been a bond between us because we are both strong women. I let Alexander believe himself master of all he surveys, but you know it isn't so."

Even Sarina's touch was comforting. And indeed, Angel had seen Sarina manipulate Alexander with a soft touch or teasing word time without end.

Sarina's voice was husky with passionate conviction. "Only you and I have the power to end this bitter feud. Drink a few sips and you'll be strong enough to do what has to be done. The sunlight won't harm you. We'll both go and get Max out of jail, and somehow, I swear, I'll make Alexander find some compromise to this bitter blood feud."

Compromise to atone for so many dead? So many innocent girls, beginning with Max's sister. So many vampires Max had killed along the way on his righteous path of vengeance. But was it so righteous? Angel knew, deep in her heart, that Sarina was right. It was up to the two of them to end this horrible violence.

Angel looked back at that frail wrist, then out at the sunshine. There was no doubt that the blood in the wine had made her stronger. Angel looked at her image in the mirror. It was almost normal.

The bitter irony of what she contemplated didn't escape Angel, but it seemed she had no choice. To help Max, she had to become the one thing he hated most. Embrace the one fate he'd do anything to save her from.

Bending her head, she sank her fangs into Sarina's flesh, piercing the sweet vein. The warm spurt of blood was the most delectable ambrosia she'd ever tasted. One sip became two, and then she was lost, drinking and drinking.

The more she drank, the more she thirsted. And the more she thirsted, the harder it became to remember why she'd begun to feed. That easily did Angel Corbett complete her transition from lonely orphan to Angelina Blythe, creature of the night.

Hungry for the power of the vampire, not the weakness of the human.

Awareness returned slowly to Max, spurred by discomfort. He was in a tiny cell with a grilled window so small that even a bat couldn't get through it. And light—light flooded down on him from everywhere. He looked at his beet-red hands. A destitute fishmonger's widow would have whiter hands, and even as he watched they began to blister. Automatically Max felt for his talisman.

His watch was gone. And he was frying in the sunlight without it.

Max rolled off the cot, looking for sanctuary from the brilliant noon sun.

There was none. Every single corner of the tiny cell was ablaze with sunlight. Max tried shading his face for a quick glance upward and he realized they'd made a special cell just for vampires. The same tight, heavy metal grille covered the roof of the cell, allowing sunlight in but no hope of escape.

The one glance seared his retinas, but even as he covered his burning face, the image of the fresh welding marks was branded into his mind. Max knew the smithy had made this cell especially for him—the vampire he considered the murderer of his daughter.

"Angel," Max whispered, but then he blanked out all thoughts of her. She couldn't help him now. If he fetched her, she could be in danger too. Besides, it wasn't safe for her to go about in sunlight. And he didn't want her to see him like this.

Max felt the skin cracking on his face. He tried pulling his shirt collar up, but he knew it was useless.

"Burn, ye ruddy bastard. Burn! It's too good for ye." The smithy poked his prominent nose against the grilled window. He pulled at the grille as hard as he could. "Ye won't escape this time. Ashes to ashes, dust to dust is too good for ye, but I'll enjoy seeing it."

Calmly lifting the heavy cot over his head as if it weighed nothing, the shield giving him a very slight respite from the terrible fire creeping over his body, Max rejoined, "I don't suppose it would do any good for me to say that I didn't touch your daughter. I was elsewhere and could prove it if you'd care to question Miss Blythe and her stable manager, Miss Holmes."

"Ye got them fooled too, like half the people in the district, especially the womenfolk. But ye don't fool me. Ye never have. Ye deserve to burn in hell for all the lives ye took, and this little hell is one I made special just for ye."

Removing his heavy coat, Max used his stickpin and the heavy gold buttons to anchor the jacket through the grille, blocking at least a bit of the sunlight . . . and the unpleasant grin that taunted him.

The tiny amount of time he took doing it turned the redness creeping over him to vermilion. He could only huddle under his inadequate shield and curse himself for never gaining the art of turning into mist. And so, for the first time in the past century since he'd embraced the worst affliction a man could face for the best reasons a man could know, Max Britton marked the passing of time. When he had eternity, hours had become seconds, years, days, for he had forever, if necessary, to capture his quarry.

Now seconds were hours. As he faced his own mortality, he could only regret that he hadn't cherished them more. Especially the hours with Angel.

Life is sweetest when it's marked in hours, he decided.

Without his watch, he'd be dead by dusk.

In that secret room that was accessed only from the walled garden, where, appropriately enough, a mechanism hidden on a huge raven statue opened the trapdoor, Alexander accepted the watch Gustav handed him.

Suspiciously he flipped it open, holding it far out at the end of his arm as if he feared the light it would emit. When nothing happened, he warily read the inscription on the inside case. His lip curled in contempt at the Watch Bearer creed: HONOR = TRUTH = JUSTICE = VENGEANCE.

"Equals claptrap." Alexander snapped the watch shut and pocketed it. "And the other?"

"The jailer confiscated it. He didn't know I had two."

Again, Alexander suspiciously appraised the inscription. "You switched them, of course, before you handed it over?"

"Of course."

Alexander carefully set the watch down; then he casually backhanded Gustav. Gustav flew across the room, the back of his head hitting the wall. He blinked, dazed, and could only sit up, half-alert, as Alexander moved over him.

With a kick for good measure, Alexander said, "I was there. I saw. Even frequent imbibing of the punch wouldn't make you as immune to that pure beam of light as you were. You're not one of us." He kicked him again.

Gustav slumped sideways, winded, almost unconscious. Vaguely he felt the snap of a leg iron about his ankle. Alexander locked him to a ring in the wall.

Then, his fangs bared and gleaming, Alexander bent over Gustav so closely that his cloak brushed Gustav's bruised face. "You're not to my usual taste, but tonight, after Britton has roasted, I think I'll offer you as a feast to my friends in celebration. Much better than a suckling pig, don't you agree?"

In for a penny, in for a pound, Gustav decided. "Don't you want to know how I fooled you?"

Alexander drew his hand back.

But Gustav finished quickly, "I'm a magician. Pulling a rabbit out of a cloak is child's play. So you see, your bloody worship, you're not quite as smart as you think. And you're certainly not smart enough to be the Beefsteak Killer."

"If you're so brilliant, then you should be able to use your prestidigitation to get out of this." Alexander rattled the chain, picked up the watch, and sauntered out.

Smiling despite the pain of his bruised face, Gustav opened his large hand and admired the gleam of the key ring he'd filched from Alexander's cloak. Then he unlocked his leg irons and sneaked out into the garden toward the stables, limping slightly from his wounds, but all the more determined to stop this coven of vampires.

Obviously, he needed help if he was to free Britton.

He'd like to believe that his revelation would shock the redoubtable Miss Holmes, but he had a strong suspicion she already knew who he was.

Shelly, however, was not in her room above the stables. Knowing today was Cook's day to mix Alexander's punch, Shelly was helping to stir the mixture, adding the spices as directed. When Cook's back was turned to fetch ingredients, Shelly removed a flask from her pocket and poured a clear, tasteless liquid into the huge pot.

When Cook turned back, Shelly was stirring with the huge spoon. "I have the stable running right and tight. I shall be happy to help you refill all the decanters about the estate."

Cook was touched and ladled the concoction into a huge pitcher, handing it to Shelly. "Don't spill a drop, mind."

"Oh, I shan't." And, indeed, Shelly carried the pitcher as if its contents were precious.

She filled every decanter in the house, and ordered a maid to carry up refreshments to Sarina and Angel.

"The mistress told me we was not to disturb her or the miss."

Shelly frowned at this. She took the tray herself and walked upstairs just in time to see Alexander enter Angel's room. As the door opened she caught one glimpse of Angel, feeding off Sarina's wrist.

Shelly was so upset she had to brace herself against the wall to avoid dropping the tray.

Then the door closed, shutting her out. If she thought it would do any good, she'd break that door down and face both vampires alone, but Angel had been perilously close to complete transformation even before she drank the poison of Sarina's blood.

It was too late.

Angel had finally succumbed to the temptation of her own hot blood. The sins of the mother had truly been visited upon the daughter, as Max had feared since the day she'd arrived in England.

Tears brightened Shelly's green eyes.

There was one slim hope of bringing Angel back: Max. She had to get him out of jail before he died.

Knocking on the door, Shelly set the tray down and leaped out the hall window, landing lightly two stories below. By the time Alexander opened the door and looked out, she was gone. He glanced back into the room.

"Did you order refreshment, my dear?"

"No, but it's almost teatime. I'm famished. Bring us both something to drink." Stroking Angel's hair, Sarina cajoled, "Enough, dear child, or I'll be weak as a kitten."

Angel still suckled.

Gently Sarina tried to pull away, but Angel's teeth were too firmly attached. Sarina pulled Angel's hair sharply.

With a wince, Angel finally let go, blood dripping down both sides of her mouth. Her brown eyes glowed redly in the shadows of the room, but they had a vague, unfocused look.

Handing Sarina a large glass of ruby-red punch, Alexander gave an admiring smile to his wife. Then, his eyes gleaming with hunger, he looked back at Angel, sipping his own wine. His fangs showed between his lips as he fixed on the throbbing vein in Angel's neck.

They kept their voices low, but they needn't have bothered. Angel was lost in some twilight world of her own, her stomach full, her mind apparently at peace for the first time since she'd arrived. Her eyes closed, she rocked back and forth.

Noting Alexander's expression, Sarina shook her head sharply. "We'll save that for Max to see." She looked back at Angel. "A pity she's no longer a virgin." She accepted the second glass of wine Alexander offered her.

"Max will be in no condition to see anything or anyone in another hour or so," Alexander stated with extreme satisfaction.

Sarina frowned. "That's not what we planned." Shoving Angel back into a chair, Sarina finished the second glass of wine, rose, and approached her husband.

"I changed the plan when circumstance offered advantage." He showed her the watch.

She looked at it curiously, and then . . . she slapped it out of his hand. It flew across the room, landing on the couch.

Alexander was stunned. He stared at her, his mouth open. He lifted his hand to hit her, but before he could strike, she was gone.

Mist. Floating like evanescent evil in every corner of the room. Massing, swirling restlessly around Angel, part protection, part hunger.

Alexander felt her covetousness and finally, too late, he understood.

Flabbergasted, he sank bonelessly into a chair. "You! It's you."

Now that she'd made her point, Sarina transformed effortlessly back into her lovely form. The limpid blue eyes, the white dress, the flawless skin were perfect, as they'd always been.

Sarina smiled that lovely, kind smile. "Do you really think your clumsy lovemaking made me stay? You've been a convenient interlude, a place to hide while I watched Britton bumble about and planted obstacles in his way. Who would expect the gay social butterfly of being the Beefsteak Killer?"

Anger had begun to stiffen Alexander's noble spine. "You used me as a decoy. Played me for a fool."

"Played you? I had no need. You are a fool. Pitiably easy to manipulate, even for a man."

Alexander rose, too brash and arrogant to fear his own wife.

"I caught Britton for you, didn't I?"

"You expect me to thank you after you've ruined all my careful months of planning? I don't want him to die so easily."

Furious at being manipulated, Alexander lunged, his claws extended, his fangs bared.

It was the last move he ever made.

With the ease of long practice and her great, unnatural strength, Sarina picked up a silver candlestick next to her on a bureau. She drove the pointed tip through Alexander's heart so hard that it came out the other side. Blood spurted all over her.

His terrified eyes met hers and then dimmed. He fell to the floor, flesh peeling back to bone, bone becoming brittle honeycombs, rapidly decaying to dry hunks of burned matter. Then all that was left of Alexander Blythe was a pile of chunky dust and ashes.

Cleaning off the candlestick and putting it back, Sarina used the fireplace broom to sweep his ashes into the grate. She dusted off her hands on her clothes with a little grimace of distaste, paying her husband's remains no more respect than she would a pile of dirt. She stepped out of her clothes and lit them in the fire. Naked, her lush body sinuous and lethal, she glided into her bedroom.

Returning a few minutes later, she was as clean and lovely as usual in her virginal white. A jaunty, wide-brimmed hat with a red sash was tied under her chin, protecting her porcelain skin. She poured two more glasses of wine, drank one herself, and offered the other to Angel.

Colleen Shannon

Angel was still rocking and keening in the chair, lost in her own world, but when the wine touched her lips, she drank thirstily. When Sarina tapped her cheek, Angel's eyes finally opened. She had to blink several times before she could focus on that lovely face. "Sarina? What happened?"

Gently, Sarina kissed Angel's forehead. "You fell asleep, exhausted after your repast. Do you feel better?"

Considering, Angel nodded her head.

Sarina opened the curtains wide. Angel shrank back, but the light didn't affect her.

"Shall we fetch Max?" Sarina asked with that lovely smile. "I know he'll be delighted to see us." She picked up the golden watch and put it in her pocket, and then she led Angel to the door.

Thinking dreamily that Sarina was the best friend she'd ever had, Angel followed her like a lamb.

And Sarina liked her lamb very rare. . . .

Shelly was packing all she would need in the leather pouch she used to tie around her neck when a knock came at her door. She hesitated, but opened it. She took one look at who stood there and jerked Gustav into the room. She eyed his bruised face, noting the way he cradled his ribs.

"They found you out, did they?"

He stared, disappointed at her lack of surprise.

Shelly laughed at his expression. "I'm only amazed it took me so long to see it. If I hadn't been so busy, I'd have noted the usual signs of a Scotland Yard detective."

"And what might those be, pray tell?"

"You're unflappable, self-righteous, and you notice everything."

"You could be describing yourself, my dear woman."

"Indeed. I said something similar the last time I turned down the Yard's offer of employment. Except I have one skill I don't believe you've ever acquired."

With a flourish, he offered her a rose out of midair. "What do you think of my hidden talents?"

She had to laugh at his droll expression despite the urgency of their situation. Before another day dawned, either the Beefsteak Killer would be dead, or Max would be dead. Even, perhaps, she, Angel, and Gustav would be dead. Shelly had no illusions about the power of the evil they faced.

That only made the lovely, dewy rose all the

more precious to her. She accepted it with a gracious nod, looking forward to Gustav's expression when she revealed her own hidden skills. "Now enough roundaboutation. Tell me what you know, and I'll tell you what I know. On the way."

"On the way?"

"To break Max out of jail."

Shelly led the way to the carriage. For once, Gustav followed without protest.

Death, Max reflected, trying to distract himself from the agony of his burns and blisters, was the most clarifying experience imaginable. His eyes were closed, the pitiful shade supplied by the cot not enough to stop the spreading of the excruciating burns. And behind those closed lids, he saw so many things clearly now.

Odd how human emotions had colored everything he did as a vampire.

He'd wielded his golden hammer like Thor, the chosen one of the gods, killing to prevent killing; such was the bargain he'd made with his own conscience when he became a Watch Bearer. But he'd only been rationalizing the terrible reality of his blood vow. He had spilled blood, whether vampire or human, to make himself feel righteous. To feed his terrible need for vengeance.

In reality, he'd almost become what he most hated: selfish, amoral, thinking of nothing but his own base needs. It wasn't the drinking of blood that made vampires so ruthless. It was the immortality, the power of knowing that even time itself could not strike them down. How difficult to think of the consequences of one's actions when one knew there would always be a tomorrow to make right the sins of today.

Tomorrow is a gift, but today a blessing. A little homily he'd spouted all his life.

Only now, when this would be his last *today*, did he truly understand its meaning.

Even his seduction of Angel had only partly been because of his vow to Eileen to protect her daughter. The truth was, he'd wanted Angel with a selfish, gut-wrenching, purely male need that had overwhelmed all else. The first time he could perhaps reason away. But the second?

He'd taken her again, let her sip of his blood, even knowing he was doing her more harm than good, for the simple reason that he wanted her with the power and selfishness of his vampire urges. And as a man, he'd probably have behaved no differently.

He gave a bitter smile. Wanted her? What a pale word for the emotions she aroused in him.

He loved her. Loved her with all the lonely store of passion he'd been hoarding for a hundred years.

No, even before that, when he was an idealistic, laughing young man who found women aplenty to bed but none to wed. Who could ever match him, he'd wondered, in intellectual curiosity, logic, passion, and courage? Such a creature, with the femininity to complement his extreme masculinity, didn't seem to exist.

Then he'd met Eileen.

Even Eileen had not shared Angel's analytical mind. However, she'd birthed in her daughter all the qualities Max had loved in the mother, plus the unique qualities he'd despaired of ever finding in one woman. If Max had taken dust and formed it into his own personal Eve, blowing breath into mud, he could not have created anyone he'd have loved more than Angel.

This, then, would be the torment and the blessing the Watch Bearer, the last Earl of Trelayne, would take into eternity with him—it was not the watch, the powers it bestowed, or even his own sacred blood vow that gave him strength to face his own mortality.

It was the love of a vampire. A vampire he'd helped create. That knowledge was both the most bitter and most liberating of his life. With every fiber of his being he longed to call Angel to him and confess that he finally cherished what he'd learned too late.

But he retained enough pride and arrogance to want her to remember him as he had been, not like this.

Yet again, Max tried to pull the cot over his arms. They were burning even through his shirt now, and he could smell the acrid stench of his own flesh burning off his bones. He tried not to think of Angel, he truly did, but she was his only comfort. "Angel," he whispered, and just the sound of her name on his lips alleviated some of his excruciating pain.

In the carriage with Sarina, Angel roused out of her stupor, feeling his presence.

"Max," Angel whispered, frowning as she tried to concentrate. She picked up the wisp of an image of Max, his face blistered, his mind at peace. She looked at Sarina across from her, smiling that warm smile, and the image faded into Sarina's magnetic presence.

Angel had never felt so blissfully empty, so free of fear, of hate, of indecision. She had no pain in the sunshine anymore, and the blood she'd so feared drinking sustained her as no feast of man ever could. She was so full. And calm. Why had she struggled so hard against this fate? Angel held her arm in the bright sunlight and it stayed fair, unburned. She felt invincible, all-powerful.

"It's wonderful, isn't it, my dearest one?" Sarina asked, her blue eyes bright even in the shade of her hat. "Embrace the night, and the night will embrace you back. You'll never know fear or hunger or loneliness again."

Angel understood at last the allure of the way of the vampire. She was grateful to Sarina for guiding her and showing her this new, bold path that seemed so much more certain than the winding road she'd traveled as a human. And yet . . . there was something else. Some cost she'd have to pay for this journey.

Why couldn't she remember?

When they passed the fork that led to the village, Angel's eerie calm was spoiled by a terrible image: Max, writhing in pain as he fried in the sunlight.

She sat up, closing her eyes to block out Sarina's smiling face, and the image grew stronger. "Max," she said loudly this time. Her eyes popped open. "You promised to take me to Max!"

Sarina's smile faded. "It's too late, my child. He'll be dead in an hour."

"No!"

"It pains me to tell you, but Alexander did

this. He set a trap for Max that worked all too well. But he's paid dearly for his hatred. Gustav, our trusted head groom, and Shelly, our stable mistress, have both been working to find the killer. I'm afraid Alexander"—and here her voice shook—"was indeed the Beefsteak Killer. He's fled. I . . . helped him pack. I could not bear for him to be captured."

Scarcely hearing the words, Angel could think of only one thing. "Max. I demand you take me to him! *Now!*"

A strange emotion flickered in those deep blue eyes, but then, sighing, Sarina rapped on the roof of her carriage and told her coachman to take them to the village. "You will not like what you see, and it's too late for us to save him." Sarina pulled two flasks from her cloak. "Drink. For strength. We'll both need it." Sarina drained her own.

Her dulled senses at last alert again, Angel merely sipped at hers and then capped it. Tensely, she stared out the window, the fog clearing further from her brain. Whether she could embrace the night or not, she wanted Max with her in that night.

The voice came to Max through a million blazing suns crawling over his body. "Move away from the window, Max." It was Shelly.

Feebly, Max crawled to the corner, dragging his pitiable shield with him. Mercifully, the sun's zenith had passed so that it didn't directly shine down into his cell anymore, but it was too late.

Flesh was peeling off his body, flaking like burned ash onto the ground. There was a great roaring in his ears, and as he hunkered against the far corner, it became a crash and a thunder of stone imploding against stone. He coughed at the dust stirred up and squinted through the haze, trying to figure out what had happened.

More stones fell aside like giant blocks as the grille, with a final groan, was pulled from the wall. Sunshine peeked through, heightening Max's pain, but that blue sky also gave him curious joy.

Freedom beckoned in that sunshine.

Shelly's face poked through the opening. Shock widened her green eyes when she saw what had happened to him. She pulled the rest of the stones aside enough to make an opening he could crawl through. He barely glimpsed a team of horses still linked to the grate, because immediately he felt her put a heavy oilcloth covering on him, blocking the sunshine.

And then the jailer and several villagers, the smithy among them, rounded the corner to see what the commotion was about. The jailer pointed his blunderbuss, but Gustav pointed two pistols, and Shelly pointed a small but lethal shotgun.

The three men eyed the man and woman and the still lump under the oilcloth. But they didn't lower their weapons. "You can't take him. He's the killer," said the jailer. "We all know it."

"Then you know in error. You have the wrong man."

"Me own daughter were in his bed—" cried the smithy.

"Planted there by the real killer. I can prove it. Give me a piece of cheese, or an apple." She nodded at the knapsack on the back of the third villager. A loaf of bread peeked out. He hesitated, then pulled off a piece of cheese.

She went to Max, lifted the oilcloth slightly, and whispered to him.

With a great effort, he managed to form fangs and bite down into the cheese. Shelly showed it to each man with a flourish, still aiming the shotgun, braced against her hip, with the other hand.

The fang marks were dead even.

"We're all agreed, are we not, that the Beefsteak Killer has a crooked tooth?" Shelly demanded.

They looked from the cheese back to the lump of oilcloth.

Guilt skittered across the smithy's face. "He still be a vampire."

"A vampire who has risked his life to protect us." Shelly removed Max's kit from the carriage and showed it to the men. "He wants the killer, too, even worse than we do. He lost his entire family to it."

They stared at the gold-handled stakes, the vials of holy water. The jailer and the other villagers melted away, but when the smithy tried to slink off, too, Shelly grabbed his arm.

"Do you have something to say to the earl?" she asked softly.

The smithy shifted his feet, mumbling, "Sorry, yer bloody lordship." And then he stomped off.

Soft laughter, and then a groan, came from under the oilcloth. Shelly peeked inside.

"I always have liked that man. No subterfuge about him. He wears his pride on his sleeve," Max said, in great pain, but still showing that curious peace.

"I'd expect you to like him. In many ways, despite the difference in your births, you are much alike." Hearing rapid hoofbeats, Shelly looked over Gustav's shoulder and saw the Blythe coach fast approaching.

Hurriedly, she unlinked the team of horses while Gustav helped Max into the back of the carriage. While Shelly's back was turned, Gustav reached into his pocket and offered something to Max.

Max stared down at it. "Alexander has the wrong watch?"

Gustav nodded modestly. "I engraved the fake he had made so he couldn't tell the difference. If he thinks to use it against you, he'll be rudely surprised."

Max frowned. "I'm not sure it's him anymore. In fact . . ."

When she turned, Shelly caught the tail end of the exchange. Shelly and Max exchanged a long look. They both suspected who the true killer was, but neither stated it. Yet.

This killer would be much harder to face, because Sarina had won Angel's liking and loyalty. Even worse, if Angel was fully a vampire now, Sarina probably had the girl under her spell.

Then Max took the watch in his burned, blackened hand, and, wincing, he managed to flip it open. Immediately, a luminous blue glow was emitted. It encased him in a healing cloud.

To Shelly's mingled delight and astonishment, Max's burns started healing even as she watched. The red splotches whitened, the blackened flesh grew firm and healthy, and the blisters faded.

Gustav whistled. "Handy little bugger, that."

Shelly got into the driver's seat and lashed the horses away from the village, back toward the Blythe estate, just as the Blythe carriage came barreling up the main street.

Gustav stared after it. "You think they saw us?"

"I hope so. Because I think Angel is in that carriage. With the killer," came Shelly's grim response.

Strong now, Max sat up. His fangs bared in a grimace and he flung off his shirt.

"No." Shelly shook her head. "Don't transform and go alone. She won't hurt Angel until you're dead. She'll use Angel against you, as she has from the very beginning."

Max hesitated, but his green eyes finally turned away. He nodded reluctantly.

"She?" Gustav glanced between them as Max put his shirt back on and checked his vampire kit. "What she? It's Alexander, isn't it?"

"Who was always asleep in her bed, conveniently alone, during the murders?" Shelly asked, lashing the horse faster until they had to raise their voices to be heard over the pounding hooves and the rush of wind.

"Who began the balls and purveyed the

punch to every vampire in the county but always imbibed an incredible amount herself?" Max asked.

"Who has a fondness for bloodred Turkish delight, an Eastern treat, and knows a great deal about Eastern ways and Eastern spices? As if, perhaps, she came from Persia?" chimed in Shelly.

"Who always wears white and invites every lovely virgin for miles around to her balls?" demanded Max. "Who never ages?"

Gustav completed, "And who was responsible for bringing Angel to England?"

Surprised, Max and Shelly both looked at him.

"I checked the lading record. Alexander didn't pay for Angel's passage. Sarina did. And when I searched, I found her name on the manifest of a voyage to New York City only a few months prior."

"She must have seen Angel and realized she was Eileen's daughter," Shelly concluded. "She's planned this day from the very beginning. That's why she flung Angel at your head, Max."

They were nearing the Blythe cemetery.

Max frowned. "I've searched every catacomb in the damn place. There are no empty caskets here."

"Then you've looked in the wrong place, my lord." Shelly drew the horses to a stop next to a grave.

Max jumped down. He stood over Eileen's grave. He closed his eyes, trying not to remember, for fear Angel would read his thoughts, but the horrid images would not fade. Eileen, the only vampire before Angel he'd ever loved.

And the only one he'd loved even as he was forced to kill her.

Inside the pursuing carriage, Angel could think clearly enough now to link with Max, to realize Shelly had saved him. He was in that coach up ahead, pulling into the Blythe cemetery. And he was having terrible thoughts.

Thoughts of her mother.

Angel closed her eyes, trying to block out the horrific sight of Max standing over her mother's coffin, pounding down with the golden hammer. The stake pierced her mother's tender heart. Blood spurted but still Max pounded. . . .

"*No!*" Angel's eyes opened to Sarina's sorrowful expression.

"I tried to warn you," Sarina said. "But it's best that you know the truth. Max will try to kill me in a few moments. And perhaps you, too, if you don't help me defeat him." Sarina put a comforting arm around Angel's shoulder, and some of Angel's turmoil faded.

"We are two of a kind, my dear Angel. Stronger than the men who think to dominate us. We can help each other, succor each other, through all eternity. Help me now, because I'm too weak to fight him alone. He killed your mother, and he'll kill us if we don't ally against him."

The words pounded into Angel's eardrums, but across the rapidly diminishing space between them, Angel felt Max's pain and his guilt.

It was true. He'd killed her mother. The one terrible truth she'd refused to face had to dictate her actions now. Looking into Sarina's mesmerizing blue eyes, Angel nodded.

For this she'd come here: to find out who her mother was, why she'd feared her own relatives, why she'd wanted to be buried in England. And who had killed her, for she realized now her mother had never committed suicide.

The answers had proved to be far worse than the tormenting questions, but Max had used her, lied to her, made sweet love to her, all the while planning to kill her aunt and uncle. Perhaps Alexander was the Beefsteak Killer, but Sarina was kind and good and honorable. Angel couldn't let Max harm her.

Besides, she hated him for his lies and his

manipulation. She'd let the killer of her own mother into her body. Angel curled her hands and watched long nails grow, felt her fangs forming.

Watching the progression of thoughts on Angel's expressive face, Sarina flung off her hat with a joyous smile. "Welcome home, Angel." She hugged her.

And then they drove through the gates of the Blythe family resting place.

Here Angel's journey to truth had begun. And here it would end. . . .

Chapter Thirteen

The carriage that had borne Max, Shelly, and Gustav was now empty. A dark, yawning hole beckoned where Eileen's simple headstone had been turned aside on a pivot.

Angel didn't hesitate to storm down into that void. If she'd held a flaming sword high over her head, she could hardly have looked more full of fury and righteous vengeance. She'd learned well at Max's side.

Smiling, Sarina swigged the last of Angel's flask. Then she followed Angel down into the blackness, her fangs glistening as saliva formed in her mouth. Her eyes glowed red with an ancient hunger.

A hunger about to be fulfilled.

*   *   *

Down below, Max looked at the plush chamber that had been carved into the earth. He'd never found it because it didn't connect to the other crypts. It was secretive, self-contained, accessible only beneath Eileen's headstone. "How did you find it?" he demanded of Shelly.

"I followed her here late one night as a wolf. She never saw me. It was then I began to suspect her."

The walls were painted with murals depicting the passage of the centuries—the Crusades, the Middle Ages, the Renaissance, the Spanish conquest of the Americas, and finally Georgian, Regency, and Victorian England. And in every panel, painted larger than the march of kings and visionaries like Leonardo da Vinci, hovered Sarina, dressed in virginal white, with that same luminous beauty.

A luminous beauty she maintained by sucking lovely young virgins into dry husks.

Even Shelly looked a bit uneasy as she, too, realized the strength and cunning of what they were about to face. "No wonder she's never been captured. Who would believe such a lovely, fragile creature so strong and evil?"

Max scarcely heard her, though he'd taken the precaution of verifying that he had his watch, his stakes, and his hammer handy. He was standing over the center of the room now.

Here stood two caskets, very ornate, very costly. Both were carved with symbols of the night: bats, wolves, moons. But the slightly larger one was glistening white, while the smaller one was bright blue.

Angel's favorite color, Max thought grimly. But it held no dirt. He looked around, and then found final proof of Sarina's plan: a crate stamped, NEW YORK, NEW YORK. He opened it. Inside was dirt.

Closing his eyes in pain, Max realized Sarina had fooled him yet again. She had no intention of killing Angel. Angel's blood was a continuous source of strength for her. She intended to enrapture her prey, turn her into her familiar first and ultimately her companion for all eternity, as evil, remorseless, and eternally hungry as she was. How many humans would Angel convert to vampire along her path?

Max fingered the stakes in his pocket, his stomach roiling as he wondered if the fate of the mother would indeed be the same as the fate of the daughter. Before he'd let Angel live that life of eternal death and decay, he'd kill her with his own hand. And then kill himself, for surely he'd rather die than live with the knowledge of what he'd done.

Shelly saw, too, and comprehended. She

looked at Max sympathetically. "It won't come to that. No matter how she's filled Angel's mind with vicious lies, Angel is too strong. She'll see the truth. We'll make her."

Max hovered over the caskets. The white one was filled with dark black earth mixed with desert sand. He ran it through his fingers, sniffing it. It even had the scent of the East. "Persian, I warrant."

He debated spraying it with holy water, looking at the vials Gustav held. Gustav offered them, but Max shook his head. "She'll have other stashes of earth. She's too careful and too devious."

Shelly agreed, but then she stiffened.

He heard it, too: the rattle of a carriage, the steps being put down. Shelly retreated to a black corner.

Gustav peered after her, confused. Max gave the poor fellow two vials of his holy water and a cross. "You're on your own. But it's me she'll want."

Gustav glanced at Max, then back at the dark corner, where green eyes glowed. A growl came that made Gustav back up, and then the soft sound of great feet.

A wolf stood there staring back at him with Shelly's eyes. It even spoke with Shelly's voice. "Sorry, old chap, but there was no better way to acquaint you with my own unique skills as an investigator of psychic phenomena than to show you." Shelly licked a paw. "Prepare yourself. They're coming."

Gustav tried for a retort, he truly did, but it was no use. He was so frightened he didn't have spit enough to bless an ant, much less talk. A werewolf on one side and vampires on the other? "I'll become a butcher if I survive the night. A clerk. A priest, even."

As footsteps approached, Shelly thoughtfully eyed the white casket filled with dirt. Then, exchanging a look with Max, she squatted over Sarina's precious earth and urinated. "I had a bit too much water today," she observed judiciously.

Max did something he'd never have believed he could do on the most momentous day of his long life. This was the reason he'd become a Watch Bearer: to face the Beefsteak Killer. And to save the only women he could ever love. Still, he was greatly amused at Shelly's audacity.

Thus, when Angel entered the crypt, she did so to the sound of Max's deep, rich laughter. She froze at the bottom of the steps, staring at him, stunned at his boldness.

There he was, showing no remnant of the burns. All bright, bold, beautiful in every way a man could be. On the surface. In truth, he was a liar, a killer, a coward.

Still, she was torn. As much as her new vampire being despised her weakness, somewhere she still loved him. Somewhere in the dwindling humanity of the heart he'd once touched, he still held sway. But now she hated that humanity, wanted to wrench it out of her breast and fling it against the wall, where it would burst with all her stupid, naive intentions. Far better to embrace the night and learn to enjoy not feeling pain or sorrow. Only hunger and power conferred the true peace she'd sought fruitlessly for all her days.

He felt her acrimony and met it with a gentle, mind-melding reprimand. That silent bonding still linked them, despite everything. *No, Angel. She's poisoned you with her lies as surely as she poisoned you with her blood. Only look around you. The paintings.*

As Sarina glided into the crypt, Angel looked at the murals. Her mouth dropped open. Sarina was everywhere, through the ages. Always in white. Always luminous with an unearthly beauty.

Sarina saw what she stared at. "He's twisting everything, as he always does. I'm older than I look, yes, because I've been Alexander's wife for close to five centuries."

"She's lying, Angel." This time Shelly spoke. "Ask her to bite this."

Gustav flung a large, juicy apple at Sarina's head. Sarina ducked it and it splatted against the wall.

"I detest apples as much as I detest lying traitors and murderers," Sarina spit. Her eyes were beacons now of red, murderous rage.

Angel looked at her and took an automatic step back.

Sarina noticed and the red glow softened back to luminous blue. "Ask him yourself. Ask him if he killed your mother."

Angel looked at Max.

And he didn't turn away. He stared right back, his green eyes glowing with a tinge of red. "Yes, I drove a stake through Eileen's heart. And I've lived with that knowledge every night and every day of my life for the past quarter century."

Tears filled Angel's eyes. "Why? If you loved her, how could you?"

"It's only because I loved her so that I could do it at all." Tears of remembrance filled his own eyes, and then a flood of memories assailed Angel's mind, flowing like a healing river from him to her.

Eileen, calling him to America. Begging him to end her torment. She'd started hungering

353

lately for younger and younger prey. No matter how much she drank, it was never enough. But she retained enough of the glowing humanity that had so enraptured Max that she recognized how amoral she was becoming. She'd turned too many young people into vampires, and she feared for the fate of her daughter. Sometimes she stood over her bed, wondering what she'd taste like. . . .

Angel physically recoiled from the sight of herself sleeping in her bed, but Max wouldn't release her until he finished the terrible communion.

Eileen's pain had been so great that Max had finally, after a wrenching argument, conceded. That next night, as Eileen lay sleeping in her crypt, Max had pulled out his kit and . . .

Finally Max spoke aloud. "She made me promise, Angel, two things. One, to bring her home so she could spend eternity on the soil of her birth. And two, to protect you from becoming a vampire. No matter what it cost me." He let her see her mother one last time.

"You're the only one strong enough, and brave enough," Eileen had whispered. "You're not killing me. You're freeing me."

Angel and Max were so intent on the exchange between them that they'd momentarily forgotten Sarina.

But Shelly hadn't. She watched the vampire with unblinking green eyes.

Sarina's eyes flared redly back, and then she noticed the smell coming from her coffin. Her nostrils flared.

Shelly smiled her werewolf smile, tongue lolling.

Giving a chilling scream of rage that only immortality could endow with such shrill power, Sarina began to transform. Her form began to dissipate and fade away, but then . . . it stopped. Sarina shut her eyes and concentrated, but she remained corporeal, not the mist she always sought as her ultimate refuge.

The shock on Sarina's face made Shelly laugh her husky wolf laugh. "Did you enjoy your wine, Lady Blythe?"

Sarina froze, so shocked that she was obviously distracted from maintaining the artifice that was second nature to her. Briefly, she was revealed in her true form: old, wrinkled, hideous, with a hank of gray hair and no teeth but two very long, sharp fangs, one crooked. Her red, slanted eyes gleamed with evil.

While Sarina was distracted, staring at Shelly, Gustav threw his holy water at her.

It hit her in the face. She screamed, the eerie rage drawing Max and Angel away from their silent communion.

Tears still filled Angel's eyes, but at least now she understood.

Max had truly loved her mother. She'd felt his pain and despair, and believed that her mother had sent him here to protect her, as he'd proved more than once.

But what did that prove about Sarina? How could someone so sweet and kind be such a ruthless killer?

Angel stared between Sarina and Max. Sarina drew her hands away from her burned face, lovely again now that her concentration had returned, but marked with burns where the holy water had struck her. Pitifully, she squinted at Angel through swollen eyes.

It's just as I warned you. He intends to kill me first, and then you. Look in his pockets. You can see the golden handles.

Angel looked. Indeed, the golden-handled stakes peeked out of Max's pockets.

"Sarina is the one who converted Eileen to a vampire, when she was just a young schoolgirl in England," Max said evenly. He spoke without vitriol or condemnation, which would have made Angel suspicious. He stated the terrible claim merely as cold, hard fact.

But then that voice Angel had heard twice before was in her head again.

He lies. He's the one who converted her. That

voice sounded neither male nor female, as if it had learned such skill over many centuries because it had absorbed so much bright life along the way. Angel remembered it vividly. It was so insidious, so tempting. Begging to be invited into Max's home. Tempting her to drink blood.

"Remember my family picture, Angel?" Max urged her softly. "Me, as a baby, on my mother's lap a hundred years ago. And I'm not strong enough to transform into mist."

Neither am I.

"Only because I put a potion in her wine that has weakened her. Believe him, Angel. He speaks the truth," Shelly the werewolf added urgently, moving close to Angel and sticking a cold, wet nose for comfort into Angel's hand.

Sarina. Patting the nose absently, Angel looked again at the pictures of Sarina on the walls. If Alexander was the killer, surely he'd be there, too. And no one had seen a trace of him for hours. His clothes were still in his room, all the horses and carriages in the stable.

Sarina had lied about helping him get away. Which meant she'd probably killed him because he was of no further use to her.

Angel stepped away from Shelly. Away from Max. Two steps closer to Sarina. It was somehow right and good that she face her mother's true killer on the ground where her remains lay buried.

"Did you kill your familiar, Sarina?" Angel asked calmly. "Or should I call you the Beefsteak Killer?"

You ungrateful little bitch. You are your mother's daughter. She was a whining moralist, too.

Just like that, Sarina changed. One minute she stood on two legs, the next on four—as a tiger, but an unnaturally large and ferocious one. Roaring loudly enough to flake paint off the walls, the tiger leaped for Angel's throat.

And if she'd had any doubt, as Angel fatalistically watched those jaws gape open and the fangs glistening, she saw that one tooth was crooked. . . .

Then Max was between her and the tiger, his stakes out. But as he tried to drive one into the heart as it leaped, the tiger swiped it out of his hand, leaving deep claw marks from his shoulder to his wrist. They began to bleed. The tiger paused, one great paw raised, and sniffed, intent now on Max, not Angel.

With a feral growl, it shoved Max to the ground and bent its great head over Max's jugular. Its fangs sank deep, and then there was the terrible sound of sucking, a smacking of delight, as if a delicacy that had been hungered after for over a hundred years was finally being satisfied.

Max struggled against the creature with all his great strength, but even weakened, Sarina was more powerful than he, especially in this form. She pinned him flat to the floor with both paws and feasted at her will.

Angel picked up the fallen hammer and a stake and ran forward, raising them over the tiger's back, but to her shock, Shelly shoved her away with her nose.

"No, Angel, wait."

Unable to bear the hideous sounds as Sarina began to drain Max of blood, Angel struggled against Shelly. But her vampire powers were still weak compared to Shelly's unnatural strength.

"Stop! I don't want to hurt you. Another minute and you'll see . . . Max will be fine."

Angel was forced to watch as the tiger slurped harder. It looked as if Max were paling, all color leaving his face. And then . . .

Then a most curious thing happened.

The tiger staggered. As it caught itself, its fangs released Max. It staggered again, this time sideways, allowing Max to squirm free. He was weak, but he managed to crawl away from the tiger's great shadow and then stand, weaving slightly, but still managing to make it to Angel's side.

He rubbed at the fang marks on his throat, but they'd already coagulated. The dark smear clearly showed the outline of one crooked fang.

It was the final proof positive, not that Angel needed any more.

Max tried to take the hammer and stakes away from Angel, but she held them tighter, still watching in shock as the tiger walked as if drunk. And then, sides heaving with exhaustion, it collapsed in a heap. The transformation came much more slowly this time, as if Sarina couldn't control it. First into a wolf, then a great dog, then a cat, then a dove, then a bat, and finally a tiny shrew, each figure smaller and weaker than the last.

Angel and Max exchanged a look. Then, as one, they stared at Shelly, knowing who was responsible for this unexpected boon.

"Later." She sniffed, her nose in the air as if she still scented danger. "You'd better kill her now while you can."

Max tried to take the hammer and stake. Again Angel resisted. She ran over to stand above the tiny shrew. She knelt, but when the stake touched the creature . . . suddenly Sarina looked up at her again with those kind blue eyes.

"I always loved you, my dear. I wanted you to be my companion for all eternity."

Angel hesitated. This was, perhaps, the first truth Sarina had spoken for the last century. Angel had to know. "How could you kill so many innocent young girls? And then you tried to turn me into a creature like yourself."

"Survival, Angel. Survival of the fittest. You are a scientist. Ask Darwin what he thinks of such a tactic. It's the same one human beings have been using since time immemorial."

"But we don't think ourselves above the moral implications of feeding on one another."

Angel set the stake against Sarina's heart. She lifted the hammer high.

Then Sarina's hand was about her throat, claws piercing her flesh.

Max grabbed the hammer and stake away, raising them, but he paused when he saw what Sarina held in her other hand: the gold pocket watch.

"Get back," Sarina spit. "Get back or I'll use it. If I die I'll take her with me." Sarina moved to open the watch.

Max casually reached in his pocket and removed his own watch. "You might get a quid for that one at a clockmaker's. But this one . . ."

He glanced over his shoulder at Shelly.

Sarina was distracted enough to release Angel. Angel staggered away.

Understanding, Shelly shoved Angel into her empty coffin and slammed the lid down.

Terrible comprehension again made Sarina's eyes glow red. For an instant she took her true form again—her face was a brilliant grid of wrinkles highlighted by the light from Max's watch as he flipped it open, softly speaking his incantation.

As the light blazed into Sarina's eyes, turning her, in her weakened state, to lobster red, Max dropped the watch and drove down with the hammer. Once, twice, thrice, and the deed was done.

Gustav and Shelly had to shield their eyes from the brilliant light, so they missed the last of what happened.

As the stake struck through her heart, hitting the stone floor with a terrible, ringing finality, Sarina reached up to Max. Strangely, her blackened hand formed no claw. She cradled his cheek, as if, too late, now that her long life was finally ended, she grasped for the tender humanity that had once been hers.

"I could have loved you," she whispered. Her red eyes faded to blue, and then they dissolved to ash in their sockets. The process accelerated rapidly, head to toe, as her hideous, bony face and form simply dissolved to ash.

Shelly and Gustav watched analytically, fascinated.

Because of her extreme age, Sarina was very dry and brittle. She left no chunks and bone remnants as Alexander had. Only a black powder so fine that all Max had to do was blow.

Dust dissipated down the corridor, a brief fog of black haze, and then it drifted out the entrance into the late sunshine, becoming one with the earth again.

Sarina was gone.

Bowing his head, Max looked truly exhausted, his face still pale from the blood he'd lost, but then he staggered over to Angel's coffin and lifted the lid. The smiling face that stared back at him helped his own color return. Tenderly, he cradled that face in his hands, kissing her cheeks, nose, and throat as she sat up.

He moved to help her out, but instead she dragged him inside on top of her.

"What are you doing, wench?"

"Fulfilling a fantasy. That's a specialty of vampire rakes, isn't it?" Angel demanded. She reached up to kiss him, but Max pulled away.

"And what would you say, my temptress, if I told you that I long for nothing more than the boring life of one human life span?"

Angel looked around the walls at the march of years Sarina had ruled over. She ran the tip of her tongue over her own tiny fangs, as if testing them and her own dedication to what they symbolized.

Her decision didn't take long. She smiled up at Max's handsome, determined face. "I'd say boredom, after the last few months, sounds delightful. We'll watch the grass grow together."

Soft laughter came from Gustav and Shelly as Max helped Angel out of her coffin. Angel looked between the coffins and Max. "But how do we accomplish that? I've never heard of a vampire choosing to become human before. Is it even possible?"

"Perhaps not in the normal way of things. But with very special people with very special talents . . ." Max's sparkling green eyes met the luminous green ones of the wolf. "You spiked her wine, didn't you? With something that began turning her human again. That's why she couldn't dissolve into vapor."

Shelly licked her paw without answering.

Max demanded, "What did you use?"

Shelly let him squirm for a moment longer before her mouth stretched into a taunting grin that showed all her formidable teeth. "You had the right theory, but used the wrong control substance. It's not Angel's blood that makes the perfect weapon against a vampire, Max. It's your own. The lifeblood of a Watch Bearer."

Both Max and Angel looked stunned. Then they looked at each another, saying, "Of course," in unison.

Shelly finished, "The Watch Bearer is the only vampire created by choice, not converted by force. As Angel was a human becoming a vampire, you have been a vampire trying to remain human. This drink, based on your own blood, mixed with a few of my own additions such as liquid silver, merely accelerated the process."

"Where did you get the blood?"

"Your own lab. Where you drew it yourself to test it with Angel's."

"You invaded my home?" A black scowl descended over his face.

She snorted, not in the least intimidated. "Without hesitation. And I should think I merited a thank-you, not a lecture."

Max was silent, his mouth sulky again. It was apparent to all three what he was really angry about: he'd not thought of it first.

With a last husky, mocking chuckle, Shelly the werewolf bounded up the steps.

Max clenched his hands, staring after her.

Angel had to cover a smile with her hand

under his glare. "You look like a sulky little boy. I wonder . . . will our children have just that look of lordly disdain?"

His eyes lit with green fire. "Aren't you being a bit premature? Have I asked you to wed me?"

"No, but you shall. I'm the only woman on the face of the planet who can stand up to you, in the lab and out of it."

Making a garbled excuse, his face red with embarrassment, Gustav followed Shelly outside.

Neither Max nor Angel even noticed that he left. They were too intent on each other. Angel stuck her forefinger in the middle of his full lower lip. "I want them to have the shape of your mouth, to pout and laugh, to make me angry and make me glad. It was your mouth, you know, that followed me into my dreams and kept me sane."

And so, in this place of death where they'd almost been buried themselves, they celebrated life. They truly buried the past. No more recriminations, no more regrets.

Standing over two coffins, they laid to rest old wrongs.

And, living up to the motto of his family and hers, beneath her eternal resting place, they gave Eileen's restless spirit surcease as they birthed a future built on the blessing of today. . . .

Epilogue

Two weeks later

With loathing, Max looked at the band Shelly tied about his wrist. "I'm feeling like a pincushion."

"Pincushions do not bleed." Shelly inserted the needle and began, for the dozenth time in the past two weeks, removing his blood into a large vial. When he opened his mouth, she added tartly, "Nor do they complain so vociferously."

His mouth snapped shut. When she'd finished drawing his blood, he rolled his sleeve down and fastened it. He was dressed now in the garb of his time, proper Victorian pants, spats over his shoes, and a plain shirt and thin tie.

Liking his more dramatic attire, Angel had complained at first, but when he'd pointed out that sedate married earls who wished to be invited to join the London Royal Society had best look the part, she desisted.

Max took the vial from Shelly and mixed it meticulously with just the right chemicals in a beaker. Then, adding the diluted blood to wine, he drank a large glass. He made a face. "I can still taste it. And the thought of drinking my own blood is revolting."

"If blood no longer tastes good to you, it's working."

"And I'm stumbling about at night—"

"I know, and you can't fly, or read minds. Poor, pitiful human."

"I can still read Angel's mind." He smiled with anticipation.

They'd wed a few days ago in a private ceremony attended only by Shelly, Gustav, and a few villagers.

Shelly laughed. "I apprehend you're anticipating your long-awaited wedding gift?"

"It was delivered to our suite today."

"And what did you give her? I've noticed no sparkling ring or necklace."

He looked at her askance. "For Angel? You

know her better than that. She got what she wanted most: the latest, most powerful microscope available, made in Germany. Cost me a pretty penny."

He poured a large glass of the elixir of humanity and started to the door with it. There, he stopped. He hunched his broad shoulders, and then he whirled abruptly. "Forgive me for not saying this earlier, but . . . thank you. We likely would not have survived without you. And we most certainly would not now be human."

Shelly thought about teasing him, but she was too touched at this atypical humility. She merely nodded her head regally. "You are quite welcome."

Max smiled ruefully. "It's been a very long time since I said this to anyone, but you, my dear Miss Holmes, humble me and make me feel quite stupid."

A smile curled about that generous mouth. "You gammon me, sir. I aver you've never said that at all. To human or vampire."

"I've most certainly never said it to a werewolf."

Shelly's smile faded under his acute green gaze. It was her turn to move aside.

A gentle hand landed on her shoulder. "And your own fate? Do you wish my aid in trying to reverse your ailment?"

Shelly sighed and patted his hand. "I've worked on a cure these last two years, so far without success."

"But do you truly wish to be cured?"

He saw more than she liked, certainly more than she was comfortable with. "The answer is . . . I have no answer."

Shelly looked at the neat notebooks filled with her handwriting, and the wine stored in casks. "But my time here is done." She stepped away from him and began packing her own things in a valise.

"Where will you go?"

"America, I believe. I have an old friend in Boston who claims to have lost a child to a witch's coven. He wrote begging for my help."

"The skills of a werewolf should come in quite handy in such an endeavor, I should think."

"Quite."

"And Gustav? Will he keep your secret?"

Shelly laughed. She imitated Gustav's deep, proper voice perfectly: "His response to that very question was something like, 'Since I've no wish to take up residence in Bedlam, I'll keep the truth of what happened to myself and say only that I know the Beefsteak Killer is dead.' And he wished me well. He will be quite a great detective someday."

Shelly hefted her bag and turned to the door, where she offered her hand. It was almost as large and strong as Max's.

He shook it. Then he escorted her out of his lab up the stairs to the hallway that passed his suite of rooms. "But you can't leave without telling Angel good-bye. She's napping."

"Keeping her up at night, are you?"

The bold Earl of Trelayne blushed. But then he grinned.

Briskly, Shelly walked past Angel's door. "Good-byes are trying affairs. Tell her . . . to enjoy the blessings of today. I'm fortunate to have known you both." And just like that, she was gone, her steps firm upon the stair treads and upon the path of her own destiny.

But Max saw the tears glimmering in her eyes as she looked over her shoulder at Angel's closed door. And then her steps faded. He had a feeling they'd never see her again.

A bit choked up himself, he took a moment to collect his emotions. Then he entered the master suite of their new mansion. The bed was empty, but he heard Angel singing in the water closet. He set her glass of wine down on the bureau beneath the family shield bearing his motto that he'd had reforged.

He was about to sneak into the water closet when she emerged, wearing only a gleaming silk robe and smelling like life, but looking like heaven. He clasped his hands around her waist. "Angel mine," he whispered, reaching down to kiss her.

Teasingly, she evaded him. "Haven't you had enough of that?"

"Your kisses are much more addictive than blood. Speaking of which . . ." He went to the bureau and offered her the glass.

She made a face, but drank it. "How many more?"

"Miss Holmes estimated another week should do it. She left enough mixed up for us."

"Left?"

Max put a comforting arm around her shoulders. "She's gone, Angel. She didn't want the pain of good-byes."

Angel flew to the window and ripped aside the curtain in time to see Shelly getting onto her horse. Shelly looked up at the house. She lifted a hand, kicked her mount, and then she had disappeared among the trees.

Tears bedewed Angel's eyes. "I shall miss her."

"So shall I."

Angel finished the last of her wine, twiddling with the stem between her fingers. Something was obviously bothering her. Max had felt her, several times since they'd wed, dance close to a sensitive subject, then away from it. But when he tried to read her mind, she blocked him.

"Your wedding gift has arrived, but before I give it to you, Max, there's one thing I must know."

Max braced himself.

Angel put her glass down. "Would you have killed me if Sarina had won me totally over to her side?"

He tried to evade her by straightening his tie before the mirror.

She turned him to face her. "Would you have taken that lovely golden hammer and driven a stake through my heart?"

"I didn't have to make that choice. I'd much rather hold you tenderly to my own heart for the span of one natural human lifetime. I've tried it, and I can tell you living forever is more of a burden than a joy."

"You're evading me. I need to know, Max."

Impassioned now, he caught her shoulders in his hands and pinioned her with his bright green gaze. "Could I have borne your blood on my hands and your scream as my last memory of you? Yes. Rather than see you become Sarina. Yes, Angel, I would have killed you if I'd had to. And then died by my own hand rather than live again with the knowledge that I'd failed the daughter as I'd failed the mother. Satisfied?" He released her, standing still, as if half expecting her to run screaming from the room.

Instead, she nodded her head solemnly. "I thought so. And there's something comforting in knowing that no matter what, you were strong enough to protect me, even at great cost to yourself. I love you, Max."

He went limp with relief, glad that at last she understood. "In the end, Sarina had a tiny remnant of humanity left. Enough for regret. I thank God every day that, with your help and Shelly's, I was spared that terrible choice. Together, Angel mine, we ended the old Trelayne inheritance."

With a shake, as if just like that he cast aside the mantle of his bitter legacy, he pulled her into his arms with a lusty laugh. "Can you tell me, my dear wife, what my new inheritance will be?"

Those green eyes had no wisp of shadow or despair anymore.

With wonder, Angel saw Maximillian Britton, Earl of Trelayne, as he had been before he took on the terrible burden of the Trelayne inheritance. Joy filled her heart. He was handsome, so vibrant with life that she knew, since the temptress powers of the night were not hers, that he'd wrap her like string around his finger for all of their lives if she didn't strengthen herself now with her logical mind.

Archly, she turned her nose up at him. "I'm

fatigued. We'll work again on our heir tomorrow, or the next day, or perhaps the next." She started for the door.

He caught her from behind, lifting her into his arms. He moved toward the bed, kissing her with all the fire of the night and all the joy of the day.

The day that now would always be theirs.

"You are my blessing, Angel," he whispered into her mouth. "And I will treasure you accordingly, for all the todays God allots to me."

Angel swallowed harshly, so touched that her surprise was almost spoiled. She kissed him back, then whispered into his mouth, "And I am ready to fulfill my duty, my very dear earl. But . . ." She squirmed free and shrugged out of her thin robe, leaving it in a gleaming silk puddle about her feet. Her skin had the same luminous glow.

With a sparkling look of mischief over her shoulder, temptingly naked, she ran into the sitting room.

Eyes alight with the joy of the chase, the earl pursued his errant bride.

Two steps into the room he froze. His mouth dropped open.

His innocent, all-too-human bride had shocked him yet again. In the middle of the sitting room sat her bright blue coffin, plushly lined with white silk.

She stood next to it, her hand out. "When we're very old, and very tired, we can sleep together in it and remember. Maybe they can even bury us together. By then we should be quite comfortable."

Ripping off his own clothes, he picked her up and dropped her inside, tackling her. "And what if I want to fulfill your fantasy instead, right this moment, when I'm still young and strong?"

She pulled his head down to hers.

Outside, the sun settled down for the night. And somewhere in the dark, vampires roamed in their eternal, lonely quest for surcease that proved ever more fleeting in their endless march of tomorrows.

But in the suite of the Earl of Trelayne, life would always be a joyful today.

And as they made love, candlelight gleamed on the motto that had brought them together and would keep them bonded through the rest of their lives. For now, through great cost, they finally understood its meaning.

Tomorrow is a gift, but today a blessing.

And while he could still think, the Earl of Trelayne realized that, as usual, Angel was right and he was wrong.

The joy of sex was all the more enticing in a coffin.

And they fit perfectly. In every way . . .